The SUMMER of GRACE

KAREN JONES

Library of Congress Control Number: 2022939465

Cover Design by: www.beapurplepenguin.com

For information please contact:
Brother Mockingbird, LLC
www.brothermockingbird.org
ISBN: 979-8-9863305-0-1Paperback
ISBN: 979-8-9863305-5-6 EBook

This book is dedicated to Patricia Miller,
Sharon Ogden, Jane Davis, and Brown Hound.
And to all my Carolina folks who loved me,
no matter what.

Jones County, North Carolina 1920

Running through the midnight woods, ignoring the pain of those first sharp bites, Marcell stumbles over a rotten log and crashes through the underbrush. The drumbeat of Elroy Simmons' words pounds in her head matching the throb in her ten-year-old chest. "Tell us where he is, girl. Come on now. You want Blue and Smokey have another bite? They sure do like the taste of pickaninnies." Laughter.

"Elroy, what you got there, Ivis' shirt? That'll have his scent. Leave her. Let's us go. We'll track him easy. Gonna get some pay back for Miss Lacy."

A fallow moon slides behind the clouds, and she slams into an oak. Stunned, she falls back to the ground but scrambles up on skinny, shaking legs. She has to get to her daddy. She runs, cautiously now, keeping her hands out in front. The moon reappears, and she sees the scum-filled ditch. Jumping it easily, she stops at the edge of the tobacco field. Bending over to slap the mosquitoes off her blooded ankle, she strains her ears.

There. Men's voices again. Dogs baying. A shout. "Look what we got!" More shouts, laughter. Vomit spews out of her mouth. She ignores its spatter and turning, races across the freshly plowed field towards Miss Emily's house. The words play over and over in her head like a prayer, "Cap'n Tom. He'll stop 'em. He'll make it safe. He'll get my daddy back."

CHAPTER 1

Tidewater Virginia, 1951

It was quiet inside the two-bedroom house, like the hush before a summer storm. The air heavy and still, the threat of lightning, muted and sullen, hidden. Waiting.

I sat outside on the picnic table, my bare feet dirty from playing in the yard, my shorts sticky from popsicle drips. When would I have to go inside? I wanted to spend the rest of the day and the whole night with my arms wrapped around Brown Hound's neck, inhaling her sweet smell. But I couldn't. It was late afternoon and time for supper. The silence broke.

"Get in here and set table!"

I gave Brown Hound a hug and climbed down. She gave a tail thump but didn't follow. She never ventured near the back door. Not since two years ago, right after my eighth birthday when she'd been caught on the screened back porch. Momma had laughed as Brown Hound belly-crawled away from the swinging broom trying to squeeze behind the washing machine. I wondered how it could be funny, but I was old enough by then to keep my mouth shut and my eyes down.

"Don't make me call you again."

I knew what that meant. My legs prickled with the thought of willow switches burning through the air. I opened the screen door, walked across the cement porch, and went inside.

"No. I don't think we should have cigarettes as favors for the card party. I don't care if Philip Morris gives them free." Momma, or "Sissy" as the family calls her, was on the phone holding up her end of civilization by arranging another garden club card party. She sat on the plastic kitchen chair, legs crossed, dress tight, and red hair in perfect waves. Clunky pearls hung from her neck. A pointed black high heel dangled from her toe, and she jiggled it back and forth. "I know Barbara Stanwick smokes, but you know how trashy those actresses are...sophisticated my foot! I'll not have it! I want you to get small pots of violets for the favors." Her red lips clamped together, and she didn't move her teeth. "Yes, you will." Her voice hardened. Blocking her out, I worked at placing knives and forks on the table.

"Euella, I'm president of the club and you do what I say, you hear?" The receiver slammed down with a crack, and I jumped. The silverware went flying.

"Look what you've done. All over the floor! Now I'll have to wash them again because of you. Pick them up right now!" She jumped to her feet, but I dodged past her hand.

"Sissy honey? I'm home." Momma paused at

his voice, her hand grabbing air as I lunged under the table. "Sugar, what's wrong?" It was Daddy. Always wondering what was wrong. Always trying to make peace. Through the chair legs I saw him enter the room. "Now darlin' what's got you in such a fuss?" His dark blue pant legs came closer. Momma's feet danced sideways like a crab getting away with bait. I bet he was holding onto her shoulders. Steadying her as usual. I stayed quiet.

"Euela wants cigarettes on the tables at the card party," Sissy's voice raised yet another notch, "and that's what trash would do. Ladies don't smoke and you know it. And then Elizabeth Grace comes in and throws silverware all over the floor." Her voice got higher and broke into sobs. Suddenly her feet stopped their skittering, and her sobs became muffled. Then both pairs of feet moved off toward the bedroom. Daddy called back, "Gracie, you wash those knives and forks while I get Momma settled."

I hate my name. Momma gave it to me because she thought it was elegant, Elizabeth Grace. Daddy says it's "high pretense", so he calls me Gracie. I think it's the only fight he ever won.

I crawled out from under the table. Moving in a duck squat, I picked the rest of the silverware up off the green and yellow linoleum floor. I ran the knives and forks under the faucet. Usually, it takes more than a yelling match with Miss Euela for Momma to get into one of her states. I wiped a knife with the dishcloth. Momma seemed to be getting worse. She'd been having her states ever since I could remember. But they were coming sharp and strong almost every day now for about the past year. It was getting hard to hide from her every minute of the day, checking her face to see if it was smiling or screwed up in a scowl.

Footsteps. But I knew they weren't hers. "You all right?"

I spoke without turning, "Yes, sir."

"Good girl."

I kept wiping the same knife. I said what I always said. There was enough trouble around here without me having a problem too. Momma's spells took up most of the air. And besides, Daddy didn't want to hear anything different. He just quieted her down. When he wasn't around and the storm broke, I ran and hid under the willow branches in the big doghouse with Brown Hound.

"Gracie, put that knife down and come over here."

I set the knife down and moved to the table. Daddy pointed and I sat, wrapping my ankles around the chrome legs of the chair. His jacket was off, and his tie was loose. He sat down in the chair, stretching his long legs under the table, and running his hands through his thick black hair. He looked like he was studying the kitchen wall for what to say. I hoped he didn't want me to say anything. I didn't have much to offer. I spent most days with Momma in the house and me outside. The only person I talked to was Brown Hound and being a dog, she didn't have much conversation.

It's been like this for as long as I can remember. But sometimes, I can think of a few moments way back when Momma smiled and laughed. I even remember her singing along with the radio. Those were times when the air in the house was so light you could pull it into your chest. It wouldn't choke you. But those times had gotten fewer. Things had changed slowly, like wisteria starting to climb a tree. You didn't notice until it had the tree in its grip and was digging into the bark for support.

Daddy gave a sigh. "Gracie, there's something Doc Johnson and I have been talking about." I froze solid. Doc Johnson. The living authority on needles. I drew myself inward, trying to be a smaller target. "He and I have been talking about your momma. He said she needs a rest."

I thought about that for a minute. "She's going to bed?"

"No honey, she's going away for a while."

My breath stopped, just like the time I fell out of the willow tree. Go away? Where? How long? I sat and stared.

Daddy continued, "She's going to a nice place Doc Johnson found. He thinks she needs some rest and that she can't get it here."

I hung my head. If she didn't have to yell at me about Brown Hound, tell me every move to make, and do everything right behind me she wouldn't be so tired. That's what she always said. I was ashamed.

"So, I'm going to take her there this week."

My chest felt too heavy to make words. I sat and stared at the tabletop.

"Don't look like that, honey. You get to go someplace, too."

I kept completely still. I heard Daddy scoot away from the table and stand up. I raised my head. His fists were jammed into his pants pockets. I waited.

"With your momma gone and school out, there's nobody here to take care of you during the day."

Brown Hound.

"So, you're going to go and spend the summer on Miss Emily's farm."

He stood silently for a moment as if I was supposed to say something. I had nothing to say. Miss Emily's farm?

His voice was impatient like he wanted to get this over with and go back to Momma. "You remember the farm in North Carolina. In Jones County? Miss Emily and Jane and Great Granny Jane?"

That last name made me jerk my head up straight. Great Granny Jane. A faint memory came of tobacco smoke and creaking porch boards.

Daddy continued, "I know it's been years since we visited there, but you do remember it?"

Years? You bet. Momma thought she was too good for the Carolina folks, so we didn't go down there much. I could barely remember the last time.

"You remember your cousin Jane? She's about your age."

I nodded my head. Not so much that I

remembered Jane but, that I knew no matter what I did or didn't remember, it had been decided. I was going to be shipped off to North Carolina and nothing I said would make one bit of difference. Suddenly my breath hiccupped in my throat. The next words I had to get out. "Brown Hound."

"I don't know if that's such a good idea, Gracie."

I couldn't get air. Daddy leaned forward and looked at me. Just once, I begged silently. Just this once, please get me nice and settled like you do Momma. I heard his sigh and waited for life or death.

"I guess one more dog on the farm won't matter. But you listen to me. The other dogs might not like her much, so don't come crying to me if she gets hurt."

Of course not. The idea of Daddy helping hadn't crossed my mind. I heard the relief in his voice as if sending Brown Hound with me made everything all better. "We'll get you packed and ready to go for tomorrow." It was settled.

Warm spring air blew through the car. I kept my eyes straight ahead, but my mind was back at the house. Momma had been quiet last evening, missing supper, staying in her bed. Daddy had given me a dollar. I'd walked to Klop's grocery and bought a blue collar for Brown Hound. When I put it on her, she shook her neck and gave me a dirty look. But it was beautiful next to her short brown fur, and it lit up her deep, brown eyes. I sat with her on the picnic table in the evening gloom and explained we were going off to my grandmama's farm where dogs had to wear collars. If I didn't have a choice about it, then she didn't either. She whined, licked my face, and forgave me. I know it must have felt strange, that stiff piece of leather around her neck. It seemed like we were both going to feel strange for a while.

In the morning, Momma said goodbye while still in bed, all dreamy with a soft voice and vague smile. I don't think she even knew it was me. Daddy came in. It was time to go.

I watched the road push into the distance, parting the deep green trees. Brown Hound hung her head out the side window, eyes narrowed to slits, ears flapping. As far as she was concerned, she was in a car and nothing else mattered. I was the one who held it all in my stomach; the leaving and the knowing that somehow this was all my fault. I glanced up at Daddy. His eyes were straight ahead. He looked tired and I could see lines at the sides of his eyes. A lick of his hair hung on his forehead, not brushed back tight like usual. He'd packed me up last night without too much to say. Once or twice, he placed a hand on the top of my head and stroked my hair. He always said my hair felt like corn silk. It looked like it too, so thin my ears showed through. After he closed my bedroom door, I went to the window and placed my mouth on the sill, digging my teeth into the soft wood. I pushed down hard. There. My teeth marks gleamed in the dark. That would show I'd been here.

"Not too long now."

We'd stopped at a gas station where I used the restroom. It was hard trying to go and not sit on the seat. The gas station man gave Brown Hound a bowl of water. Daddy bought me a candy bar and an Orange Crush. I'd noticed the air was warmer and wanted to ask Daddy about it, but I kept still.

Brown Hound's head still hung out the window. A happy look danced in her eyes. I wanted my eyes to look like that. I wanted to feel like that, but I couldn't. For Brown Hound, it would be all new doggie friends and places to explore. I didn't know what it would be for me.

"You remember Granny Jane, don't you?" I jumped at the sound of Daddy's voice. He kept his eyes on the road pretending he was paying close attention to his driving but, I knew he just didn't want to look at me. He continued, "Do you remember?"

I leaned my head back and closed my eyes. A gnarled hand, the smell of tobacco, a cane whipping out and flicking a fly from a porch railing. My stomach eased a bit. "I remember her."

"Well, she'll be there. But older, must be in her late eighties. She's my grandmother and your great-grandmother." He glanced over at me. "She was married to old James. He's long gone, but she's still here. They had your grandmama, Miss Emily. Miss Emily married Cap'n Tom and they had me and your Aunt Sally."

I let that sink in. The first hint of things to

come. I thought of that fly twirling off the porch railing. I hoped being older hadn't hurt Granny Jane's aim. I waited for the next bit of information to bounce off the windshield.

"And Jane."

I stayed quiet.

"She's about your age. She's a good girl. You remember her?" Nothing came to mind. I lifted my hand and rubbed Brown Hound's fur to fill the empty space.

"No, I guess you don't. You were both young, about four, five? I remember because it was when Sissy got so sick, we had to carry her back home."

That didn't help me any. I could count back to when I was five years old, but I didn't have enough fingers for counting all the times I'd heard about Momma coming home sick from North Carolina. Maybe there was something in North Carolina that made Momma sick. Maybe it would make me sick, too. Maybe I would go there and get sick, then Daddy would have to come and carry me back home. I sank deeper into the seat, maybe I would die. I sat up straight. A small, satisfied feeling danced in my stomach. Yes. I would die, and they would feel bad for sending me to a place they knew was unhealthy for me. I could see the gathering in the church. Everyone would be talking about what a bright and promising child I was. I could see my parents sitting in the front pew. No one talked to them. People marched right past, looked in the casket, and reached down to pat Brown Hound sitting faithfully beside it. My stomach lurched. If I died, I would lose Brown Hound. I yanked myself out of the casket and looked at her sitting at the window, ears flying, smiling widely. I sat back.

"Who's Jane's momma and daddy?" Daddy gave me a quick, sideways glance. I knew there was something bad about them but couldn't quite remember.

He looked back at the road. "They're dead. Her momma, my sister Sally, and Dave, her husband, were killed in a car wreck when Jane was just a baby. She's been living on the farm with Granny Jane and Momma ever since."

A car wreck. I tried to ignore how fast the trees were flying by my window. I let the words softly out of my mouth "Miss Emily?"

Daddy eased back in his seat, "Your grandmother."

"Is she nice?"

Daddy smiled for the first time since starting the car. "Oh yes, she's very nice."

I was glad he was thinking about her and not Jane's parents smashed in a car. "Will she like Brown Hound?" A pause. I could tell he was gonna make it up.

"Sure, sugar, she'll be happy Brown Hound's coming to stay."

I changed the subject. "What about your daddy?"

"Cap'n Tom? He had a bad heart. He died a

long time ago sweetheart before I went into the war. I was right about your age. Even your momma didn't get to meet him."

I thought that Momma was probably glad. I'd just about run out of questions, and I could see Daddy was getting tired of answering. "Anybody else?" I could see him struggle silently for a minute.

"Marcell." He snapped his mouth shut.

"Who's Marcell?"

Daddy shifted in his seat. " Nobody." He cut his eyes over at me, saw the next question and headed it off. "She's just someone who comes in and helps on the farm. You won't be paying her any mind."

I could tell I wasn't supposed to ask anything else about her, so I let it drop. I sat back and thought about Jane. A good girl, Daddy said. I had visions of petticoats, white gloves, and church hats. Then suddenly in the back of my mind I heard a giggle as that fly shot off the porch railing. I sat back hoping, for what I wasn't sure. I watched Brown Hound sniff the coming territory.

Chapter 2

She was the first thing I saw when the dust settled around our car in the farm's driveway. I didn't see the chickens in the yard or the unpainted boards of the farmhouse. I only saw the colored woman. Through the haze of Carolina dust, she moved slowly, gliding with purpose, not glancing right, or left but keeping her gaze on something or someplace I couldn't see. Her hair was bound tight to her head and a faded purple print dress pushed against her legs. Brown Hound gave a soft whine. I patted her as I watched the woman glide past the car and on out to the road. Daddy was busy switching off the engine, setting the brake, and fiddling with his shirt. He took in a deep breath. I couldn't tell if it was for courage or if he was inhaling the sweet Carolina air.

"Robert, bring that child up here this minute." The voice was commanding and cracked through the haze.

Daddy looked over at me. Reaching out, he brushed my hair smooth with his hand. "That's Granny Jane. Now mind your manners. No, leave the dog in the car. Windows are down, she'll be fine. I just don't want a dog fight first thing."

I pushed out of the car shoving Brown Hound back. Two dogs came out from under the front porch, trotted over and stood, tails stiff with curiosity. I shut the car door carefully.

"Bring her on up here."

Daddy took my hand. I looked back to Brown Hound for comfort then turned to the porch. It was unpainted like the rest of the house and stretched the whole front length. We climbed the three steps, and there she was like an old bird just ready to peck. Her white hair was pulled firmly into a bun at the back of her head, her body was ramrod straight in a black dress, and she was thin as a stick. I looked for the cane. There it was, beside her rocking chair. Suddenly I remembered how it could whip out and take a bite out of you faster than lightning. I edged a bit out of reach, but the old woman ignored me and talked with Daddy.

"It's better she's here with your people. Not much for her up in Virginia with Sissy, the way she is." The words were direct and cutting. I hoped they were truthful, the part about it being better for me here. I looked out at the car. Brown Hound was holding court hanging her head out of the window as the other dogs danced with impatience for the first sniff.

"Child, come over here." A bird-like claw motioned me to her side. As I got into range her hand snaked out and grabbed my wrist. I stood still, my heart beating with a flutter and a hitch. "Cat got your tongue?" I nodded my head. She made a small humming noise as her eyes raked me up and down. I glanced up at Daddy. He looked down smiling. I didn't see anything to smile about.

A sudden yowl filled the air. Jumping a foot high I switched around and saw Brown Hound taking to the woods, the farm dogs in hot pursuit. In the dust beside the car door, her hand on its latch, stood a girl just about my age. She'd opened the door. Brown Hound had escaped and was running for her life. Yanking my arm from the old woman's grasp, I flew from the porch and raced to the car. Skidding to a halt, I gave the girl a shove, pushing her to the ground. I turned and ran towards the woods.

"Young'un, get back here!" The words had no effect. Brown Hound was in trouble. I had to save her. The other dogs would eat her alive. I slid to a halt at the edge of a big ditch and listened hard. No barking. No howling. Maybe they had already killed her and were eating her! I jumped over the ditch and raced ahead.

"Robert, go get that child. She'll kill herself in those woods." Granny Jane's words chased after me. I shook them off trying to hear the dogs. I took off to the left, crashed through a bush and hit the ground. Looking up I saw a tangle of fur, noses, and tails. Then, a familiar snout. No blood! I grabbed Brown Hound hard around the neck. She shook me off, scrambled to her feet, and pretended to nip the nearest dog. He leaped in the air then landed, rolling on the ground. I froze in position, my arms with no dog in them. Playing. Jumping, rolling and rear-end sniffing. They were having a fine time.

"Gracie." Daddy had followed me into the woods.

"I'm right here." I stood and brushed the dirt from my shorts. I remembered the girl who'd opened the car door. I hoped she was dirty, too.

"Gracie!" His voice dropped a notch. I could tell he was disappointed. I walked slowly over to him. He looked down at me and without a word, put his hand on my shoulder and guided me back through the woods and over the ditch. I kept my eyes to the ground. I saw the bumper of the car and then two feet in tennis shoes. Daddy pulled me to a stop.

"Gracie, tell Jane you're sorry you pushed her."

So, this was Jane. The girl who'd opened the car door and let her dogs get to Brown Hound. No matter that instead of biting and killing, they were rolling and rear-end sniffing. She'd let my dog out without asking me. I raised my head and saw curly, black tangled hair, a tilted nose with freckles, and coal black eyes.

"Tell Jane you're sorry."

I wasn't sorry one bit. I glared to let her know this while the correct words mumbled out of my mouth. She grinned in reply and wiped her nose on the front of her arm. Her eyes danced. I tried to muster up some hate but couldn't. I heard another yelp and knew Brown Hound was having a glorious time.

"Robert, bring them up here." The harsh voice cut through the air. No one dreamed of ignoring it. The weathered boards creaked as I moved to stand in front of Granny Jane. Jane took a casual stance, one tennis shoe slouched out to the side. I could see it was an act.

"That dog of yours going to cause grief?"

"No, ma'am."

"See that it doesn't."

Brown Hound was not an it. I shifted my feet but kept still. We turned at the slap of the screen door. A soft voice drifted through the air. "Dinner's ready."

Daddy spoke with a smile in his voice, "Gracie, do you remember Miss Emily?" I pulled away from Granny Jane's eyes. I thought I remembered her. Or maybe it was just the smell of her I remembered. The smell of kitchens, food frying, and warm biscuits.

"Yes, sir." I looked up as she gazed down with a smile. A small woman, low to the ground and a bit wide. Her gray hair was loosely piled on the top of her head. She was like a soft cloud you wanted to touch.

Daddy leaned over and gave her cheek a kiss. "Hi Momma." Miss Emily wiped her hands and patted his face.

"Robert. Glad you're here." She looked down at me again. "And glad you're here too, Gracie. Now y'all come in to dinner." I looked back towards the woods.

"That dog of yours'll be just fine. Come on in." Miss Emily led the way, giving me the tour.

For a farmhouse it wasn't large. Just one story with a living room you could walk straight through to a big back porch that ran the entire length of the house.

There were five bedrooms, a large dining room, and kitchen. I glanced around. Where was the bathroom? The excitement of Brown Hound's adventure had worked the Orange Crush straight through me. I entered the dining room and saw a door. I went towards it and Jane warned me away. "That's Granny Jane's."

Easing back over to Daddy I tugged on his shirt. "Where's the bathroom?"

Daddy looked down at me and chuckled. "You don't remember? Well, that's something you're going to have to get used to, Gracie. The bathroom's there." He pointed outside. His eyes laughed and I sank into myself, angry he would tease me on such a hard day. Usually, it was Momma who did that.

Miss Emily walked over and put her hand on my shoulder. "Come to the kitchen, child. I need some help." I followed her, my stomach cramping with the effort of holding it in. Leading me into the kitchen, she stopped at the back door and pointed. I looked up at her and she smiled. "See that little house right there past the chicken coops? That's where we go to the bathroom. We call it the outhouse." She gave me a pat on the shoulder. "Go on. There's nothing there to bite you."

Walking across the dirt-packed backyard, trying not to step on chicken poop, I eyed the outhouse. It was wood, had a door, and a sloping roof and a little chimney. What was that for? It looked too small to have a fireplace. I walked closer and opened the door. There was a wooden box at the back that had a hole in the center. Cautiously I stepped through the door and moved toward the hole. Leaning over, I dared a glance and swiftly jerked back. White toilet paper mixed with black things. So, this really was the bathroom! I couldn't imagine sitting on that nasty, wooden box. But I couldn't go out and pee in the bushes either. They would see me. Momma was right. These people were hicks. I stood for a second then made my decision. I wasn't going to give them anything to laugh at me about, and I wasn't going to give Daddy anything to tease me about. If I was down here with hicks, I would just have to pee like one.

Edging my underpants down to my ankles, I scooted up on the box. I tried not to think about spiders swinging in the dark. The thought made my pee stop. I closed my eyes and concentrated. Brown Hound's bark echoed in the woods. The smell of biscuits from the kitchen drifted in through the crack in the door. I relaxed.

Fried chicken sat heavy in my stomach as I waved goodbye to Daddy. Miss Emily was in the kitchen, Granny Jane had gone to take a nap, and Jane was seeing about the dogs. I guess they wanted to leave me alone with Daddy to say goodbye. They shouldn't have bothered. He couldn't wait to get back to Momma. I'd seen the way he'd fidgeted during dinner, and the way he kept looking at his watch. Momma could reach him even this far into enemy territory. Now he was gone, and I was left on the porch with my two suitcases.

"So, why'd they send you away?" I hadn't heard Jane come back. I opened my mouth. Nothing came out. She continued. "Granny Jane says I'm not supposed to ask. Did you do something bad?"

I shook my head no.

"What? They just up and sent you away? "

I nodded my head. I was too full up to talk about it. And I didn't want Jane to know I'd made Momma sick. She'd never play with me. She put her hands on her hips giving me a funny look. I turned my face and stared out at the front yard. Jane followed my gaze.

"Look at the way she walks." Jane pointed at the colored woman I'd seen earlier. Her shoes didn't seem to touch the ground at all.

"What's wrong with her feet?"

"It's not her feet. It's her drinking." I gave Jane a quick glance, and she continued, "Uncle Will says it's because she's so drunk most of the time she can't feel the ground."

I took that information in and watched the woman glide closer to the house. I lowered my voice. "Why does she drink?"

"Don't know. She just does. And a lot sometimes."

"What's her name?"

"Marcell. She lives down by the tracks."

The woman Daddy didn't want to talk about was colored. I felt a small thrill in my stomach. Marcell glided past the oak tree and headed to the back of the house. As she passed, she avoided our eyes but gave us that kind of side and down glance coloreds were supposed to do when encountering whites. Even children. I felt a shiver up my back and Jane laughed.

"You scared?" I stayed silent. Jane continued, "She can't do a spell like Miss Charity Frazier. And she doesn't have a cane to hit you like Granny Jane."

Taking that in, I ventured a question. "Who is Miss Charity Frazier?" Jane stopped midway picking up a suitcase, pleased at my ignorance.

"She lives in the swamp past the tracks." Jane continued in a low, spooky voice. "She can conjure people." I looked puzzled and she poked me in the arm. "She lays spells on folks," Jane gave a satisfied nod at the widening of my eyes. "And you have to be real careful of her and watch the road."

"Why? Does she drive fast?" I was thinking of Brown Hound.

Jane gave an exasperated sigh. "No. She draws conjures on the road with magic powder. If you step on one, you're dead." She gave a wicked grin. "And Confederate Johnny's on the road too. But only at night and with his face blown half-off, looking to give you the kiss of death." Still grinning, she picked up both suitcases and headed into the house. I followed.

The moon, dulled with the mist of an early Carolina summer, hung in the night sky. Jane was curled in a small ball, the flowered sheet pulled up to her nose. I thought about her. She was nice. Well, not really nice but at least she hadn't made fun of me or called me stupid. And she'd stopped asking why I'd been sent away. I thought back over the day. Jane and I unpacked my suitcase then she showed me the farm, the chicken coops, the barn, and the pasture. The farm dogs showed up with Brown Hound and were introduced as Black Jack and Sassy. Supper had been quiet. Granny Jane, tired by the events of the day, skipped the meal and went to bed. I was glad not to have to eat under her gaze. I kept expecting the mysterious Marcell to come in the dining room, but she didn't make an appearance. I was disappointed. I wanted to figure out why Daddy wouldn't talk about her. Jane chattered about the farm, the fishing hole, and the train tracks.

I sat up in the bed hugging my knees. Granny Jane didn't seem too bad. Well, really, she did. But I thought I could keep away from her. Miss Emily. I liked her. She didn't smother me with kisses or anything, but she was kind.

Marcell. I didn't like the way she'd given me that glance. And then there was something about her Daddy didn't like. And Jane talked about her but didn't really say anything. The woman gave me pause.

Momma. The word bit into me, and I took a quick breath. Daddy was most likely home by now. He hadn't called to say, but then I guess he was too busy getting her ready to go to the place where she'd get better without me around. The words danced in my head, and I turned to look out of the bedside window. Silhouetted against the sky, Brown Hound trotted along, leading Black Jack and Sassy down the dirt road.

Jane made a soft, snoring sound. I closed my eyes and pulled up the sheet.

CHAPTER 3

"Breakfast on."

The words jolted me awake. Heart thumping, I looked around. I was at Miss Emily's farm. I saw Jane's butt sticking up in the air as she snuggled deeper into the mattress.

"Said breakfast on." The deep, flat words came from Marcell. Close up she was dark brown, like the chocolate Momma dribbled on her lace cookies. She gave no sign she'd seen me. "You best get up now, you hear, Jane?" No answer from the mattress, but I nodded yes. Marcell slowly turned her eyes to me. "Dog of yours's a yapper."

Brown Hound! I scrambled across Jane and looked out the window. There, chasing Black Jack and Sassy was Brown Hound. She was only barking because she was having fun. I looked up at Marcell and knew when to keep my mouth shut. She walked out of the room without another word.

"Jane." No response. "Jane!"

"What?" Smothered and grumpy.

"Get up. Marcell said to."

Jane gave me the evil eye then climbed out of bed to begin the day.

Breakfast was in the kitchen. The heavy wood table with its plastic green and white checkered tablecloth was a far cry from Momma's kitchen table. Breakfast was a far cry, too. Instead of frosted flakes and milk, there was bacon, eggs, and biscuits. Biscuits you could hold up in the air and they'd float back down one thin layer at a time. I watched in fascination as Jane did this, then I cautiously followed suit.

"Girls, I need some help out at the chicken coop. I thought I'd make a nice pot of soup for supper," Miss Emily said.

I slipped from the chair and took my plate to the sink. "Breakfast was good." Miss Emily smiled and dropped a soapy hand on the top of my head. I stood still. It felt fine. We helped cleaning up and then Miss Emily led us out to the yard.

"Gracie, your daddy says you're a real good helper. Now I know this is just your first full day, but it's time to start seeing how things are done around here. You and Jane go on in the pen and get me a chicken."

Get me a chicken? I looked at Jane. She closed her eyes. I looked up. Marcell stood silently. Miss Emily walked to the pen, opened the door, and pointed.

"That biddy over in the corner. The one with the red feathers."

We stepped into the pen and stood still. Momma bought chicken at the store and cooked it up. It was good, but it was never an animal.

"Jane, show Gracie how to do it. Go on now, I don't have all day."

Jane moved toward the chicken. I followed behind for protection. What if it bit me? What if it flew up in the air and landed on my head and clawed my eyes out? I edged closer to Jane for cover. She stepped back and tripped on me. Grabbing at each other, we fell into a heap, arms and legs flailing. The biddy bolted by us to the other side of the pen. We heard Miss Emily sigh. Not wanting to disappoint her, I jumped up and ran after the chicken. Jane followed. We closed in as it flew over top of us. We squatted covering our heads.

"Stand up!" Marcell said.

We leapt to our feet. She walked into the pen. Going over to the biddy, she clucked and scattered grain. When it started eating, she picked it up by the neck. I stood there astonished. Jane gave a groan as Marcell headed out of the pen and over to a big stump with a hatchet buried in its side. The biddy hung from Marcell's hand.

"Miss Emily, say you need to learn this."

I pulled my eyes from the hatchet and saw Miss Emily walking back to the kitchen, her mind already on other things.

"You put the head here," Marcell placed the biddy's head on the stump, "and you hold the body down here." The chicken was stretched over the stump and flapping.

"Pull the hatchet," Marcell directed.

Jane's hands were behind her back. Silently and with great stealth, she'd backed a step or two away. Marcell looked up from the biddy and fixed her eyes on me. A sudden thought held me steady. Maybe if I did this, she would like me and then wouldn't say anything to Miss Emily about Brown Hound's yapping. I looked down at the biddy. It had stopped flapping and was clucking.

I reached out and grabbed the hatchet. I pulled. My hands slipped. I stumbled back then gathered myself and approached again. I pulled harder. The look in Marcell's eyes gave me strength. The hatchet yanked free.

Marcell nodded down to the chicken. "Go on."

I looked down. The biddy had gone still. A small crooning sound came from its throat. I held the hatchet and swallowed. My head hurt and I felt sweat beneath my undershirt. I couldn't. I had to. My hand shook.

"Marcell!" Miss Emily's voice cut through the air. "Marcell, you want to lose a finger?" Miss Emily hurried down the porch steps drying her hands on her apron. "Gracie doesn't know a thing about hacking the head off a chicken."

"Should learn," Marcell muttered. Then louder, "You said she needed to start helping out."

"Yes, but not by chopping a chicken head off the first day! Jane doesn't even do that."

Miss Emily was beside me now and lifted the hatchet from my grip. "Here, give me that." And without so much as another word she turned and gave the chicken a mighty whack. And off flew its head.

"Oops." Marcell let go of the biddy and it fell off

the stump. Leaping to its feet, it began to run, without its head. I gagged. Jane giggled. Miss Emily gave a sigh. Marcell moseyed after it as it ran in circles. My stomach flipped again. But then true horror. Flying around the corner of the house roused by the commotion came Brown Hound, Black Jack and Sassy, their eyes latched on the running biddy.

Marcell's voice rang through the air. "No!"

The farm dogs skidded to a stop, twirling and yelping. They knew that voice. They knew what it meant. But Brown Hound didn't. Still at a full run she swept by us, grabbed up the biddy, and flew out towards the barn. I froze. Jane clapped her hands over her mouth.

"Kill that dog." Marcell turned and started toward the barn.

Howling, I jumped into the air and made a grab at her. She side stepped. I went after her again.

"Stop!" Miss Emily yelled. I teetered back and forth on my feet; eyes glued to Marcell's back. "Marcell, you too."

Marcell stopped, keeping her back to us for a moment then spoke, "Dog gets a taste of chicken, never stops killing."

"She didn't kill anything. The chicken was already dead." I was frantic.

"Don't matter. Taste is what does it." With that Marcell continued toward the barn.

Miss Emily spoke to Marcel's back, "Marcell, I'll take care of this. You go on and get us another chicken for tonight."

"Yes, ma'am." Turning and walking past us like we didn't exist, Marcell headed back to the chicken pen.

Kill Brown Hound? Momma had yelled at her and beat her but never tried to kill her. I turned and faced Miss Emily. Had Marcell already told her Brown Hound was a yapper? Part of me strained toward the barn and my dog, and part wanted to stay and beg. Miss Emily watched Marcell grab another chicken and chop off its head. She didn't drop it on the ground this time.

"You pluck the feathers. I'll be along directly," said Miss Emily.

Marcell moved past us like we were smoke. Miss Emily watched her for a few minutes then turned her gaze down to me. I felt a movement at my back. Jane was edging out of firing range.

"Gracie, dogs are hard to break once they get a taste for chicken."

I nodded my head in misery and waited.

"If you want to keep her, we have to get the biddy away from her and show her it was a bad thing to do. You come on with me now."

Jane followed as we walked to the barn. My stomach hurt, but at least Marcell wasn't gonna kill Brown Hound. I smoothed my shirt with sweaty palms and kept pace with Miss Emily.

Pushing the heavy barn door open, my grandmother walked inside. Brown Hound was happily tearing bits from the biddy's stomach. Miss Emily walked over to a big wood box, leaned in, and picked up a riding whip.

Jane was behind me whispering. "It's what they use with the mules. Looks worse than it is." I started forward, but she grabbed the back of my shirt. "Shhh."

Miss Emily walked over and put her foot on the biddy. Placing the solid end of the whip on Brown Hound's throat she pressed in, pushing the dog away. Brown Hound looked up bewildered.

I started pleading, "See, she doesn't know any better. She doesn't know she was wrong."

Jane gave my waistband a fierce yank and the breath shot out of me. I struggled but Jane held firm. Miss Emily kicked the chicken to the other side of the room then let up on the whip. Brown Hound made a dash for the biddy and the whip snapped though the air. I felt my skin burn. Yelping filled the barn. My knees gave way, but Jane held me up by my shorts. Brown Hound whirled around, licked at her back, then went for the chicken again. The whip snapped. Jane let go. I fell to a heap then scrambled up and forward. She stuck out her foot. I tripped and fell. Jane dropped down beside me clamping her arms around me holding me still.

"Quicker she learns, less she'll get the whip, either that or they'll kill her," she whispered.

I shut my mouth and shrank as the whip cracked once more through the air. Sounds floated through the barn: my gasping, Brown Hound's yelping,

Miss Emily's hard breathing, Jane's whispered words.

Suddenly, there was silence. Brown Hound stood in the middle of the barn quivering. Miss Emily walked over to the biddy and kicked it toward the dog. Brown Hound backed away. I held my breath. Miss Emily did it again. The dog crouched back once more. She kicked it a third time. Brown Hound backed against the far wall and whined.

"That'll do. Jane, get the biddy and put her down the outhouse." Walking over to me, Miss Emily tried to put a hand on my head, but I shrank away. She leaned lower, made contact, and said, "Your dog'll be fine." She put the whip back in the box and walked out of the barn.

I jumped up and ran to Brown Hound. She yelped when I tried to hug her and wiggled away. I sat still for a moment. What if she thought I was part of the whipping? The idea made my heart hurt. After all, I brought her down here. If it wasn't for me making Momma sick, we would be up in Virginia safe on the picnic table.

Jane crouched beside me giving instructions. "You're hurting her. Don't hug her, it pulls the cuts. Miss Emily's got some salve. Let's fix her up."

Jane went to a cabinet and got supplies. Kneeling beside Brown Hound, we talked to her, telling her what we were doing as we gently smeared the salve on her cuts. She looked me right in the eye, and I knew then she didn't think it was my fault. Jane held her still while I wrapped long strips of cloth around her. The bandages wouldn't stay on long, but it made us feel like we'd done something for her. She strained away from us, and we let her go. Trotting out of the barn, Brown Hound ignored the biddy on the floorboards. Jane picked it up and headed for the outhouse, swinging the chicken by its feet as she went.

The next day Jane and I sat on top of Old Man Bob Ridley's grave across from the house. The cement hump rose about three feet out of the ground and made a fine place for an argument.

"She's mean."

"No, she's not. That's just the way she is."

"She wanted to kill Brown Hound."

"Well, Brown Hound tried to eat the biddy. Lots of dogs are shot for that."

I could see Jane wanted to push the conversation away from Marcell, but I wanted it to stay there. I wanted to pick at it like a sore. Yesterday's beating still stung as if it'd been me who stole the chicken.

"She hates me."

Jane gave a sigh, "No, she doesn't. Most likely she doesn't even think about you at all."

"Then why does she give me that look every time she walks by?"

"She's only walked by you a couple of times. And anyway, she gives everybody that look."

"Everybody? Even her momma and daddy?"

Jane hopped off the grave and faced me. "Her momma died when she was born, and her daddy died when she was a kid," Jane said. "Look, are we gonna do something today or sit around talking about Marcell?"

That's just what I wanted to do. Talk about Marcell. Talk about why she could speak sharp to Miss Emily and not get yelled at. Talk about why my daddy avoided mention of her. Talk about how she didn't like Brown Hound because she was a yapper. And she didn't like me because Miss Emily fussed at her about the chicken.

I didn't know a lot about colored people. Mamma never let me get too near one except for Mamie who cleaned our house. One day when I was little, I picked up some gum Mamie had parked on the counter during her lunch. Mamma shrieked when she saw me chewing it. My mouth burned for days from the soap scrubbing. I knew then something must be wrong with colored people but didn't know what. And now one was gunning for my dog.

Miss Emily calling from the porch broke into my thoughts. She waved us back and we walked to the house.

"I just heard from Miss Victoria Simmons. Her handyman has taken sick and is over in Jones County Hospital. He's going to be there for a spell, and Miss Victoria has some chores for you girls to do."

"For money?" Jane eyed her grandmother.

"Shouldn't you do it as a Christian?"

"Not for old Miss Victoria!"

Miss Emily laughed. "She said she would give you some compensation."

Jane smiled and gave me the 'let's get out of here' look. We did.

Walking down the dusty road to the old woman's house, Jane explained the rules of the day. I was going to mow, and she was going to supervise. I kept silent while the rest of the summer played out in my head. Jane giving orders and me doing all the work. I didn't like it one bit. Suddenly, a thought came to my rescue. Miss Emily hadn't sent me back to Virginia because my dog grabbed the chicken. I felt a small flame of courage, took a deep breath, and said, "I'll tell Miss Emily if you make me do it alone."

Jane gave me a glare. I could see her struggle with it then let it go. Her attempt to push me around had been half-hearted at best. She punched me in the arm, and we walked on.

Hours later, sweating, dusty, and mad at what Miss Victoria had given to us as compensation, we walked back to the farm. Spying Granny Jane sleeping in her rocker we tried to silently slip by.

"Come up here." She hadn't been dozing after all. Slowly Jane and I walked up the steps.

"What's in that basket?" Granny Jane leaned over and looked. There, hiding as best he could, was our compensation. A foot-tied chicken rooster. "Miss Victoria gave you this?"

We nodded our heads in misery. We'd wanted money for comic books. Granny Jane grabbed him up by the neck and gave him a look.

"He's cockeyed!"

Jane and I began to twitch. We'd examined the rooster on the way home and already knew.

"Untie his feet. See if he can walk."

We did, but the rooster just sat. I picked him up and rubbed his legs. He stood for a minute and swayed back and forth.

"Looks like Marcell after she's been drinking," Jane said.

Granny Jane shot a look, and Jane snapped her mouth shut. The rooster refused to walk. Granny Jane cracked her cane on the porch railing. He didn't move. I feared for his life. She pulled herself out of her rocker. "Take him out back. We'll see if he can do his business."

At the chicken pen, Granny Jane waited while Jane stepped through the door and set the rooster down. He stood and swayed. Suddenly a sassy looking biddy skirted past. The rooster straightened up and started after her. Sideways. He cocked his head to the side, twisted it up and moved his feet one over top of the other, sidestepping as fast as he could. All three of us hollered with laughter. The rooster was stepping sideways just fine but taking corners bad. The biddy turned to the right and the hopeful rooster went tail feathers up and beak down. Jane and I fell on the ground howling.

"What's this noise?" Miss Emily came down the steps smiling followed by Marcell. Granny Jane wiped her eyes. Jane and I continued rolling on the ground. All three of us pointed at the chicken pen. The rooster recovered and was once again in hot pursuit. Everyone was laughing. Even Marcell. It was the first time I'd seen her do anything but frown.

Jane jumped up, wiped the dirt from her legs and explained, "Miss Victoria Simmons gave him to us for cutting her grass."

The laughter died and I saw a look pass between Miss Emily and Granny Jane. It was one of those adult looks. Jane missed it completely. I jumped to my feet.

Marcell began to turn away, but Jane grabbed her arm. "Look Marcell, watch him. He's gonna go butt up again!" Her words ended sharply as Marcell shook her off. Jane stumbled back and almost fell. I caught her arm and steadied her. Without a word, Marcell walked back to the house. Jane stood still for a minute rubbing her elbow then drew in on herself. I tried to pretend I wasn't there.

"You girls certainly have yourselves a prize there," Miss Emily said, picking up the thread.

Jane and I nodded and kept our eyes on the rooster. Granny Jane turned without a word and made her way back to her rocker on the front porch.

Miss Emily walked over to Jane and stroked her hair. "Come on now. Why don't you and Gracie go get me some of that wild asparagus growing down by the tracks?"

Jane nodded without a word and walked away. I followed but kept my mouth shut. I watched Jane work, trying to learn how to snap the stems without asking. Jane seemed to be snapping stems harder than she needed to. A cloud scuttled over the sun and the late afternoon became still. Jane straightened up.

"I thought it was you that Marcell didn't like," Jane said. She turned back to picking.

CHAPTER 4

"Gracie?" Miss Emily called, checking on me.

"Ma'am?" I was sitting in the kitchen with Jane eating breakfast. The day was as calm as the past few days had been. Brown Hound had settled in and wasn't yapping with excitement. And Miss Emily hadn't asked for help catching chickens for dinner. If Jane would only perk up, life would be fine.

I watched as Jane went out to the yard and started scattering grain in the chicken pen. The chore had fallen to her since Marcell wasn't around. She'd been gone for a couple of days, right after she'd pushed Jane. Nobody talked about it, and I didn't ask. The older women went on like nothing was unusual. Jane kept to herself. I kept to Brown Hound.

In between chores of setting table for each meal, hanging laundry, and sweeping the house, I sat under the tree in the front yard with my dog. It was like sitting on the picnic table at home except there wasn't anybody yelling at me. I looked at Brown Hound. She was fine and loving her life. She'd learned the lay of the land and seemed destined to be the queen of the yard dogs, bossing both Black Jack and Sassy when the mood took her. The wounds from her whipping had healed, and you could only see one or two ruffles in her fur where she'd been hit. I thought back to Marcell saying my dog needed killing. I was happy she wasn't around even if we did have to do extra chores. And then there was the way she had pushed Jane.

Brown Hound gave a low growl and I looked towards the road. Trudging down the dusty lane had to be the infamous Miss Charity Frazier. I bet she'd been drawing a conjure on the road so someone would die. I held on to my dog while the colored woman headed toward the tracks. I buried my nose into Brown Hound's fur, smelling the wonderful doggy smell. I wished Jane had something to make her feel better like I had Brown Hound. I looked up and saw Miss Charity disappear into the swamp. Suddenly I reared back and looked into Brown Hound's eyes. She looked back.

What if Miss Charity Frazier had a spell that could make Jane feel better? What if I could help make Jane happy again? The thought scared me. Then excited me. I took a deep breath and kissed Brown Hound on the tip of her nose. She sneezed.

I started to wipe my face when a sudden thought made me go still. What about getting Miss Charity to put a curse on Marcell instead. A shiver of warning climbed up my spine. Spells sometimes ricocheted back. I didn't want that. But if a spell for Jane came back on me, it was just to make her happy. I thought back to our conversation one night when Jane explained where Miss Charity lived. It was down the tracks, over the trestle, into the swamp and along a path with blue conjure bottles. It couldn't be that hard to find. Wiping my face, I got up and told Brown Hound to wait. I headed to my room. Daddy had given me some spending money. I scooped it into my pocket. I had no idea what a spell cost but figured I'd take it all.

Jane had finished with the chickens and was down at the barn. Granny Jane was over at the graveyard having a visit with her husband James Earl.

Nonchalantly, I eased out of the back door, peeked around the front of the house, and softly called Brown Hound. Giving her a pat on the head to follow, I headed to the train tracks. Glancing back to check that no one was looking, I high tailed it, down the tracks, over the trestle and down into the swamp. I leaned over, hands on my knees, catching my breath as much from daring as running. Brown Hound danced, ready for adventure. I could barely believe I was doing this. I'd never been this brave before, but my anger at Marcell pushing Jane was driving me hard. The look on Jane's face when it happened was like how Momma made me feel. Jane was keeping to herself like I did on the picnic table. And Jane didn't have Brown Hound to make her feel better. I took a deep breath and started forward.

The path to Miss Charity's was marked by the blue bottles hanging beside carvings on trees. I stopped to look at each one. A shiver went up my back. One was two stick figures, a man and a woman. Another showed a cross and a star. I walked a few more feet and saw three blue bottles making a triangle on the ground. I swung wide past these. The trees closed in, and it felt like the sun was hiding from me. Brown Hound gave a yip and nosed at some small bones arranged on a patch of moss. Another blue bottle sat at the end of it like a headstone.

Too soon, there was Miss Charity's cabin. It was old and saggy, made from all sizes of dark, dingy boards. A big black pot sat in the front yard with a fire under it. The contents were boiling, and steam was rising. I didn't want to know what was in that pot. Suddenly the door flew open. Out walked Miss Charity Frazier. Three hundred pounds and the color of midnight. She walked down the porch steps and over to the steaming pot. Picking up the ladle, she started stirring. "What you want?"

"Well, Miss Charity, I'm Gracie."

"I know who you is. What you want?"

She knew my name! I couldn't speak. I grabbed Brown Hound by her collar for safety. She tried to pull away and I gave her a yank. Sensing my fear, she gave a small whine and sat. I gathered my courage.

"I want a spell." The words came out too soft, and I had to repeat them.

"Uh huh. On who? That dog?"

"No! Not her. Not on anyone, but for anyone." I was scared and not making sense.

"Jane then."

I was stunned. She'd read my mind. She'd been teasing about my dog. She was a conjure woman for sure if she knew about Jane. I nodded my head.

"You want her sick?"

I jabbered, scared she might cast the spell before I could clear things up. "No. Not sick. See. Marcell pushed her and she's sad."

"Then you want Marcell sick?"

I gasped, "No!"

Miss Charity nodded her head. "She plenty sick enough."

I looked at her blankly.

"Corn liquor."

"Oh." I didn't know what to say.

"Easing pain. Dead momma, dead daddy. Wants to be with ghosts 'stead of live folks."

I didn't care. I pushed Marcell from my thoughts. It was Jane I was worried about. "Please. Can you make Jane happy again?"

Miss Charity held out her hand. Making sure Brown Hound stayed put, I eased forward and put two quarters into her palm. Nodding, she dropped the money in her apron pocket and began stirring the pot. She started mumbling and began to sway. I backed up a step then another making sure Brown Hound stayed behind me. She mumbled and swayed some more. Suddenly, the air went still. She drew a small vial of white powder from beneath her apron.

Walking over to an old cypress tree, she crouched and picked up a stick. Brown Hound started forward at the sign of a game, and I lunged after her, throwing my body onto hers. She squatted to a stop and looked back at me like I'd lost my mind. I put my arms around her, and we both stayed low. Ignoring us, Miss

Charity drew a large circle in the dirt then stood in it. She chanted. She stepped out of the circle and drew lines inside of it. Dropping the stick, she uncorked the bottle and marked the lines with magic white powder. I clung to my dog for dear life.

"She be better now." Miss Charity turned and walked past me, up the steps of her cabin and shut the door. Brown Hound wiggled from under me. Cautiously, I stood and dusted off my shorts. What had I done? I'd had a spell put on Jane. It was a good thing to want to make someone happy, wasn't it? Brown Hound whined and I agreed. Quickly we turned and ran from the clearing. I moved fast through the swamp and Brown Hound followed, not even stopping at the chicken bones.

We made it safely back to the backyard and I started breathing easy. I wondered when Jane would perk up. I didn't go looking for her, afraid I might disturb the working of the spell.

"Gracie?" It was Miss Emily calling from inside the house.

"Ma'am?"

"Gracie, your daddy's on the phone."

Jumping over Brown Hound, I ran to the porch and up the steps. Daddy was on the phone, and nothing mattered but talking to him. Racing into the living room, I screeched to a halt then shifted from foot to foot with impatience.

"She's doing just fine. And so is that dog of hers."

My heart sang at the words. We were fine. The dog was good. We were doing all right. Miss Emily handed the receiver to me.

"Hi, Daddy."

"Gracie, your grandmother says you're doing good."

"Yes, sir." I wanted to tell him about Marcell, Jane, Miss Charity, and the chicken rooster, but he interrupted.

"Your mother is doing good, too." I tried to speak, but he kept talking. "Seems like the rest has done wonders for her."

The knot came back in my stomach. I hadn't even realized it had gone. But it must have because now it was back and biting.

"In fact, the doctor says she is doing so good she might come home next week."

The knot bit deeper. I was doing good too.

"I know you're glad to hear that, aren't you?"

"Yes, sir."

"Since you're getting along so well, I think we'll let you stay down there a bit longer. When your mother comes home, she's going to need peace and quiet."

And me not around to make her sick.

"Gracie, you there?"

"Yes, Daddy. I'm glad she's better."

"That's my girl. Tell the rest of the folks I said hello. I'll call once your momma's home."

"Ok, Daddy. Bye."

I placed the receiver in the cradle and stood

in the middle of the room. Miss Emily gave me a look. I gave her a bright smile. "Momma's better."

"Well, that's real nice."

"Yes, ma'am. Daddy wants me to stay here a while longer."

A soft hand came to rest lightly on the top of my head. "We're glad to have you here, Gracie. We'd like you to stay as long as you can."

"Marcell doesn't want that." The words were out before I knew it.

"Gracie that's not true."

How could I tell Miss Emily she was wrong? Marcell did all the chores for her, and I was just an added burden. I'd come out on the short end of that stick, but I couldn't help it. "I think she hates me!"

Miss Emily looked down at me. I waited for her to yell. Or even worse, laugh. Instead, she gave a heavy sigh and spoke, "Gracie, she does not hate you." The words were evenly spaced like she was talking to a baby.

"Well, why does she look at me like that and fuss about my dog? She wanted to kill Brown Hound."

I could see Miss Emily struggle for an answer. She closed her eyes, then opened them and said, "Marcell hates dogs."

"She doesn't hate Black Jack and Sassy."

"They mind her and stay out of her way."

I thought back to the headless biddy. But I still wanted to know. "Why does she hate dogs?"

"You're here with our family now Gracie, and we're happy to have you. But they're some things that don't need to be talked about. You go on out to the porch and sit with Miss Jane. She's just come back from the graveyard so don't you bother her with this." The words were final. There was no room for discussion.

I walked out onto the porch. Granny Jane rocked in her chair, smoking her pipe, her eyes narrowed against the afternoon sun.

"Was your daddy on the phone?"

"Yes, ma'am. He says Momma's better."

Granny Jane stopped rocking and pointed the pipe stem at me. "That woman won't ever get better." Nodding for emphasis, she put the pipe back into her mouth and began rocking. I ran down the steps to find my dog.

CHAPTER 5

"Breakfast on."

The familiar words jolted me awake. Marcell. I sat straight up, and we came face to face. She stood quietly at the foot of the bed. I slid my foot over and poked Jane.

"Y'all get up now. Miss Emily's expecting you to set table. Don't want to be late for church."

With that, she walked out of the bedroom just like she hadn't been gone for days. Just like she'd never pushed Jane. I pressed my teeth together. I'd had a bad night. Granny Jane's words played over and over in my head, "That woman won't ever get better." Did she mean Momma wouldn't get better because I would always be around? And now Marcell was back. I wasn't going to let her mess with me, Jane, or my dog. After facing Miss Charity, I felt ready for battle.

"Jane. Wake up. That was Marcell."

Jane sat up irritably. "I know who it was."

"She's back."

"I know she's back. Shut up."

I wondered if my quarters had been wasted. Jane was still grumpy. Maybe Miss Charity's spell wasn't working after all. Silently, I bunched up my fists.

I wanted to poke Marcell in the nose but knew I never would. It just felt better to think about it.

"Girls." It was Miss Emily calling and time to get a move on. Throwing on our Sunday dresses, we dashed to the kitchen to help with breakfast.

"Running late. We're running late!" Miss Emily said as she fussed, rushing us through" the meal.

"Ease down. The Lord'll wait." Granny Jane sat at the table with us.

"Yes, but the preacher won't," Miss Emily snapped.

I was amazed. Miss Emily almost never snapped. Jane and I finished eating in record time and rinsed the dishes.

Out front, Uncle Will and Aunt Viola sat in their 1948 blue Plymouth. Granny Jane had explained who they were during one of our lazy afternoons on the porch.

"You'll be meeting your aunts and uncles soon," she had said. "So you'd best learn how they fit." She'd hauled herself up out of her rocking chair and gone down the porch steps to the dirt driveway. Making marks in the dust with her cane, she explained who was who.

"After I inherited the farm, I married James Earl and we had two boys, Carl and Tom. Carl died in the 1900 flood along with James Earl, and that left just Tom and me. Tom later married Emily and they are your grandparents. They had two children, Robert and Sally. Robert of course is your daddy. Sally married Dave and they had Jane, who is your cousin. Sally and

Dave died in that terrible car crash."

"Who are the aunts and uncles?"

Granny Jane made more marks with her stick. "You know my sister Evelyn had two daughters named Grace and Sarah. Grace passed before she had children, but Sarah married and had your aunts, Viola and Martha." The old woman paused to give a chuckle. "Those two couldn't be more different. Viola married your Uncle Will and Martha married your Uncle Ben."

"Did Aunt Viola and Aunt Martha have babies? Do Jane and I have cousins from them?"

"Viola had a baby named Bess who died, but Martha never had children. So no, no children on that side. You and Jane are doing just fine for all of us."

Jane's voice yanked me back from remembering. "Let's go!" Bolting from the house, she jumped in first to claim the window seat.

"Ladies behave yourself."

Sitting in front beside Uncle Will was Aunt Viola. It was my first look at her, and I didn't like what I saw. She had a thin nose pointed in the air like she smelled something bad. Tight, brown curls swirled all over her head. I bet she thought she was cute. But what wasn't cute was a small, nasty looking dog squirming in her arms. It snarled and bit the air.

"There, there, Miss Garson," Aunt Viola crooned to the rat-tailed thing. I looked at Jane and she crossed her eyes. I clamped my mouth and tried not to laugh. Miss Emily slid into the back seat with us.

"Viola, you remember Robert and Sissy's girl, Gracie?"

Aunt Viola turned, gave me a look, and smiled. I didn't like her teeth. They looked like she stole them from the mules out back.

"Hello, Aunt Viola." I was my most polite. She was unknown territory. I kept a close eye on those teeth. They made me uneasy.

"Scoot over, Viola. You keep a grip on that dog." Granny Jane commanded. Uncle Will jumped out, ran around to the other side of the car, and helped Granny Jane aboard. I wondered what she thought of Aunt Viola's teeth, but knew I'd never ask. Shutting the door, Uncle Will turned, and bending down looked into the back seat.

"Howdy Miss. You sure have the look of your mother."

I gave a smile to Uncle Will. He seemed nice enough. He was tall like my daddy, but it stopped there. His bald head gleamed, and he had a big round belly that looked like it was held up by his suspenders. His face was round, too. Smiling back, he got into the car. We were off to church.

Jane and I pushed each other trying to look out the window, and Miss Emily gave us a look. I settled down and Jane won.

"Heard Marcell flat tied one on this past week."

"Now Viola maybe you shouldn't bring that up." Uncle Will watched the road as he spoke. Miss Garson squirmed and snarled. Granny Jane glared at it. I bet she wanted to hit it with her cane.

"And just why can't I say that?" Aunt Viola twisted around to the back of the car.

"Listen here, Emily She's getting worse, and you know it. I don't know why you keep her around. She drinks something awful. My friends in the Dorcas church class were just saying this week how Marcell's carrying on is a bad influence on Jane. It's the scandal of the county."

"I reckon there're a few things a bit more scandalous, Viola." Granny Jane's words flattened on the windshield.

Aunt Viola whipped around to the front and stared straight ahead; her face flushed. Granny Jane's comment put a clamp on the conversation. It set me to wondering. Granny Jane didn't put up with foolishness from anybody, but here she was turning the conversation away from Marcell. I sank back into the seat thinking. Why? Did Marcell have something on her? Maybe Granny Jane had killed somebody. Marcell knew and was holding it over her head. Seemed unlikely.

Aunt Viola's next words interrupted my thoughts. "Emily, I know you feel guilty about Marcell's father, but it wasn't your or Tom's fault. Everyone knows the family did their best to protect Ivis. The whole thing was old man Elroy Simmons' doing."

Granny Jane's voice was firm. "Viola. There are young ears here. We all have our reasons for doing what we do, and I don't care how much the county clacks its teeth about us."

I wondered if she said the teeth thing for

meanness or if Aunt Viola's teeth were so much of a presence that they just slipped into Granny Jane's mind. I gave Jane a questioning look, and she shrugged her shoulders then stared back out of the window. Marcell wasn't her favorite topic right now.

At church Jane and I tumbled out of the car. Uncle Will helped Granny Jane, and Aunt Viola took her time instructing a small colored boy about the care of Miss Garson.

I was glad Daddy packed my good Sunday dress. Miss Emily introduced me to more people than I could count. I shook hands and smiled when they said I looked just like Momma. I was tired by the time we slid into the pew. Granny Jane first, then Miss Emily and Jane, followed by Uncle Will, then me. I looked around for Aunt Viola. I saw her come out of the side door by the pulpit, walking like best friends with Miss Beulavine Simms. A self-satisfied smile framed those fearsome teeth as she made her way to the pew and slipped in. Miss Beulavine sat in front of us. Aunt Viola smoothed her dress over her knees and picked up the hymnal.

It was just like my church except there were a lot more colored people up in the balcony fanning themselves against the rising heat. Once the hymns had been sung, the money collected and announcements made, we settled down for the sermon.

Preacher Hollins began, "My message today was one that came to me as a gift just now, from two ladies of our flock. Proverbs Chapter 23 Verse 19 and

20." People turned to look at Aunt Viola and Miss Beulavine, then picked up their Bibles.

The preacher quoted, "Hear thou, my son, and be wise, and guide thine heart in the way. Be not among the winebibbers."

Electricity cracked down the pew arcing from Granny Jane smack onto Aunt Viola. I shrank back against the seat amazed my aunt hadn't gone up in flames. Miss Emily gave a slight cough. Uncle Will stared straight ahead. Jane's eyes danced for the first time in days.

Aunt Viola looked expectantly at the pulpit. I dared not glance at Granny Jane. I didn't want to be fried.

The preacher continued, "If we harbor these sinners, give comfort and aid to the winebibbers, are we not as bad as they?"

I craned my neck and casually looked at the congregation. I could see women's hats bobbing up and down in agreement and men leaning over, whispering to each other.

The preacher saw the congregation in agreement with him and said, "Proverbs asks us 'Who hath woe? Who hath sorrow? Who hath redness of eyes?'"

Jane leaned over Uncle Will and mouthed "Marcell" to me, and I stifled a laugh. Maybe Miss Charity's spell was working after all. Aunt Viola's bony hand reached, out grabbed my shoulder, and yanked me back. My head whacked the pew. It hurt. I was just glad she hadn't used her teeth.

Words thundered from the pulpit. "You know who takes deadly liquor into their bodies. You know who suffers from losing friends and families," his voice lowered dramatically, "and their Lord."

Miss Beulavine turned around and gave a nod of satisfaction to Aunt Viola. I thought Granny Jane was going to leap up and land on her like an avenging angel coming home to glory. I shivered with excitement. The preacher looked like he was just getting warmed up.

"And we know what happens when others enable these lost souls drowning in drink. They are as much sinners as those lost in the depths of drink." I waited for him to point his finger directly at Granny Jane. I snaked my hands up to my ears in case of explosion.

More heads began to nod in agreement. A slight murmur came from the balcony, and I tried to turn and look. Aunt Viola's bony hand hovered. I faced forward.

"Yes, friends. Proverbs says drink biteth like a serpent, and stingeth like an adder."

Jane leaned past Uncle Will again and bared her teeth like fangs. I snorted, jammed my hands over my mouth, and smashed myself against the pew before Aunt Viola could. But she wasn't paying me any mind. She was gazing up at the pulpit with a satisfied smile.

"I end my message today with the words of James from the New Testament. 'Blessed is the man that endureth temptation: for when he is tried, he shall receive the crown of life."

"Amen!" Aunt Viola said loudly. With her eyes closed and tears sliding down her cheeks, she looked like she was in a rapture. I inched away from her. The choir burst into "Nearer My God To Thee." In the shuffle to stand and open hymnals, I slipped by Uncle Will and stood next to Jane. I leaned over and tried to get a glimpse of Granny Jane.

"Are you crazy?" Jane hissed and yanked me back. By this time the back of my dress had a permanent pucker. I straightened up and sang along. After the first verse, Uncle Will leaned past Jane and me and spoke to Miss Emily.

"Emily? Viola is a bit overcome. I'm going to take her out before the doxology and get her on home."

"That's fine, Will," Miss Emily said. "We'll get a ride with the Franklins. You two go on now."

Jane and I looked at each other in vast disappointment. We were waiting for Granny Jane to fry Aunt Viola. And here Uncle Will was leading her out of the line of fire.

"Bless be the tie that binds our hearts in Christian love." The doxology was being sung and people were moving out of their pews. Miss Beulavine turned to pay her respects to Miss Emily and Granny Jane. I thought the woman must have complete faith in the protection of the Lord.

"Emily, a fine sermon."

Miss Emily just smiled and raised her chin. I guess that was her way of an insult. Miss Beulavine turned her words to Granny Jane, "Miss Jane."

Granny Jane nodded back, "Beulavine. And how is that niece of yours doing?"

Miss Beulavine smiled. "Linda Mae is doing fine. She's due next month."

Granny Jane interrupted without seeming to. "Emily and I have been talking and we would be delighted to host a baby shower for her."

Miss Emily's mouth dropped open. Granny Jane stood leaning on her cane; eyes boring into Miss Beulavine. Jane and I looked at each other in astonishment. Not only had Granny Jane not launched herself at Miss Beulavine, but she was also offering to host a party for the woman's niece.

"Well, Miss Jane, that's mighty nice of you but, I don't think…"

"It's settled then. I'll tell those I see before we leave today. We'll plan on next Saturday at two. You can help Emily with the calls." Granny Jane pushed a frozen Miss Emily out of the pew. Jane and I scampered behind not wanting to miss a thing. Miss Beulavine just stood there. She'd been bushwhacked by the person who protected the winebibber and was trying to figure out her injuries.

It was an astonishing spectacle. Granny Jane smiling as she walked down the aisle, nodding to people and telling ladies about the forthcoming baby shower. Miss Emily moved silently behind her. Jane and I lagged a ways back since there wasn't going to be bloodshed.

I asked Jane, "So Granny Jane is gonna make

people who are talking about Marcell come to that girl's shower right?"

"Yep."

"Jane, come here." Miss Beulavine looked like she'd recovered. The woman put her hand on Jane's shoulder.

"You're growing into quite the young lady. Seems a shame to keep you where you have to be exposed to Marcell and her drinking." Miss Beulavine reached out with her other hand to smooth Jane's hair. I wanted to swat it away but held still. "You know your Aunt Viola would just love to have you come live with her."

Jane looked like a frog flattened on the road. Miss Beulavine continued.

"And it's about time to give Miss Jane and Miss Emily a rest. They've had you on their hands since you were a baby. Never had any choice. I bet they're getting tired."

"Jane. Gracie." Granny Jane's voice cracked down the aisle. Jane yanked away from Miss Beulavine. I followed right behind. Granny Jane and her cane were safety for sure. We didn't look back to see if the fat woman was following.

The ride home with the Franklins was quiet with very little discussion about the sermon. Dinner was the same. We helped Miss Emily since Sunday afternoon was Marcell's time off. After that, we peeled out of our Sunday dresses. I hopped on the bed and sat Indian fashion. Jane curled her legs under her and waited for me to start.

"Miss Beulavine looked like she was gonna eat you for Sunday dinner." I was trying for a laugh.

"It's none of her business where I live. She doesn't have a say about me." Jane snapped.

I nodded my head up and down firmly. No way would Jane ever have to leave the farm. Not like me leaving Virginia. I pushed the last thought down far and waited.

"Here's what I think," Jane said. "Granny Jane was nice at church so she could get everybody who's upset about Marcell's drinking to come to the house. Then she's gonna do something."

"What?" I couldn't see Granny Jane smacking Aunt Viola with her cane although I'd sure like to.

"I don't know. But something."

Granny Jane's voice floated into the bedroom as she headed to the back of the house, "Emily, you in the kitchen?"

Jane gave me a look, and we were off the bed like a shot. Quietly easing out the front door, we carefully circled the house, and reached the back kitchen window. We looked at each other and gave a sigh. If they were talking, we couldn't hear.

Silently scrounging under the house, we found an old box and carefully moved it to the window. Jane stepped up. It creaked. We froze several minutes then began to breathe once more. We tried again. Cautiously we raised ourselves as if the slower we went, the less chance it was that we'd be seen. Our heads cleared, then our eyes. We gazed into the kitchen.

We were right. Miss Emily and Granny Jane were both there. But there was no talking. Everything was put away, the dishes draining, the food covered, the stove cooling. It was the strangest thing. Miss Emily was sitting at the table with the rolling pin in her hands. Just sitting. Not writing lists or reading a cookbook or cutting vegetables. Just sitting. And looking off into space.

We shifted our eyes. Granny Jane was standing, her hand on the back of the kitchen chair. Her cane in her other hand. A bulge in the front pocket of her day dress meant the pipe wasn't going to be smoked. This was a bad sign. I'd learned Granny Jane usually had a good story up her sleeve when she took out her pipe.

"Emily, you know I'm right."

"I know. It's just that I don't want any more fuss than we already have."

"We'll get Marcell dressed in a good black dress and have her serve. She'll do just fine and that'll shut them up."

Miss Emily turned the rolling pin over in her hands. "Isn't anything going to shut them up unless we can get Marcell to quit going off on her binges. This last time was bad. I'm just glad Woodley Franklin saw her in town and took her back home before she could cause a scene."

Granny Jane pulled out the chair and sat.

"Emily, I don't know if anyone or God can stop

her drinking. Marcell's got too many ghosts in her head. She was just a child when it happened. And she saw it. And she still has scars on her ankles from the bites. We have to try to somehow keep the gossip down."

"You're right. It's just I'm tired of it. And I feel responsible," she held up her hand to stop Granny Jane's words, "I know, we didn't do anything. And Tom tried to save Ivis. But it happened here on the farm. And I believe we owe her."

"So, do I. That's why we're going to have the baby shower for that trashy niece of Beulavine's and Marcell is going to serve."

Miss Emily slowly nodded her head in agreement. Suddenly, she gave a laugh. "Butter didn't melt in your mouth this morning."

Granny Jane smiled back. "I was in church. The Lord was watching. Good thing." Turning, she walked out of the kitchen.

CHAPTER 6

Jane and I eased ourselves down from the window. Cautiously we stepped off the box and silently headed to the barn. We settled in the loft where no one would bother us.

"What happened to Marcell and her daddy?" I opened the conversation.

"I don't know. Nobody ever talks about it. I just know it was something bad, something about him getting killed."

"Well, they said something about bites on her ankles. That she'd seen something."

"Look" Jane switched around and gave me a hard glare. "I hate secrets. You heard them in the kitchen. They didn't even say what the secret was when they were talking about it. I've tried to ask plenty, but they just shut me up. I know not to ask anymore."

"Well, maybe the bites on her ankles have something to do with her being in pain."

Jane gave me a blank look. I continued, "Least that's what Miss Charity said, that Marcell's in pain."

Jane's mouth dropped open. I tried to eat my words, but they hung in the air.

"What you mean, Miss Charity said that?"

I didn't answer. Jane glared at me. "You talked to Miss Charity? When?" She said the words like each one was a sentence. My stomach fell to my feet. There was no way out.

"I saw her right after we got Miss Victoria Simmons' chicken rooster."

"Why didn't you come get me to go?" Jane demanded.

I tried to figure out what would be best to say. I was sure Jane would kill me for asking Miss Charity to put a spell on her. On the other hand, maybe she would think I was brave. It was the best I could hope for.

"Well, you were moping around and sad about Marcell pushing you, so I went to Miss Charity and asked her to make you happy again."

"What? You got her to put a spell on me?" The last word went right up to the top of the barn. Jane launched towards me and shoved her face into mine. "Don't you ever, ever, ever do that again!" Her words came out in a rush like one word, and I nodded, unable to speak.

"Ever!" She sat back on her heels and rubbed her hands against her eyes. "I can't stand people doing things without me knowing. Promise you'll tell me when you do stuff. I hate secrets."

"Okay. I promise," I dared a question, "But why do you hate secrets so much?"

Jane scrubbed at her eyes again then looked at the other side of the loft. "Because they never told me about Momma and Daddy for the longest time. When I got old enough to ask, they told me they were gone on a trip to be with Jesus. And then one day a girl in Sunday School told me they'd been smashed up in a car. She said they didn't go on a trip to Jesus because they didn't go to church, so they had gone to hell instead."

I felt like I'd been shot. I opened my mouth, but Jane beat me to it.

"And now, you know back in church? Miss Beulavine talking about Granny Jane and Miss Emily being tired? I thought they took me because they wanted me. Now it looks like they took me because they didn't have a choice. So there."

Her voice didn't sound like herself. But I knew the tone. It was the same one Daddy used when he refused to talk about Momma. I kept my mouth shut. It looked like that was going to be the thing to do today.

Jane asked, "What'd she do?"

"Who?" My mind was still on Granny Jane and Miss Emily having to take Jane.

"Miss Charity." Jane's voice sounded shaky. I guess I'd be shaky too if I knew I had a spell hanging over me. I hadn't really thought about it that way. I'd just wanted to help her and make her feel better.

I began to babble, "It was only a small spell. I asked her to make you feel better and,"

"What'd she do? I need to know exactly."

Questions about her momma and daddy slid away as the problem of the spell loomed bigger. I closed my eyes and thought back. "Well, she stirred that big pot and mumbled for a few minutes."

"What'd she say?"

"I don't know I couldn't understand her. Anyway, then she brought out a bottle. Then she drew a circle and stood in it."

Jane listened with fierce concentration.

"And then she jumped out of the circle and sprinkled the powder."

Jane's hand flashed out and grabbed me. Her voice was urgent. "Did she put the powder inside or outside the circle?"

I knew this was life or death. I answered honestly, "Inside, on some of the lines."

Jane gave a yelp and released me. She had her hand on her heart. I thought she was going to die in front of my eyes. She put her other hand to her mouth. I moved out of the way in case she got sick. My guilt only took me so far.

"You know what that means don't you?"

I shook my head dumbly and in shame.

"It means the power of the spell is fierce. It's not weak from being outside the circle but strong from being all locked up inside the circle."

I looked at her in amazement. I had no idea spells worked that way and I said so.

"Of course, you don't know." Contempt battled with fear in her voice. Fear won out. "You know what we have to do, don't you?" her voice was hoarse.

"No."

"We have to break the spell."

I thought for a minute. "Do we get Miss Charity

to do it?"

Jane gave me a pained look. "No. If she tries to undo it, it will just bounce to another person. We have to get it undone by somebody different before something awful happens."

Her drama was getting to me. After all, I didn't put a curse on her and I heatedly told her so.

She shook off my reasoning. "Doesn't matter. Miss Charity's power is on me. And you said yourself you didn't hear her words. We have to remove whatever she did and do it right now!"

Put that way I could see her point. "What do we do?"

Jane sat a minute then said, "I only know one person who might be able to get rid of it."

"Who."

"Marcell."

Time stopped. Boards creaked in the barn, and a rooster crowed in the distance. We looked at each other. I shook my head no. Jane nodded her head yes.

I shook my head 'no' again. "We can't go to Marcell. She's the reason I got the spell on you in the first place."

Jane stared me straight in the eye. "Marcell's a root doctor, least that's what people say she was before she started drinking hard."

"Root doctor?"

"Like Miss Charity, but instead of powders, she uses body things." Jane ignored the next question forming in my mouth and grabbed my arm, "Listen, you did this to me. If you'd left things alone, I wouldn't have the power all over me. Now who knows what's gonna happen? You have to come with me and help undo what you did."

Once again, I could see her point, but I didn't like it one bit and told her so. "Maybe we could get Miss Emily or Granny Jane to come with us."

"And have them know you went into the swamp by yourself to see Miss Charity?"

I thought back to Miss Emily's words to Daddy. She's doing just fine. And so is her dog. I couldn't disappoint Miss Emily. Then a flash of hope. Brown Hound! She would protect me from the colored woman.

"Then we have to take Brown Hound."

Jane shook her head no. "You know Marcell hates your dog."

I was firm. "Well, I'm not going without protection, and you can just have the power all over you for the rest of your life." I may have been wrong going to Miss Charity in the first place, but Jane needed me with her to undo the spell. I was sticking to my guns.

Jane gave a weary sigh then spoke, "All right. But we need to get going. We gotta get back before supper." It was settled.

I'd never seen Marcell's cabin. Jane had been to it but never gone inside. We walked down the hot dusty road in silence. I knew this was my fault. But my intentions had been good. I paused for a moment leaning down to pat Brown Hound on the head.

"You know that dog is just gonna piss her off."

I was shocked at Jane saying piss. Only men said that. I took it as a sign of her unease and tried to make things better.

"I can hang back, so Brown Hound doesn't come near Marcell. Or tie her up if you need me to come close."

"You're gonna come with me every inch of the way." That was that, and we continued on. We rounded a bend and were suddenly there. It was a small cabin set back from the road with dark, weathered boards, a sagging porch, and a rusted tin roof. The yard was beaten down by generations of feet. A few chickens scratched and pecked at the dirt. There was a tree that didn't have any leaves, and the high sweet Marcell smell came to us on the soft breeze. We paused in the middle of the road.

I was having second thoughts, "You sure you want to do this?"

Jane nodded her head. Then she swallowed. I couldn't, my spit had dried up.

"Hello?" Jane gave the usual country call. You never stepped foot on somebody's property without making your presence known. Silence met the call. She tried again, "Hello?" Still no answer.

Shrugging her shoulders, Jane jumped the ditch beside the road and walked toward the cabin. I grabbed onto Brown Hound's collar and followed. Stopping beside the tree, I got ready to tie her up and realized I didn't have anything to tie her with. Maybe I'd forgotten on purpose. No matter. It was all right with me that I had an excuse to keep my dog at my side. Brown Hound danced a bit and I put my hand on her head, giving her a pat. I pushed on her rear, and she sat. I joined Jane and we stepped up on the porch. Jane and I looked at each other. She nodded her head. I knew I was doomed. We put our sweaty hands on the screen door and slowly pulled it open.

"Hello?"

I almost slapped Jane. "She isn't here!"

Jane ignored me and pulling the door open wider, we both stepped through. We stood, silent and still. We were taking it in, surrounded by her presence. She had a little bed with a patched, frilly cover. Her good coat for church days hung on the closet door. The dresser was covered by a bit of lace tablecloth. On the dresser was a small bottle of perfume that had dried out, but she kept the pretty bottle anyway.

We walked in a bit and saw a couple of books. Some had been read and one looked new. There was one about cowboys and one about romance with a lady and a man straining and looking in pain on the cover. And the Bible, darkened by age and handling. We saw some flowers, pressed and dried with age, framed and hung on the wall near the iron sink. We saw slippers. We saw a torn petticoat with needle and thread placed on the chair. There were plates on the table, clean and looking like they had been set up for the evening meal. There was only one place setting.

Jane and I looked at each other. Marcell ate food, mended holes in her clothes, and read books. Marcell suddenly became a person.

"What you want?"

We climbed the air like it was a ladder. Marcell stood; arms folded across her chest like a wooden Indian. She could have been one too, because she didn't say anything else, and her face was hard. I eased backwards a step leaving Jane front and center. I nudged her in the back. She should be the one to speak. After all, the spell was on her not me. Ignoring the small voice reminding me that I'd been the one to go to Miss Charity in the first place, I slid back another inch or two.

"You in my home."

Jane nodded agreement and I kept silent. Marcell waited. I nudged Jane once more. She wiggled away from my touch then spoke.

"I need your help bad."

Marcell remained quiet.

"I've got a spell on me, and I need to get it off."

"Miss Charity?"

"Yes."

"How it get on?"

"Gracie."

Marcell fixed her eyes on me. Her voice was low. "You and that damn dog."

Brown Hound! Whirling, I jumped for the door and flew onto the porch. My dog was nowhere to be seen. Racing out to the road, I looked both ways. No dog. Marcell'd killed her. I knew it. Running back to the house, legs shaking in terror but engulfed in fury I flew through the screen door.

"Where is she, where is she, where is she, where is she?" I grabbed at the woman screaming over and over. Marcell calmly and with powerful hands plucked me off like a tick. Stunned, I stumbled back and sat hard on the floor. I tried to breathe. Jane stood unable to move. The only sound was my gasping for air.

"Done nothing to that dog."

Terror for Brown Hound made me lose my reason and I yelled, "You did too. You're probably too drunk to remember."

Marcell slowly walked over to me. She looked down. I tried to hug the floor with my butt.

Jane began to chatter, "Marcell, never mind that dog. Marcell, you hear me?"

Marcell turned to look at her. Jane and I waited.

"How'd she put the spell?" Marcell asked Jane, finally turning away from me like I was nothing.

"She drew a circle and then put powder inside it on the lines."

"What the spell for?"

"To make me happy."

"Happy?"

Jane looked uncomfortable and said, "Yeah happy."

"You been sad?"

I wanted to yell yes, and it was you who'd made her sad. But I knew when to keep my mouth shut.

"Yeah," Jane admitted.

"We gotta know why to take back the spell."

Quietly I wiggled out of range then sat straighter, hugging my knees, afraid to make a run for the door. Jane stood silently. Marcell fixed her with a piercing look.

"Can't undo the spell 'less I know."

I could see the struggle inside of Jane. The fear of the spell against the fear of Marcell when she told the truth. For me, fear of Marcell would win hands down. But Jane had known Marcell all her life, so that counted for something.

"Because you pushed me. I thought you liked me, and you pushed me."

"When?"

"At the chicken pen with the rooster." Jane stood with her fists clenched although I couldn't tell if they were clenched in fear or to keep from crying.

Marcell stood for a moment with her eyes closed looking like she had a pain. Quietly reaching out her hand, she plucked a few hairs from Jane's head. Then she walked over, bent down, and pulled a few hairs from mine. I froze with terror.

The woman stood and, holding up strands of my hair, spoke, "In the dark night, while the moon spins, I light a white candle and burn the maker, so the spell'll be brought out." She then held up the strands of Jane's hair in her other hand and continued, "then I burn the receiver, so the spell'll be broken. I do that tonight, Miss Jane."

I'd never heard Marcell call Jane that before. It had always been Jane or child or young'un but never Miss. She only did that with Granny Jane and Miss Emily. Jane looked up at her.

Marcell spoke again, "Sometimes it washes over me, and I can't help what I do. Didn't know I pushed you. Won't do it again."

Jane gave a nod and turned for the door. Jumping to my feet, I stood in front of Marcell quaking but firm. Giving me a flat look, she spoke, "Dog's under the house."

Pushing past Jane, I flew across the porch and hopped to the ground. Kneeling in the dirt, I looked under the porch. Brown Hound saw me and yawned, stretching out her front paws. Wiggling out from under the house she shook herself and smiled up at me. Grabbing her, I hugged her neck until she protested at the lack of air.

Jane came down the steps. We didn't look at each other. Silently, we started for home.

CHAPTER 7

Things settled down to normal during the next days. Jane was feeling better knowing the spell had been lifted. She regarded me with new found respect now that her terror was over.

"How'd you ever get the guts to do it?"

"I don't know. I just knew I had to."

Jane punched me in the shoulder. Rubbing my arm, I smiled in return and the event was put aside.

What wasn't put aside was the situation between Marcell and me. For my part, I vanished like smoke wherever she was around. That is if I could. Miss Emily was forever throwing us together for chores, but Granny Jane seemed in particular need of me that week. I found myself fetching and carrying for her more than usual.

Jane, Marcell, and I were busy cleaning the house, polishing the furniture, and the few small pieces of serving silver the Yankees hadn't stolen. Miss Emily wanted the house to be perfect for Linda Mae's baby shower.

"You don't have to say anything, just hold the tray in front of them." Granny Jane was instructing Marcell. Jane and I watched from the crack behind the door of the dining room. Marcell gave Granny Jane a look that would have cut the head off anyone else, but the old woman pretended not to see.

Granny Jane continued. "If you make eye contact with them, just look down. You don't have to speak to them if you don't want to." A snort pierced the air. Granny Jane ignored it and kept her eyes fixed on Marcell.

The colored woman backed down with a small smile on her lips. "Miss Jane, I'll be fine."

I noticed Marcell used better words than she did when she spoke to us. It must be respect. How could someone not respect Granny Jane? Or at least be scared enough to talk good in her presence. Granny Jane smiled back. "This is going to be just fine. Maybe it'll shut Beulavine and Viola up once and for all."

"Not even God could do that Miss Jane."

"That's true but you can go a long way in helping."

Marcell kept quiet. Granny Jane's tone had turned serious, and Jane and I tried to disappear. We couldn't without drawing attention.

"Marcell, you know why Miss Emily and I are having this party, don't you?"

"Miss Jane, if it has to do with those last three days..."

"Yes, it does."

"I heard about the flap in church. That Miss Viola. Guess her mouth has to be big to fit them teeth."

Granny Jane nodded her head but kept serious. "She wouldn't have been able to stir things up if there hadn't been something already in the pot. We need to show the ladies that they're wrong about you."

Silence. Then, "I try not to drink."

"I know, Marcell. But you have to try harder." Granny Jane fixed a hard eye on Marcell and continued. "You and I know why you tied one on. Jane talked about getting that rooster from the Simmons."

Silence.

"And you pushed Jane." Granny Jane said.

"I told Jane I was sorry."

"Well, that was only right but Marcell, you have to get over the Simmons. I know what happened to you and your daddy is hell on this earth, but you're not punishing anybody but yourself when you drink like that."

Marcell lifted her head and looked Granny Jane in the eye "I don't know I can change."

"You can. You apologized to Jane." Granny Jane nodded firmly as if that would set things in stone. "So, you can change and you know it. Look here, just come to Emily or me to talk when you want to drink."

Jane and I glanced at each other. Talk? Granny Jane could likely just scare the drinking out of Marcell if she wanted to.

"Yes ma'am, Miss Jane. I'll try to do that."

"See that you do."

Together they walked from the room.

It was Saturday. We were up early and doing a final dusting, waxing, and general straightening up. This was the first time either of us had been to an adult lady's party and we were feeling our oats. Not to mention that it might be like the showdown at the O.K. Corral between Miss Beulavine and Granny Jane. If it came to that, and we both hoped it would, our money was firmly on Granny Jane.

Kneeling on the bed, looking out the bedroom window, we pushed each other for a better view of the ladies arriving. They all seemed to come at once like a plague of locusts in flowered, silk dresses.

Leading the pack was Aunt Viola's favorite, Miss Beulavine, resembling a complete field of wildflowers. Tagging in her wake was the reason for the party. Linda Mae Stocks, who, it was whispered, got herself knocked up. Behind Linda Mae came Aunt Viola. She held the small struggling Miss Garson in her arms. I watched the small nasty thing snarl and bare its teeth. I bet Black Jack could kill it in one bite.

Jane pointed out a woman. "That's Aunt Martha, Aunt Viola's sister. They don't like each other very much. Aunt Martha can't wait to meet you."

I grimaced at that. The first aunt I'd met had declared war on the family by means of the preacher. I wondered what this one would do. She looked soft and had a nice smile. Jane and I left the window and slid into the living room, standing against the wall. We watched the ladies squeal hello, jostle for chairs, and pat Linda Mae on the belly.

"Ladies," Uncle Will poked his head into the room. "Us men are going over to Edward's store for a spell. Y'all be fine?" I looked up at him in astonishment.

Fine? If they'd had these ladies in the war, we'd be singing Dixie as the national anthem. The screen door slapped shut behind him and the cars faded down the road. Jane and I stayed against the wall hoping to remain unseen, but it was not to be.

"Elizabeth Grace, Jane, come pay your respects." We obeyed Miss Emily. Side by side we made the rounds of the seated ladies. They smiled and recalled Sissy and Robert and how lucky Miss Jane and Miss Emily were to have me on the farm for the summer. I met Aunt Martha and I could see why Jane liked her. Her eyes were a violet blue and they smiled all on their own. Her short white hair was fluffed in waves around her face, and she had the softest skin I'd ever seen. She gave me a kiss on the cheek and patted my face. I was hers forever. I moved on quickly avoiding Miss Garson who snarled from her prison under Aunt Viola's chair. I could see approval gleam in Miss Emily's eyes.

Aunt Martha spoke, "Linda Mae, honey, how is your confinement going?"

Jane and I stepped back to the wall and folded our hands. We shot each other a look. 'Confinement'. Secrets were about to be revealed. We stayed quiet as we could. Linda Mae sat on the sofa in a powder blue dress that looked like a tent. A big white bow was tied at her collar and the ends draped over her huge chest. Her titties were the size of baby pigs. Jane must have thought so too because she began whispering the names of the piglets out back. Granny Jane shot us a look and Jane shut her mouth. Linda Mae took a deep breath, expanding her bosom farther than I thought possible. I feared an explosion.

"It's been fine but for Tommy. He just doesn't respect my condition."

'Respect'. Jane and I looked at each other in recognition of an adult term used so young'uns wouldn't know what they were talking about.

"You mean he's not leaving you alone?"

I figured that this 'leaving alone' was probably in the same category as 'respect' and stored that information for Jane and me to examine at our leisure.

"No, he just doesn't leave me alone. He still wants to do it."

Jane and I cut our eyes at each other. Here it was. At last, we were going to learn something shocking. 'Do it', Jane mouthed at me, and I stifled a giggle.

Aunt Viola bared her teeth, "Why honey. You should just do what us ladies have always done. Just tell him that his advances are no longer welcome."

"Yes indeed," chimed in Miss Beulavine, "just cut him off."

Jane looked at me and crossed her eyes and I almost died. Cut him off? How? All I could think about cutting was Miss Emily cutting off chicken heads and that didn't seem to be what you could do to Tommy no matter how no-count he was.

Jane read my mind and got to shaking. I saw tears come in her eyes and I crammed my hand in my mouth. It didn't work. Jane gave a stifled snort and we began slowly sliding down the wall. Granny Jane shot a look at us.

"Elizabeth Grace! Jane!"

We snapped to attention.

"It's time for you to go help Marcell serve."

Thankfully, we made our curtseys to the ladies and fled the room.

"I thought we were goners." Jane whispered. We headed to the kitchen. Everything was ready. I knew Miss Emily was fretting, and I wasn't sure how relaxed Granny Jane was for all her show.

"Here," Marcell handed the napkins to Jane. "Go pass these out to the ladies." Jane grabbed at them. Marcell yanked them back.

"Don't wrinkle them. Miss Jane'll have my hide. Look, hold 'em like this."

Jane left the kitchen balancing napkins on her outstretched hands like she was holding the crown for the Queen of England.

"Let's see," Marcell stood in the kitchen slowly turning around. Her new black dress bought for today by Miss Emily swished against her legs. Her hair was neatly combed and pushed into waves against her head. I saw her frown but didn't worry. This time the frown wasn't for me. She didn't even know I was there. Her mind was busy double and triple-checking, taking Granny Jane's words to heart. It was a strange sight, seeing Marcell, want-to-be-killer of dogs, remover of spells, chicken murderer, worried about making a good impression on those fat, white ladies. I watched her silently mouth the list of things she needed to remember.

She nodded her head. "Let's go. You hold the doors for me. After we serve these cookies, we come back for the tea."

I opened the kitchen door and preceded her along the back porch. The floor boards creaked and I knew the ladies heard us coming. The smell of cookies drifted through the afternoon. My mouth watered and I could almost taste the icing. Suddenly, a flash of brown whipped past me and leaped. Turning in horror, I saw it happen. Brown Hound flew through the air, smashing straight into Marcel. Cookies soared to the ceiling, then rained down. Marcell landed hard on her knees. Sassy and Black Jack appeared and began snapping up cookies.

I stood, stricken dumb. Marcell stayed on her knees just looking at the dogs. With a flash like a shard in my heart, I knew there'd be no forgiving this. Brown Hound had ruined Granny Jane's plan to redeem Marcell. It was my fault. I wondered where I would be sent this time. I hoped they'd let my dog come with me.

I waited for Marcell to leap up and go looking for the hatchet, but she didn't. She just stayed still. Her eyes had a tired look in them. The look I'd seen in Daddy's eyes when Momma fussed.

"Marcell? What was that noise? Do you need help?" Miss Emily called, trying for calm.

Marcell didn't answer. I rushed to the screen door desperate to save myself and my dog. Poking in my head I gave my best Sissy and the club ladies smile. "Cookies'll be here in a minute."

Smelling disaster, Aunt Viola jumped up, pushed past me, and leaned out the door. "It's Marcell." Viola's voice held a pleased note. "Beulavine, it looks like she's had an accident."

I hated her. I hated the way she'd made Miss Emily feel bad. I hated that she wanted to take Jane away from the farm. I hated her fat friend. I hated the way she was getting ready to make fun of Marcell. I hated the way Marcell sat on the floorboards. I hated that my dog had done this. I hated the entire world. Brown Hound and I were doomed. But maybe I could at least save Marcell.

I called out, "It wasn't Marcell. It was Brown Hound."

Aunt Viola looked down at me. I pushed my body against her, making her step back. I moved inside the living room and pulled the screen door closed behind my back.

"It was Brown Hound, Miss Emily. She saw the cookies and jumped right up on Marcell and knocked her down. They're dogs all over the porch eating cookies."

Miss Emily stood up. "Elizabeth Grace, you should have locked that dog up. Poor Marcell. I'll go and help. Jane, you stay here and help Miss Jane get the games started. Gracie and I will be back in just a minute." Hurrying across the room she flashed a gracious smile at both Aunt Viola and Miss Beulavine who were forced by good manners to take their seats. I followed Miss Emily out the door.

Marcell was gone. The dogs circled the tray nosing it for crumbs. Miss Emily kicked them away and they bounded from the porch. I watched them go with Brown Hound in the lead. Miss Emily broke into my thoughts.

"Take this tray," she held it out to me, "clean it up and get the extra cookies." I looked at her blankly. My mind was already packing my suitcase and walking towards Daddy's car. "Hurry up child. I've got to find Marcell." That made me move. Grabbing the tray, I raced to the kitchen. In a few minutes I was handing the tray around, keeping my eyes and words to myself. Jane hovered in the background.

Aunt Viola's words punched through the lady chatter, "Well, look who's here."

Marcell stood at the door holding the good silver tray with cups and the teapot. Lowering my head, I continued to pass my cookie tray.

"Marcell, I hope you're going to take a whip to those dogs," said Aunt Viola. I wanted her dead. "You know if a dog can't mind, there's no place for them on a farm." She sat back and took a chomp out of her cookie.

"Viola you're right about that." Miss Beulavine shifted her large bottom in the chair, searching for comfort. "My daddy always said a dog was better dead than misbehaved."

"That's the truth. My husband Will's father once had three of his dogs shot for killing chickens," Aunt Viola nodded her head. "It's a small jump from cookies to chickens in my opinion."

The words shot out of me. "You and your big teeth just leave my dog alone!" I dropped the tray. Cookies once again hit the floor. I high tailed it out of the house and ran to the barn. Heedless of my good dress, I wiggled into a pile of straw and listened hard. I didn't hear anyone running after me.

My breathing steadied. I was surely done for, right along with Brown Hound. Tears flowed, and I wiped my nose on the hem of my dress. Well, there you go. I'd gone and ruined my dress but so what? That was a small thing next to ruining Marcell's chance to look good in front of the ladies and my yelling at Aunt Viola. Nothing I could do would make up for today. The tears came faster. Suddenly they were being licked away by a tongue. Brown Hound! I grabbed her by the neck and held on hard. Just like when we were on the picnic table at home. Seemed like nothing was ever going to change. I cried harder.

"I think that's the last of it." Miss Emily straightened up and put her hand to her back having retrieved yet another pink and blue ribbon. Granny Jane sat in the living room rocking chair. She pulled out her pipe. It was early evening, and I was crouched below the window on the porch, listening and sneaking peeks. Jane hadn't shown up to tell me anything and I needed to know where Brown Hound stood.

Granny Jane lit her pipe, puffing. "A fine party."

Miss Emily gave a laugh. Tiredly she sank to

the sofa and absently curled a ribbon around her finger. "If we wanted to stop the talking, looks like we did the opposite." Shoes clunked to the floor. "I hate high heels. Even these low ones. Don't know why women wear them." I could tell Miss Emily was talking until she could lead up to talking about me.

Miss Emily repeated my words, "You and your big teeth!"

Granny Jane cackled with laughter, "I liked to choke. Funniest thing I've heard in a long time. I thought Viola was going to explode."

Maybe if they thought this was funny, they wouldn't send me away.

Granny Jane turned serious. "That damn dog is going to be the death of us yet."

My heart stopped. Tears ran out of my eyes, and I rubbed them away.

"I know," Miss Emily said, "but what can we do? The child will die without that dog."

"I know that, too. Seems like she didn't have anything else up in Virginia."

"That's the truth. I don't know why Robert married Sissy. I could tell she wasn't right first time I met her. High strung."

Granny Jane shook her head. "If Robert had any sense, he'd have stopped her foolishness a long time ago. I don't know why he puts up with it. I'm just glad we have Gracie here with us for a while." Granny Jane's voice became flat, "but that dog." They were back at the starting point. Brown Hound. "Marcell hates that dog."

"Marcell hates any dog, and you know it," Miss Emily replied.

"After today, she's going to hate this one even more."

Miss Emily sighed and put her hands on her knees, "Oh I know." She straightened up wincing at the cracking in her back "I'll talk with Marcell. I just don't know how we're going to fix this."

"Didn't speak to her before she left?"

"No. She cleaned the kitchen and was gone by the time we got everyone out of the house."

"That was pretty fast seeing how those women couldn't wait to get the gifts opened and get out of here. I can just hear telephone wires burning, and talk over supper tables. You and your big teeth." Granny Jane went off in another gale of laughter.

"Laugh all you want Miss Jane. We've got to do something about that dog and Marcell." Miss Emily turned and walked out of the room.

I stayed on the porch swatting at mosquitoes, my mind churning. Granny Jane thought today was funny but called Brown Hound a damn dog. Miss Emily was worried about Marcell. I was sure Marcell would win over me and Brown Hound. Just like Momma always did. I rubbed my hand against my eyes. I was tired.

"Come on inside."

My hand stopped. Granny Jane!

"Said come in. Wasn't a question."

Stepping into the living room, I looked around.

"Jane's gone to spend the night with your Aunt Martha and Uncle Ben. Always was their favorite. Looks like Emily's gone to bed. Marcell's gone home. Just you and me." Smoke drifted from her pipe. "Why don't you sit down?"

I sat on the sofa, waiting. Granny Jane rocked and puffed at her pipe. The only sounds were peepers in the swamp and the rumble of a far-off thunderstorm. She began, "Quite a day."

I didn't know what to say.

"Stirred things up, you and that dog."

I was tired of people calling her 'that dog'. My dog was my friend, and she had a name just like me. The words were out of my mouth before I could stop them. "Her name is Brown Hound."

Granny Jane pulled the pipe from her mouth and pointed the stem at me.

"Don't you get sassy with me, young lady. I'll lay my cane on you as fast as you can say jackrabbit."

I shrank. She continued, "I've been thinking, and I believe we need a little break from your Brown Hound."

My heart slammed to a stop but I already knew it was coming. They were going to get rid of us. It was just a matter of how quick and where to. I looked at the floor. The little spurt of defiance sputtered out and I sat quietly, a hole in my stomach.

Granny Jane sat silently, rocking, and watching me. "You want to go back up to Virginia?"

The question made me feel sick. I wanted to go,

but I didn't want to go. I wanted to see Daddy but then Momma was there. And he said she was better, but what if I went there and she got sick again? How could I explain this to Granny Jane? Better to say nothing and wait.

"No, I guess you don't want to go there right now. How about we do this? Child? Look up here at me."

I raised my head and waited for the blow.

Granny Jane leaned back and gave me the once over with her eyes. Nodding to herself she continued, "Jane is with Martha and Ben. How about you and Brown Hound going into Kingston to be with Jane and your aunt and uncle for a couple of days?"

I stared at the old woman. Not Virginia? No going back to Momma? The hole in my stomach eased a bit. Then the important question, "Do they like dogs?"

"Well-behaved ones they do."

"Brown Hound can be well-behaved."

A great puffing on the pipe was the only response.

"She can."

"Well, she won't have much of a chance to be otherwise. They have a fence. It'll do that dog good to not run around. I think the freedom here has gone to her head."

I nodded in agreement. Anything to get Brown Hound off the hook. My stomach was feeling better. Still empty, but it was from lack of supper more than anything else.

The old woman read my mind. "Go on. Get us some cold chicken from the Frigidaire and biscuits."

I jumped from the sofa and headed to the back door. We were home free. I wanted to dance like Brown Hound. I heard the rocking chair resume as I went for our food.

CHAPTER 8

"Gracie, time to get up." Miss Emily stood at the foot of the bed. Marcell was nowhere to be seen and I couldn't have been happier. "Breakfast is on. Why don't you eat, and I'll get you packed."

I guess they wanted me out of the way before Marcell came back. With no one watching to comment on my manners, I shoveled the eggs and biscuits. In record time I was on the porch, the rope to Brown Hound's collar in one hand, and Miss Emily's small overnight case in the other. A cloud of dust came down the road. It was Uncle Will's car.

I looked up at Miss Emily. Aunt Viola was his wife. She smiled down at me. "You just pretend yesterday didn't happen. Will's got too good a manners to bring up what you said about Viola." I hoped that would be true and turned out it was. Uncle Will was polite if a bit distant on the ride into town. That was fine by me because I had my hands full trying to keep Brown Hound from jumping out of the window.

Jane was dancing impatiently on Aunt Martha's porch when we arrived.

"Whoo Hoo! Hurry up. We're going to the pool!"

I ignored her for a moment and looked around.

The porch was a far cry from the farm's. This one sat in front of the gray house all tidy and looking like it had on a Sunday dress. There was wood lace at the top corners and a big white swing with blue cushions. Aunt Martha came out of the house smiling.

"Quit hollering like a stuck pig. Let Gracie get in the house." Aunt Martha hurried down the steps to welcome me. "Gracie, nice to have you here. Will, want to come in for some iced tea? Jane take that dog and put her in the back yard." She managed us without effort. Before I could turn around twice, Uncle Will was on his way back home, Brown Hound was sniffing the back yard, and Jane and I were in our swim suits holding towels.

Aunt Martha smiled down. "Girls, I won't be coming with you to the pool." I gave a sigh of relief. I worried I'd have to see her in a bathing suit. I didn't think they made bathing suits for bosoms like hers.

"Miss Ginny's boy, Dan is going to carry you down and bring you back. You girls mind the lifeguard."

"Yes, ma'am."

I'd never had a day such as this. Dan was a dreamboat. Jane took the seat beside him, and I had a fine view of his eyes in the rearview mirror. The pool water was an astonishing blue, better than the ocean. All those swimming lessons were paying off now because I got to go off the high dive. Jane was busy showing off for Dan. The water was cool, and the lifeguards were cute. Jane was happy, I was queen of the high dive, and Brown Hound was safe. Clearly, the world was a fine place indeed.

That evening I met Uncle Ben. He was tall, thin, with deep brown eyes. What was left of his hair was shaved close above his ears. The best part about Uncle Ben, besides the cigar in his mouth that got smaller even though he wasn't smoking it, was he was as nice as Aunt Martha. He didn't have to sit and listen to us tell all about the pool, but he did.

Later, with Jane in the big bed, the electric fan blowing, I raised up on my elbow and looked out the window. The night was soft. I imagined Brown Hound lying in the backyard on the old blanket Uncle Ben put there, her nose on her paws, her eyes closed. I closed mine, too.

Aunt Martha was giving orders like the organized general she was. "Your Uncle Ben's pulling in the driveway. Girls, you come in and set table for supper."

Earlier that day, Jane had gone down the street to play with an old friend. I stayed behind, having met enough new people for a while. Aunt Martha gave me a Bobbsey Twins book and I spent the afternoon on the front porch swing, reading and recovering from the past few days.

"Hurry with the table now." Aunt Martha called as she went out of the front door. I started to follow. Jane stuck out a hand and stopped me, pointing at the door. Aunt Martha had pulled it a bit closed behind her. She and Uncle Ben were whispering. We went still and listened.

"...just glad I was able to get to her before she made it into town. If Will had got to her first, that damn sister of yours..."

"Ben! Little pitchers, big ears!"

Aunt Martha pushed the door open. Jane and I jumped, bumping into each other. Knives and forks went flying. Aunt Martha gave a sigh. Jane and I snatched up the utensils and began squabbling over who would put what where. It was for show. I could see Jane's mouth get tighter, but my mind was on Brown Hound. Granny Jane and Miss Emily hadn't been able to talk Marcell out of drinking after the cookie disaster. I was glad we were in Kingston. Uncle Ben washed up and we finished the table.

Supper eased the tightness in the air. Aunt Martha didn't fuss when we left spinach on our plates, and Uncle Ben told funny stories from town. You could tell by Aunt Martha's laughing he made most of them up. We were digging into the banana pudding when Uncle Ben leaned back, hitched up the waist of his pants, and proposed the evening's entertainment.

"You girls know the carnival's in town?"

Jane and I darted hopeful glances at each other but kept quiet.

"Ben, you know how trashy those things are."

Uncle Ben continued without missing a beat. "I wonder if you girls would be interested in going out there tonight?"

Our eyes almost popped out of our heads. The carnival! I'd never been to one but had heard about them. They were supposed to have a Dog-Eared Boy and the fattest lady on the planet. Aunt Martha and Uncle Ben started going eye to eye. I was hoping Uncle Ben would win but anyone with a brain would put money on Aunt Martha.

The first cannon shot was fired. "Ben."

"Now Martha." The responding shot. Uncle Ben's voice was soft. He smiled at her. He gave her a wink. My mouth flew open. Uncle Ben was flirting with Aunt Martha! I didn't know adults carried on like that. I wondered what was next.

"Oh you." That sure didn't sound like a cannon shot to me.

"You don't have to go, Martha. I'll watch them."

"Well, maybe I should."

"And have someone tell Viola?"

"Well, there is that."

Uncle Ben pushed back from the table, stood, and slapped his hands together. "Girls. Get this cleaned up. Shake a leg!"

"Gracie and Jane?" We stopped mid-skid to the kitchen and stood at attention. "You girls go on. I'll clean up. Now you mind your Uncle Ben."

Her last words were lost in the race to the bedroom for our shoes.

Dying from excitement, we climbed into the car. Jane sat in front as usual and led the conversation. "Uncle Ben?"

"Yes?"

"Uncle Ben, have you ever been to the Freak Show?"

"Well," he chewed thoughtfully on his cigar. "I can't rightly say I have."

We took that to mean he probably had but didn't want to say.

Jane persisted. "What's in it?"

Another pause as the unlit cigar became a bit smaller. "I've heard tell there're some terrible sights." He kept his eyes carefully on the road. Jane got up on her knees, faced backwards and whispered, "the Man-Woman Thing."

I nodded eagerly. Just because we'd never been to a carnival didn't mean we didn't know how to read a poster. And carnival posters in town featured the Freak Show with the Man-Woman Thing. We were dying to find out just what men had down there. We'd seen pigs and Miss Victoria Simmons' bull, but none of that looked like it would fit on a man. Tonight, we'd get answers.

Uncle Ben interrupted my thoughts. "I don't think you girls should go."

"Uncle Ben." Jane and I dragged out his name as long as we could. If he could flirt with Aunt Martha, we could flirt with him. He managed a smile with the cigar in his mouth.

"Now don't you go begging. I don't think you're grown up enough to see the Freak Show."

Jane sat back down facing the front. I leaned

forward and tried to see Uncle Ben, but the darkness concealed his face. We arrived at the carnival and climbed down from the car in a flurry.

"Girls."

We stopped and turned. Uncle Ben curled his finger, and we walked back to him.

"Now," he dug in his pocket. "Here's some spending money. I trust you to mind what I've said. If you need me, I'll be at the horse shoes."

We gazed at him in disbelief. He was giving us money and setting us free. In that minute we grew taller. Instead of dashing away, we politely said our 'thank yous' and walked away in style. Money in our pockets, no one holding our hands, and the Freak Show ahead. We tingled with excitement.

The night was hot and clingy like a wisp of cotton candy. We walked to the midway and were suddenly assaulted by the smells. Wonderful smells that went in our noses and rolled around on our tongues. They were popcorn, cotton candy, hot dog, wood shavings, horse manure, and plastic melted on light smells. And the lights themselves were bright and hard, trying to be elegant but only glaring from their dust-coated surfaces. It revved up the blood; these smells and sights did. It promised something other than what you were given to live every day.

"Come see. Come guess," the voices called. It was wild, wishful, and it worked.

Jane wanted a chance at the milk bottles. Picking up the slicked baseball, she tossed it up and down judging the weight, then threw. And missed. Then missed again. Jane had a good arm, but no matter how hard she threw, those bottles wouldn't budge. Giving a sigh she turned and walked away. I trailed behind entranced with the sights.

"No skill. Just luck. Try Lady Luck." The bone-thin young man saw Jane and me approaching. "Lady Luck favors young girls. Yes, she does. Girls come here and let Lady Luck shine on you."

Yellow and pink plastic ducks bobbed and swirled on the water. All you had to do was let Lady Luck shine on you and pick up the right duck. You could win the big teddy bear hanging from the ribbon around his neck. I wanted to win him so I could get him down from being strangled. Jane and I peered earnestly into the mirror at the bottom of the fake blue stream. We tried to read the numbers pasted on the duck bottoms as they swirled by. Jane shook her head and putting her hands in her pockets stepped back. It was up to me. I paid the man then, squinting hard, saw the teddy bear's number. Sixty-six. I grabbed the duck and triumphantly handed it to the barker.

"Ninety-nine," he called out. I stood there aghast.

"No. It's sixty-six."

The man looked down at me with a bored expression. "Ninety-nine." Turning he fished inside the box marked 'ninety-nine' and came up with a set of Dracula teeth and held them out to me. There was no arguing with him. Dropping the teeth into my hand, he began his call for more customers, "No skill. Just luck. Try Lady Luck."

Jane shook her head in disgust, and we ambled over to the bumping cars. We watched teenage boys slam into each other. Morons. We walked farther down. We bought cotton candy, pink and dripping with dark beads of sugar. We walked and nibbled. But what we were really doing was waiting for the other one to say it was time for the Freak Show. We ambled a bit farther in an offhand but calculated direction.

Suddenly, there it was. The Freak Show. Right on the midway. But then how could you expect such a wonder to be anywhere else? Dropping our cotton candy in the trash, we approached the ticket booth, dug in our pockets, and laid our money down.

"One?" The woman had no teeth. I wondered if she was a reject from the show. Jane dug me in the back, and I spoke, "Two please." I was standing as tall as I could stretch. I didn't want her to ask how old we were. The old woman pushed the tickets through the slot with her greasy hand. Jane moved past me like lightning and snatched them up. Clutching our tickets, we walked to the tent and waited. Jane looked at me and grinned. I grinned back. We were on the loose at the carnival and going to see the freaks.

"Ladies and Gentlemen!" The hawker came out onto a platform. "Tonight, you will see things that will amaze you. And," he lowered his voice and bent forward, "frighten you." Jane grabbed my hand.

"This is no place for the timid or the weak." He

nodded solemnly to the crowd. "Men, keep a grip on your lady's arm. There's liable to be fainting."

Jane and I giggled then went still, not wanting to draw attention.

"Come in and be amazed. See the Dog-Eared Boy. See the fattest lady in the world. See the man who is a lizard. And see the one creature God forgot, the Half-Man-Half-Woman."

The crowd shifted and made for the tent. The hawker held up his hands. "Don't push. There's room for all. Give yourselves some breathing space. You're gonna need it." He hopped off his stand and followed us through.

The tent was hushed, dark, and smelled like decaying leaves in the fall. The hawker hurried to the first small stage. The curtain rose with a swirl of dust. The hawker announced with a flourish, "The Dog-Eared Boy!" For a moment everyone stood in awe. Suddenly the silence broke.

"Those ears are strapped on his head. Look at them. You can see the buckle." A large man was pointing. Jane and I stood on tip toe and the man was right! This was no freak, just a tired looking, dirty boy with fake ears. The crowd gave a mumble of disappointment. I sagged back and shot Jane a look of disgust. Jane nodded in agreement.

The crowd shifted, unsatisfied with the first weak offering. The curtain closed and the hawker bustled over to the second stage. The faded yellow curtain parted. "The World's Fattest Lady!" Well, he was right about that. This was the fattest lady I'd ever seen in my life including Miss Charity Frazier. This was more like it. The Fat Lady's arms were the size of Jane.

"Give us a dance, sweetie." It was the same big man in the crowd. He grinned with bared teeth and hard eyes. On his arm hung a woman whose dress was so tight you could see her garter snaps. My momma would have said she was trash. And Momma would have been right.

The barker nodded to the huge woman. Parting her robe and showing only a shiny white slip underneath, the fat lady did a quick shimmy dance, her flesh swinging with every step.

Moving forward a bit to get a better look, I saw the bottoms of her feet. They were dirty. And her legs had black hair growing all over. I backed up a step and rubbed the palms of my hands on my shorts. She shimmied over to her chair.

"Now this chair had to be specially built for her by Watermark Boat Builders of Maine," the hawker was trying to interest the crowd, but they didn't care. They were ready for more. Quickly, he lowered the curtain and moved to the next stage.

"The Lizard Man!" he trumpeted.

Jane tugged on my arm. "That's no lizard man."

She was right. He didn't have scales, just skin folded in wrinkles that hung over other wrinkles. He was skinny and dried up and looked like the fat lady had sucked everything out of him.

"Aw heck. I want my money back." It was the big man again with the trashy woman.

The hawker was fast footing it. "This man is the real thing. Just look at him. Those are scales all over his body. Just come up here. Come on up here and feel him." His eyes searched the crowd and landed on Jane.

"Come on little lady. How about you come up here and feel his scales?"

Jane shook her head.

"I paid good money. You let Doreen feel him." The big man pushed his lady friend to the front.

Doreen and her garter snaps gave a wiggle that matched the fat lady's dance. The crowd chuckled. The hawker knew when he had a good thing. He let Doreen stroke the old man. She gave a small shriek. He pulled her away and led her back to the big man. "Better keep a good hold of her now. This next bit is hard even for men to take."

The hawker moved to the final platform and the crowd surged forward. Jane and I shoved in between the adults pushing our way to the stage. The crowd hushed. The hawker let the high drama of the moment draw out. Then, with dramatic fanfare he slowly raised the curtain.

"The Man-Woman Thing!"

There it was. We strained to see through the dim light. People tried to take our places, but we held firm. We wanted to see from every angle.

A spotlight shined down on it. It had a full beard and mustache, but its hair was all done up like a lady with curls and bows. It had on red lipstick and earrings. Well, that didn't tell us much. We waited for more.

Slowly the Man-Woman Thing undraped the shawl covering its chest. There was a sound from the crowd like bees at a hive. Yep. Here was the woman part. She had titties all right. They were withered like two little sacks of dried beans. It was nothing for us to get excited about, but the men liked it. There was sweat on their foreheads and one or two shoved their hands deep into their pockets. I looked over at Doreen. She and her tight dress were rubbing on the side of the big man. It made me feel a little sick. I turned back to the stage.

The Man-Woman Thing's hands began to move lower. Jane and I stood transfixed. We were gonna get some answers now. Slowly the baggy red pants began their descent. We saw curly black hair. Its hands paused. The crowd gave a sound like a dog going for a bone. The thing looked at the hawker, and he nodded his head. Jane and I glanced at each other and then back at the stage. The pants moved slowly lower. Suddenly, from under the tight waistband popped up a tiny thing that looked like a finger. The pants lowered a bit more and the finger-looking thing bounced against two little red round balls that looked like wrinkled bird eggs. Jane and I looked at each other. This was it? This is what men had down there? It wasn't anything like the pigs in the pen, that was for sure.

"Oooh!" It was Doreen again. This time she

had fallen into a faint. The big man was squatting down next to her, his pants pulled tight. I looked but didn't see any suspicious bumps pushing at the cloth. So, it seemed like men's finger-looking thing really was that small.

"Make way. Make way. I told you to hang on to her." The hawker moved forward. The crowd clustered around Doreen, but Jane and I turned back to the stage.

The Man-Woman was pulling up its pants and tucking the little finger thing back under its waistband. Leaning over, picking up the shawl, it paused, eyes level with ours. The three of us looked at each other, unmoving.

"Are you really both?" Jane whispered.

The Man-Woman slowly nodded its head.

"Give her air. Give her air," the hawker yelled, pleased with the excitement. I looked back at the crowd clustered around Doreen. Someone had unbuttoned the top of her tight dress. The crowd no longer cared what was on the stage. When it came to titties, Doreen won hands down.

The Man-Woman held our gaze for a moment longer, then slowly straightened up. Turning, it walked to the back of the stage and disappeared.

"Let's go!" Jane had me by the hand tugging. "We're never gonna get a chance like this again."

One quick look back showed the crowd still absorbed with Doreen and her unbuttoned dress. We snaked along the front of the stage then pushed through the canvas opening. Suddenly, we were in another tent. This one didn't have the fancy curtains and the shaded lights. This one had hot bright lights strung from the top and big dirty electric fans stirring up more dust than cool air. There were tables and chairs that looked like rejects from a church picnic. But we barely noticed.

What held us frozen was the Fat Lady, the Lizard Man, the Dog-Eared Boy minus his ears, and the Man-Woman all sitting at a table eating supper. Just like that. They had plates with fried chicken, cornbread, and beans. There was a platter with a one-layer iced cake and pitchers of sweet tea. They were sitting just like family, eating and quietly talking. Jane and I looked at each other like we'd landed on the Moon.

"Want some?" The Fat Lady waved a chicken leg in our direction. We looked around. She was talking to us.

"No ma'am. But thank you." Jane said.

The courtesy brought a chuckle from the freaks.

"You can come closer. We won't bite. We're too busy eating," said the Fat Lady. More chuckles but they weren't mean chuckles. I had been listening hard, not knowing how freaks would act or what they'd say.

"Bet you'd like some cake," said the Lizard Man. He looked tired, but maybe it was just all those wrinkles sagging on his face. "If so, you'd better speak now before Bedeliah here lays a tooth to it." Laughter. Still nice, not like the ladies at Linda Mae's party.

Jane answered politely, "That would be fine, please."

I looked at her in astonishment. First following the Man-Woman into a strange tent, and now she wanted to eat their food? They were freaks. Maybe their food had special potions that turned them into freaks. I put my hands behind my back then quickly moved them in front. I didn't want to look rude.

"Come on then. Sit down." The Lizard Man leaned over to cut some slices of cake and the Dog-Eared-Boy scooted his chair to make room. I watched Jane walk over. Her courage flowed around her like a cloak of bravery as she sat next to the Dog-Eared-Boy. I wondered what Granny Jane would say. But then Granny Jane wasn't here to see it was she?

Suddenly it hit me. No one was watching. No one could tell me what to do. It was my choice. The freaks were absorbed in their meal and small conversations. Jane was accepting a piece of cake. I was on my own. I sucked in a breath remembering I'd made the decision to go to Miss Charity by myself. The Man-Woman looked up and gave me a smile. He looked better with the lipstick off. I nodded to him and stepped to the table.

"Where're you from?" He started off making polite conversation. I told him about Virginia, Brown Hound, and Miss Emily's farm. Jane was at the other end of the table chattering about our side-stepping chicken rooster, and the Fat Lady was laughing fit to die.

"Well, I'm from Cleveland." The Man-Woman began telling how he'd been an orphan, and nobody wanted him, "I always knew I was different. Didn't figure out why until I was older."

I looked at him in amazement. Not so much at his story, but that I was sitting right next to him.

"Ran away when I was fourteen and joined the carnival." He paused to take a bite out of his piece of fried chicken. "These here are my friends," he gestured with the chicken wing, "none of us fits in out there, but we all fit in here."

The hawker walked through the flap and spied us. "You kids. Get outta here."

Jane and I jumped to our feet.

"Scat. Go on. Shoo." He waved his hands at us.

For a moment, we stood our ground. After all, we had to mind our manners.

"The cake was very good." Jane was at her party best.

"Thank you," was all I could manage.

The hawker took a step toward us. We ran to the other end of the tent and made a quick exit through the flap.

Jane and I sat together in the front seat as Uncle Ben drove us home. "You girls are mighty quiet."

"Yes, sir."

"You have a good time tonight?"

"Yes, sir we did." Jane answered for both of us. I held up my set of Dracula teeth for him to see.

"My, my. Those are some fine teeth." He glanced away from the road and looked down at me, grinning through his cigar. I knew he was thinking about Aunt Viola but was too polite to say. I smiled up at him then sat back against the seat. Behind us the carnival lights faded into the dark and dust. I tried to take it all in and hold it to me.

Uncle Ben said casually, "I saw Will tonight. He said he thought he saw you girls coming out the tent behind the Freak Show."

Jane and I looked at each other. It was a moral dilemma. If we told the truth, Aunt Viola would have more ammunition saying Jane was running wild.

"Uncle Will must be seeing things," Jane said firmly. She poked me in the side, and I took on my share of the lie.

"I think we saw him near the cotton candy." It was a weak offering, but the best I could do.

"Well, that's mighty good because your Aunt Martha and I would be real disappointed if you disobeyed."

I slid down in my seat feeling lower than a snake. Jane hunched over beside me, and I figured she was feeling bad too. Aunt Martha and Uncle Ben were wonderful and here we were paying them back by going to the Freak Show and lying about it. We kept silent, feigning tiredness. Uncle Ben chewed on his cigar and kept driving.

Aunt Martha opened the door. "You girls have a good time?" I began to answer but paused for a second. Her mouth was smiling but there was something in her eyes. Maybe Aunt Viola had already been on the holler.

My stomach hurt.

"Yes ma'am," Jane said.

"Well, that's nice." Aunt Martha turned to Uncle Ben, "Ben, see you in the kitchen?"

Jane and I tried not to panic. Everybody knew 'see you in the kitchen' was adult secret code.

"You girls go on and get in the tub. You're covered from head to foot with dust. No telling what germs you picked up." She and Uncle Ben headed to the back of the house.

The bed sheets were cooler and more comfortable than any two girls who lied to their aunt and uncle had the right to expect. The small bedside lamp lit the room with a violet glow. I wished we had a view of the backyard. I wanted to see Brown Hound. I hadn't had a chance to tell her goodnight.

"Girls?" Aunt Martha said, walking around the bed and sitting on my side. I shifted over to give her room. Jane turned on her side facing us and propped her head on her hand.

"Gracie, I got a phone call tonight."

I went completely still. Daddy. Momma.

"It was from your daddy."

I felt a bit better. He wasn't dead.

"He said your mother is feeling well enough for a small trip," she paused, "they're coming down to the farm tomorrow."

My stomach flipped. Not now! Not when Brown Hound and I had just been banished from the farm for knocking down Marcell.

Jane flung herself on her back and gave a groan then suddenly popped back up. "I don't have to go back, do I? Can I stay here with you and Uncle Ben?"

"No. Both you girls are going."

Jane flung herself back down then turned her head and shot me a dirty look.

"You girls get a good night's sleep. Tomorrow is going to be a big day." She gave us a smile and left.

For a few minutes, I just looked out the window, not wanting the news to be real.

"Now, I'll never get back to the pool with Dan."

I closed my eyes as if that would block Jane's voice. Momma must have wanted to come. Daddy would never bring her otherwise. She didn't like anybody down here, so she must be coming for me. The thought had me rolling out of bed and heading to the door.

"Where you going?"

"Outside."

Aunt Martha'll skin you alive."

"Don't care." I stomped out of the room.

"Little bit late to be outside don't you think?" Uncle Ben closed the kitchen screen door behind him and came over to the edge of the back porch. I didn't answer, just scooted over to make room dragging Brown Hound with me. The moonlight gleamed off Uncle Ben's blue and white striped pajamas. He eased down beside me. His leather bedroom slippers dangled from his feet in the soft night air.

"Tomorrow." He let the word hang in the night for me to examine.

"I don't want to go."

He nodded silently and gazed at the roses on the fence. They looked black in the moonlight.

"You don't have a choice." He put the words out there for me.

"I know. But if I go Brown Hound has to go and everybody hates her!"

He turned and raised one eyebrow. I took that for a question and vaulted into a heated explanation of the recent events at the farm: the biddy chicken, the yapping, the cookies. Sensing my despair, Brown Hound tried to lick my face.

"So, you think it'd be better if Brown Hound stayed here?"

I looked at him in amazement.

"Now don't go getting excited. I have to clear this with your Aunt Martha."

"Clear what, Ben?" Aunt Martha stood at the screen door in her bathrobe. "What are you two doing out here? Gracie, you should be in bed. Ben, you know better than to encourage the child. Gracie, let go of that dog. Go inside and wash your face and hands and get back into the bed." A pause, "Ben?"

Jumping up, I leaned over and gave Uncle Ben a kiss and whispered a thank you in his ear. I hurried to the door. Aunt Martha opened it.

"I'm sorry about being outside. I'll wash up and go back to bed." I stood on tiptoe and kissed her cheek. She swatted my behind softly as I walked past. I took that as a good sign.

"What's goin' on?" Jane mumbled from under the sheet.

"Shhh" I stood beside the half-closed door. My aunt and uncle had come back inside.

"Ben, it's out of the question. You know I'm not fond of dogs and this one will only mess up my backyard."

"I haven't seen her dig up anything yet."

"Well, there's always the chance, and I've worked so hard on my roses. All it will take is one raised leg."

"It's a girl. They don't raise their legs."

"You know exactly what I'm talking about. I don't want that dog here for any longer than we have to. Its mess will be all over the yard. I'll be stepping in it, and we'll be smelling it each time it rains."

I wrapped my arms around my stomach and my heart hurt. She didn't like Brown Hound.

"Martha, for a good-hearted woman you've got a hard head."

"Ben." Her voice held a warning note.

Uncle Ben continued. "You know how much that dog means to Gracie. It's the only thing she's ever had up in Virginia. That dog is her world. And the damn thing's caused plenty of trouble on the farm. Let's keep the dog here while Sissy visits. You know how she is. If the dog is there, someone will tell tales and Gracie will get the blame. They're only going to stay a day or two. I'll take the dog down after they're gone. Now," he paused, "come over here."

A shuffle of bedroom slippers on the floor and the sound of rustling clothes. I was hoping it was a hug. A few more moments of silence, then, "You win this one, Ben."

I heard them move off in the direction of their bedroom. Uncle Ben's words drifted back, "And to the victor goes the spoils." I heard Aunt Martha's soft laugh.

I didn't know what he meant, but I had a pretty good idea that they were friends again. I stood up and walked over to the window glorying in the night. The scent of gardenias drifted on the breeze like a blessing. Suddenly it came to me. When Momma and Daddy fought about Brown Hound, Momma always won. Daddy always gave up. But Uncle Ben didn't give up. He just kept at it until he won. He'd said that it was important to me, and he'd made Aunt Martha see that. I turned from the window and walked back to the bed.

CHAPTER 9

Once again, I was in a car headed to the farm. Uncle Ben wheeled into the drive and came to a stop.

"Ben," said Granny Jane from her rocking chair. "Girls. Where's that dog?"

We hopped out as Uncle Ben got our suitcases from the back seat. He answered as he came up on the porch, "She's going to continue her vacation with us for another day or so." Setting the bags down he walked over and gave Granny Jane a kiss on the cheek.

"Go on with yourself." She gave him a small shove away and he straightened with a smile. "Girls have been just fine. We've enjoyed having them with us. We want them to come back real soon."

"You girls have a good time?"

"Yes, ma'am," We said together.

"I expect to hear all about it but not now. Go on in and see what Miss Emily needs you to do. We're expecting Robert and Sissy anytime."

My fingers dug into the bedroom windowsill as the car pulled into the driveway and came to a stop. Momma's voice rang though the air, "Robert, there's so much dust."

"Aren't you gonna go see them?" Jane sat beside me on the bed.

"I guess." With that I slid off the bed and walked out onto the porch.

Granny Jane hissed at me, "Go over and say hello."

"Here's my girl!" It was Daddy. I went to him, and he scooped me up giving me a great big kiss. "Let's say hi to your momma." Putting me down, we walked around the car and he opened the door.

"Elizabeth Grace, how's my best girl?" Momma pulled herself from the front seat and gave me a hug and kiss. I returned both then stood back watching.

"Robert, I do believe this place is more dilapidated than the last time if that's possible." She straightened her skirt. "I guess I'm still going to have to use the bathroom out in that shed."

"Honey," he said low and soothing, "let's go say hello."

I trailed behind them. Daddy had his arm around her waist like she needed to be steered. Granny Jane didn't call to them from the porch like she did with everybody else. I looked up and saw Jane watching from the bedroom window. She gave me a small wave.

"Granny Jane." Daddy bent over and kissed the old woman.

"Robert. Nice to see you again. Sissy, you're looking well." Granny Jane sounded awfully formal.

"Robert, Sissy," Miss Emily said, stepping onto the porch, wiping her hands on a tea towel "How was your drive down?" Tilting her head up for Daddy's kiss, she reached out and squeezed Momma's hand. She drew them into the living room and out of Granny Jane's firing range.

Jane came through the back door. Walking over, she gave Daddy and Momma a kiss then sat beside me whispering, "We should be at the pool." I smiled and nudged her. She gave me an elbow in the side. We were back to being friends.

Marcell came through the back door carrying a heavy tray.

"Here's Marcell with some iced tea. Jane, why don't you help?" Miss Emily said.

This was the first time Marcell and I had seen each other since the flying cookie calamity. I sat very still. Marcell held the tray while Jane handed out the glasses. Everyone quietly sipped tea. Marcell left the room. I was glad Brown Hound was in Kingston.

"What have you been up to, young lady?" Daddy teased me.

"She hasn't been any trouble, has she?" Momma broke in, and I saw Daddy put his hand on her leg.

"Gracie has been a joy to have around." Miss Emily spoke softly, but it had a firm edge to it. Miss Emily didn't often get that firm edge in her voice, just sometimes with Aunt Viola.

"Well, she can certainly be a handful at home."

"She hasn't been a handful here." Again, the soft with the hard.

The back door opened. Marcell came in and began presenting a tray of cookies. The conversation flowed around her. Momma paused and looked around "Where is that dog?"

"With Martha and Ben," Miss Emily replied.

"What'd she do wrong now?" Momma's voice held a satisfied note.

"She didn't do a thing," Miss Emily said. Marcell paused and looked me squarely in the eyes. Miss Emily continued, "Gracie and Jane were visiting and just came back for your trip. It's easier to leave the dog there."

"Thank heavens for that. That dog's a waste of table scraps."

Marcell straightened up and turned her look on Momma.

Miss Emily broke past Marcell's gaze and spoke, "I expect you'll want to get settled. Robert, you can take the back bedroom. Marcell has it all made up."

Momma took a last bite of her cookie and washed it down with the sweet tea. "Marcell, go get those suitcases. My red dress is packed, and I just know it's wrinkled to death. Iron it. I want to wear it tonight. Miss Emily, the trip was a bit tiring. I think I'll take a nap." With that, she stood and walked out the back door. As her footsteps faded around the back porch, silence settled over the living room.

Daddy's voice came a bit too loud, "That's ok, Marcell. I'll get the bags." Smiling at no one, he hurried out of the front door. Miss Emily and Marcell paused for a minute just looking at each other.

"Miss Emily, I'll be needing that iron."

"Yes, indeed." The two women walked out the back door and headed to the kitchen.

Jane broke the silence "Well, looks like Marcell hates your dog and your momma, too."

"Miss Emily, I keep forgetting how much I love your biscuits." Momma smiled and stretched her arms over her head. Granny Jane frowned. You didn't show your underarms at the dining room table.

Miss Emily shot a glance at Granny Jane trying to warn her off and replied, "Thank you, Sissy."

Robert jumped into the conversation. "Gracie, I hear tell you went off the big diving board at the pool in Kingston."

I turned to him. "Yes, sir."

Jane continued the sentence for me saying, "and the lifeguards let her because she had her swimming badge. And they don't let kids our age do that." It felt good to hear.

"That's a pretty big honor young lady," Daddy began, "I've been swimming in that pool many a time and know for a fact it takes a special person for the lifeguards to..."

"Didn't Marcell do a nice job with my dress?" Momma's voice overrode Daddy's, and everybody looked at her. She was smiling up at Marcell who was handing out plates of pie. She usually didn't stay this late. Miss Emily needed help with the extra company. Marcell didn't look happy about it. "Marcell, I said you did a good job with my dress."

"Yes, ma'am." Marcell turned and walked to the kitchen.

"I don't know why you put up with her insolence," Momma threw her words at Marcell's back, making sure she heard. Daddy reached out and covered her hand with his.

"Gracie, your mother and I are real proud of you for going off the big board. Did you tell the lifeguards you got your badge swimming in the ocean?"

"Yes sir." I kept my answer short.

"Yoo Hoo!" A shrill voice pierced the air.

"That'll be Viola and Will," Granny Jane said. "I expect she's here to get the next round of gossip about y'all's visit." She shoved back and stood up. "We best get on with it."

"I didn't mean to get you up from the table." Aunt Viola's teeth proceeded her into the dining room. Uncle Will trailed behind. "Sissy, come here. You look just fine. She looks just fine doesn't she, Will? Yes," she answered the question herself.

"Let's go into the living room." Miss Emily led the way. Aunt Viola grabbed Momma by the arm to stop her for a minute and shot us a look. Jane and I fled to the kitchen but hovered right outside the door.

"Sissy, this might not be the best place for Gracie right now."

Jane looked at me and mouthed, "Brown Hound".

Aunt Viola kept talking. "It's that Marcell. She's been drinking worse than usual, wandering the road, falling in ditches. Your girl doesn't need to see that type of thing." Aunt Viola kept going. "And Jane doesn't either. Beulavine and I have been talking with the ladies at church. We think Jane needs to come live with me. It's obvious that neither Emily or Miss Jane is in control. They've had their turn with Jane. Lord only knows they must be tired, women their age having a child around. And it shows too, with them not stopping Marcell from drinking. It's a crime to sit by and watch Jane being raised in these conditions."

I looked at Jane. She was dead white. I grabbed at her arm. She shook me off and leaned her head against the wall.

"You just think about it, Sissy. You might want to take your daughter on home."

My chest squeezed. I felt a movement above me. Marcell stood silent, one hand rubbing her forehead and the other braced against the wall. Her eyes were closed. She heard the whole thing. My mind churned. Jane sent away? Me go back home right now? And Marcell heard it was her fault? Marcell went back to the sink. I opened my mouth to speak but Jane put her fingers to her lips.

Drawing in a deep breath Jane spoke in a normal voice, "You need any more help clearing?"

Marcell turned from the sink. "No, you go on out there with the adults. Show you know how to act, even if they don't." Jane and I looked at each other in astonishment.

"You can have a stomach ache if you want," I told my cousin, "I'll be okay by myself."

"No. I'm going in the living room, too."

"...there were cookies all over the porch and I thought I'd laugh fit to dying."

Jane and I walked into the middle of Aunt Viola telling about Brown Hound and the cookie calamity. I wanted her to die choking on one of her big braying laughs. Jane gave me a knuckle in the back and I moved into the room.

"It wasn't all as bad as you're telling Viola." Miss Emily was on the defense.

Momma spoke right up, "Oh, don't tell me how bad it wasn't, Miss Emily. I have to take care of that dog all the time. She knows just what she's doing, let me tell you."

I sat on the sofa and listened to Momma tell tales about Brown Hound. Between her and Aunt Viola in full holler, my dog was the topic of the evening. I looked over at Miss Emily and she gave me a smile. I looked at Daddy and he was looking at Momma, a worried frown on his face. I felt eyes on me, and I looked up. Uncle Will was staring straight at me with a guilty look.

Jane leaned over and whispered, "He knows and he's told. Remember? He told Uncle Ben he thought he saw us coming out of the Freak Show tent."

I froze solid. If Momma and Daddy thought the story about flying cookies was bad, when they heard about the Freak Show no telling what would happen. If Aunt Viola knew, she would never let it pass. It was just too good a story and would prove her theory about Jane's living at the farm. Never mind that Uncle Ben took us to the carnival. It would still be Miss Emily's fault.

Uncle Will's guilty look proved true at Aunt Viola's next words. "That dog isn't the only thing that's been running wild around here." She sat back, folded her arms, and smiled. Miss Emily looked at her hard. Uncle Will shifted in his chair. Jane's fingers crept across the cushion and held onto the bottom my shirt. I waited.

"What?" Momma looked at Viola, then Miss Emily, then Daddy. "What's she been doing?"

It wasn't clear if she was talking about Brown Hound or me. I didn't see it made much difference.

Aunt Viola took a pleased breath and said, "Will saw the girls at the carnival."

"Uncle Ben took us yesterday evening." Miss Emily slowly turned her head in my direction and gave me a quiet look.

Granny Jane thumped her cane on the floor beside her rocker. "So, Ben took them to the carnival. I don't exactly call that running wild. He was there with them the whole time."

"Well, Miss Jane," Aunt Viola spoke triumphantly, "if Ben was watching them how come Will saw Jane and Gracie come out of the Freak Show's back tent?"

There was dead silence all the way around. I

saw a shadow at the back door. It was Marcell with the coffee. She stood still, blending with the night, watching.

"Elizabeth Grace, you did what?" Momma's voice rose up to the ceiling. She began lifting herself out of the chair. I knew a slap was coming and I braced myself. Daddy grabbed her arm. She remained in a half stand, straining against him. "What's wrong with you? Why can't you behave? It's no wonder my nerves are shot."

I shrank back against the sofa. Seemed like I made her sick even when I wasn't around. I waited for Daddy to loosen his grip and her hand to come swinging through the air.

"Sugar, there's no need to get yourself in a fuss." Daddy's voice was low and soothing. He was hanging onto her hard. Momma looked at him then around the room. Everyone was watching her. She eased back down in the chair. Daddy released her arm, and she folded her hands in her lap. I wasn't fooled for a minute.

"Girls? Is this true?" Miss Emily questioned.

I started to plead for mercy when the picture of Uncle Ben on the porch in his pajamas came to mind. He stood up to Aunt Martha. He took us to the carnival over her protests. He argued with her about Brown Hound. I couldn't let them know he turned us loose at the carnival. It was my turn now. I was going to keep Uncle Ben safe.

"Uncle Will, I saw you walking past when we

were running to get cotton candy. That's right beside those tents. Uncle Ben was just down beyond watching bumper cars.

"He said he saw you." Aunt Viola's voice was firm.

Granny Jane cut in, "That true Will? You saw them come out of that tent?"

Uncle Will squirmed in his seat. I knew at once he hadn't actually seen us run out of the tent. If he had, he'd be backing up Aunt Viola one hundred percent. He probably caught a glimpse of us near the tent and thought he'd make Aunt Viola happy by stretching the truth. But right now, he was torn between keeping Aunt Viola happy or keeping Granny Jane from killing him.

"I could have sworn I saw them run out of the tent." He was talking fast, trying to make both sides happy.

"Well, it was dark. You'd probably been playing horseshoes and taking a little nip of 'shine," Granny Jane said the words with a laugh, but there was a knife in it. Aunt Viola eased back in her chair when she heard the old woman's tone.

"Miss Emily, you get the door?" Everybody jumped a mile. It was Marcell with the serving tray. Coming through the door, she shot Jane and me a look. Bounding up we helped her pass the cups. The adults let the anger drift out of the room by being busy with the coffee. Jane and I passed the cream and sugar while Marcell poured.

"Sissy, how long are you and Robert going to stay?" Aunt Viola was pretending she hadn't tried to stir up a mess.

"We're headed home tomorrow," Daddy answered her.

"Is Gracie going back with you?" Her words were like a haystack with a hidden pitchfork.

I clutched the cream pitcher in my hand. "Brown Hound," I whispered to myself.

"Robert, she's having a good time and we're enjoying her. No need for her to go back now." I loved Miss Emily better than anyone. I looked over at Daddy and my heart sank. He looked relieved. He sat there patting Momma's hand. She was smiling. I looked up and Marcell was watching them both.

Daddy turned to Miss Emily. "If she's not a bother, that'd be nice Momma."

"Help me bring these things to the kitchen," Marcell ordered. Jane and I jumped. She usually didn't give orders in front of company. But she was doing it now.

"Gracie, Jane, you go on and help Marcell," Miss Emily said. Jane and I followed Marcell into the kitchen. We handed her the cream and sugar and helped put the cookies away. She loaded the cups into the sink then turned and spoke. "You all getting silly. I expect you too tired to stay up. Go on to bed. I'll tell the folks I sent you straight without letting you say g'night as punishment."

My mouth dropped open. I had never heard

her say so many words at one time. Jane grinned and grabbed my hand.

"Thank you, Marcell." Jane sounded almost formal as she pulled me to the kitchen door. Quietly, we tiptoed through the dining room and into the back hallway. Moving past the attic stairs we made it safely to our bedroom. Jane sat on the bed holding her pajama top in her hands, twisting it in knots.

"What if she does it?"

I knew she was talking about Aunt Viola wanting her away from the farm.

She tried to sound brave, "I'm not gonna leave. Granny Jane won't let me go. And stupid Aunt Viola can't make me." Her voice trailed off as her eyes met mine. I shrugged my shoulders. Here I was, living proof that adults could do anything with you they wanted.

I tried to sound reasonable. "Marcell was good tonight, handing around the coffee. Nobody could say she was behaving bad." I could tell Jane wanted to hope but saw herself in the back of Aunt Viola's car waving goodbye. I continued. "And she got us out of having to kiss everybody goodnight so maybe she is better."

Jane replied, "Yeah but what about Aunt Viola and your momma in the dining room talking about Marcell..." her voice trailed off.

"We have to get her to stop drinking completely," I said.

"How? Granny Jane and Miss Emily can't even do it."

"Well, Miss Charity says she drinks because

she is sad and wants to be with ghosts."

"And just how're we gonna fix that?" I could see tears in Jane's eyes. She really thought Aunt Viola could do it. A sadness came over me. I pulled on my pajamas, turned off the light, and climbed in beside her.

The old bed creaked as Jane settled into sleep. There was a murmur of voices from the living room. Tomorrow, Daddy and Momma would be going back. A small weight lifted from my chest. I could stay for a while, and I'd saved Uncle Ben. Now we just had to fix Marcell. I closed my eyes.

"We're going to get an early start to avoid the heat." We were at breakfast and Daddy was explaining their early departure. "The heat always makes Sissy sick, and she's not feeling so good today anyway."

Momma wasn't at the table. Neither was Granny Jane. Miss Emily said she was having another one of her spells, but was nothing to worry about. I could see Jane trying hard to believe her. Daddy was anxious to get on the road.

"We're sorry you couldn't stay longer. I know everyone would love to see you in church tomorrow. And Gracie has missed you both." Miss Emily smiled as she spoke. It was only half-truth. I missed Daddy but not Momma. I'd hoped she'd miss me and start to like me. The image of her starting to leap up from her chair to slap me rose in my mind. I put down my fork.

"She's so delicate. This might have been more

than the doctor thought it would be. Seeing everyone at church will just add more strain. I need to get her back home."

I guessed the doctor hadn't counted on stories about Brown Hound knocking over Marcell and me going to the carnival. It was obvious my doings made her too sick for breakfast. I raised my head and looked around the dining room. Miss Emily was smiling and talking to Daddy. Jane was gulping down her eggs and reaching for another buttered biscuit. A thought stopped me cold. They weren't sick. I'd been here for weeks, and I hadn't made them sick. Well, Granny Jane was having a spell, but she'd been having them for some time, so they weren't my fault. I concentrated on these new thoughts. Nobody on the farm was sick. They didn't have to go to see the doctor because I was here. I felt something flicker inside. I tried to figure out what it was, but Miss Emily interrupted.

"Well then, let's get you on the road. Marcell, you make up a basket in case Sissy gets hungry on the ride back. And put in a jar of sweet tea. Girls, go get in your clothes so you can say a proper good bye. Robert, do you need any help?"

"No, Momma. I'll just get our things ready, and we'll be out of your hair."

With that, we all went to do our duties and soon were standing under the oak tree beside the car.

"Take good care of yourself, Gracie." Daddy bent down to kiss me goodbye. I felt a little grab of sadness as I kissed him back.

"Try not to get into any more trouble." Momma leaned over and gave me a kiss. I wanted her gone. The thought astonished, then scared me. I reached up and threw my arms around her neck. She gave a small laugh, unhooked my hands, and climbed into the car.

"Let us hear from you," Miss Emily called to them. She moved to put her hand on my shoulder. It felt good. I leaned against her as the car drove away in a cloud of pale Carolina dust.

CHAPTER 10

Back in Kingston, Sunday afternoon at the pool was heaven. Walking up to the high dive, I jumped into the cold blue water and washed away the past two days. It felt clean and good. Thoughts of Daddy and Sissy faded as I plunged in over and over, drunk with chlorine and lifeguard approval.

"You look like you've been drinking Marcell's liquor." Uncle Ben teased us at supper. I smiled at him. "Red-eyed as a coon dog," he continued. Jane snapped up her head.

"Ben, hush about Marcell. Girls, looks like it's an early night tonight. What do you have planned for tomorrow? Pool's closed on Mondays."

"What do you mean Gracie has red eyes like Marcell?" Jane's voice had an edge to it. Uncle Ben sat back and gave her a sharp look. I glanced at Aunt Martha. She gave Uncle Ben one of those 'I told you' eyeballs.

"I'm serious Uncle Ben. What did you mean?" Jane's voice was defiant, but I heard a tremble.

Aunt Martha must have heard it too because she got up from her chair and went over to stand beside Jane. Placing her hand on Jane's shoulder to settle her down she spoke, "Ben, Marcell is part of Jane's family, and it's not fair to joke about her."

"We joke about Viola's teeth and she's your sister."

"Yes, but we don't particularly like Viola." Aunt Martha replied firmly. I agreed with that but kept my mouth shut.

"Martha," Uncle Ben's voice was firm, "I was just teasing. And anyway, it's no secret that Marcell drinks too much. It's just a shame it's such a problem for Miss Emily and Miss Jane."

"It's only a problem 'cause of Aunt Viola and Miss Beulavine!" Jane said, shrugging off Aunt Martha's hand, defending Marcell.

Aunt Martha took Jane's dismissal with good grace and moved away saying, "Honey, Marcell does drink too much. You know she does." Jane started to rise out of her chair in indignation, but Aunt Martha held up her hand for silence. "Yes, Viola and Beulavine are taking advantage of a situation, but they couldn't make trouble if there was nothing to talk about."

I saw Jane's face get red and I knew that look. She was ready to bust, and I didn't want her to ruin our stay. I tried to redirect the conversation and began to babble. "Miss Charity said she drinks 'cause she wants to be with ghosts." Well, that stopped the room right there.

"You've been to see Miss Charity?" Aunt Martha zoomed in on me like Brown Hound finding clean laundry. I was trapped by my big mouth and good intentions. Counting on the kindness of a woman who let my dog stay and poop in her yard, I braved it out. "Yes, Ma'am."

"When?"

Maybe I had been too hasty relying on that kindness. Her voice was frosty. I looked over and Jane's face was still red. I continued, "I went to see her to get a spell on Jane, so Jane wouldn't be sad."

Aunt Martha and Uncle Ben looked at each other in amazement. Uncle Ben asked, "Why was Jane sad?"

"I wasn't sad. Gracie's stupid." Jane was defending Marcell, not wanting them to know Marcell had pushed her. It was time to shut my mouth. I folded my arms across my chest.

"Now Jane," Aunt Martha began. It was time to look for cover. Jane's voice overrode our aunt. "I hate Aunt Viola. She keeps talking about how Granny Jane and Miss Emily aren't raising me right. She talks mean about them all the time and says Marcell is a bad influence."

Aunt Martha spoke calmly, "Ben, you and Gracie clear the table. I think Jane and I need a little talk."

Jane looked like she had swallowed a frog. Aunt Martha held out her hand and together they walked to the front porch. I could hear the swing settle. Leaning over the table, I picked up the salt and pepper listening hard but trying to look like I was doing my job.

"Go on in the kitchen and start washing. I'll

clear the rest of the table," said Uncle Ben.

Foiled, I dragged into the kitchen, pulled the step stool up to the sink, and turned on the water. Uncle Ben and I dried and put up the dishes in silence. He looked preoccupied and I was still straining to hear what Aunt Martha was saying to Jane.

"Gracie."

The word startled me, and I looked up at my uncle. He was standing there staring down at me with a strange look on his face. "We're finished here. Let's go outside."

We settled down on the concrete back porch just like last time, our legs dangling over the edge. Brown Hound danced up the steps to be with us and after much tail wagging and face licking, she quieted down.

"If you're going to be here a while, there's some things you should know." I stayed still. He continued, "I don't know what Martha's saying to Jane, but you should know some things about Marcell."

"What about her?" Jane's words shot through the air and gave us a start. She stood beside the screen door, holding it open for flies. Aunt Martha stood behind her rubbing her forehead.

"Jane have a seat. I'm about to tell a story about Marcell."

"Ben, do you think…" Aunt Martha's words trailed off. Jane stepped through the door and plopped down beside Uncle Ben. Aunt Martha came out to the porch and sat in one of the plastic chairs. Brown

Hound thumped her tail and thought all the fuss was about her.

"I'm going to tell you something. This is grown up talk. And I want both of you to promise you won't tell anyone else."

"Even Miss Emily?" Jane asked.

"Miss Emily and Granny Jane already know. It's the reason they keep Marcell on at the farm and let Viola and Beulavine go on with their talk." Here Uncle Ben paused and gave us a stern look. Jane clutched her hands in her lap, and I pulled Brown Hound close. This didn't sound good.

"Ben, you sure the girls are old enough to hear this?"

"Martha, they were old enough to go to the Freak Show."

Jane and I stared at each other in astonishment. Uncle Ben intercepted our look and nodded his head. At that moment, we loved him above all else. He continued, "And I expect Gracie here has seen a few things we don't know about." He looked at me and gave a soft smile. I buried my nose in Brown Hound's fur. "So, I expect it's time they know about Marcell and the Simmons."

"Miss Victoria's people?" Jane asked, focusing completely on Uncle Ben.

"Yes. But this isn't about Miss Victoria, it's about her father, Old Man Elroy Simmons."

We sat quietly and looked up at him. We were ready. At least we thought we were. Uncle Ben took a match out of his pocket and dragged it across the concrete. Seemed like for once he was going to smoke his cigar instead of chewing it to death.

"It was about thirty years ago. When Marcell was just a girl." He looked at us. "Right about your age." I tried to imagine Marcell as anything but who she was right now. He continued, "I remember it was right around August when it happened."

"When what happened?" It was Jane. I kept quiet. I figured Jane was the one who had the right to ask questions.

"Piece of white trash girl named Tillman. She was about sixteen years old. Her people lived in the swamp. A no-count tart."

"Ben. That's not necessary"

"You're right, Martha. Anyway," he paused to take a drag on his cigar. "Nineteen twenty was a bad year. Coloreds were raising a fuss about their people being hanged and killed. Lots of white folks didn't like that fussing one bit. Anyway, one June evening this girl, Lacy Tillman, came running into town hollering about somebody forcing her."

I heard Aunt Martha stir in her plastic chair, but she kept quiet. I knew about forcing. I'd heard Sissy and her club ladies talking when I should have been outside. Jane and I'd never talked about it, but I could see she was easy with the term too. Uncle Ben looked at us and we nodded we knew what he meant.

He continued. "She was crying and carrying on all the way to the sheriff's office. When they finally quieted her down, she said that Ivis, Marcell's father, had caught her in the cornfield near their house and forced her."

Uncle Ben looked at us to see how we were taking it. Seeing we hadn't passed out from shock, he kept going. "The sheriff back then never did have any sense. He told Lacy to go on home. That he'd get his deputies together and bring Ivis in. Well, word spread like a wildfire. Lacy'd been sure to let everybody within a mile hear her. People started talking before she even got out of town. Half the people believed Lacy or wanted to, and half knew Ivis well enough to know Lacy was lying. That damn lazy sheriff!"

"Ben!"

"Sorry, Martha. That no good sheriff didn't bother to get his deputies. Said later he thought he'd wait and deal with Ivis the next day. Frankly, I think he was waiting for the Grand Tigers to take care of it for him. And that's what happened."

"The Tigers. They killed colored people like the KKK," Jane said.

"Yes and no. The Grand Tigers started off doing good. Doing things that needed to be done for both white folks and colored. It just got out of hand. Like it always does when people think they don't have to follow rules.

The Tigers decided to go after Marcell's daddy that night. Your granddaddy Tom was in town that day ordering seed and heard about it. He warned Ivis on his way back to the farm. Later that evening Tom met

The Tigers on their way to get Ivis. He tried to talk them out of it. Didn't do a bit of good. By then Ivis had run to hide. Was just him and Marcell. Her momma died when she was born, you know. Anyway, the Tigers got to the cabin with Old Man Elroy Simmons in the lead. What an old bastard he was."

"Ben!"

"I know. I'm sorry, Martha. Forgive me, girls. I shouldn't talk that way about Miss Victoria's father but telling brings it back." He gave a sigh, held up his cigar and inspected it. Brown Hound stirred restlessly, and I scratched her behind the ears. Jane didn't have that comfort. She sat, hands twisting in her lap. Uncle Ben took a few puffs on his cigar. "The Tigers broke into the cabin and asked Marcell where Ivis was. She had no idea where he'd run to. That's when Old Man Simmons let the dogs have a go at her."

Uncle Ben stopped and took another deep inhale off his cigar. Jane's hands went still. I thought back to Granny Jane and Miss Emily talking about the bite scars on Marcell's ankles. My hands dug deep into Brown Hound's fur. She didn't complain. She'd felt me do this to her long before now.

"Hear tell, her legs were torn up some. Could've been worse."

I tried to imagine being torn up by a dog. I looked down at Brown Hound. I'd seen her snarl at other dogs but beyond that, I'd never considered her an animal. Uncle Ben puffed away in the silence. I heard the plastic chair squeak with Aunt Martha's shifting weight. I loosened my grip on Brown Hound's fur and got a small tail thump of thank you. I looked over at Jane. Her hands were still clamped together.

Uncle Ben broke the silence. "Anyway, they took one of her daddy's shirts and gave it to the dogs for tracking. And Marcell, even being hurt, lit out to find her daddy. The men tracked Ivis down through the swamp and onto the railroad tracks beside Miss Emily's farm." He gave a look over at Jane. Reaching out he put his arm around her shoulders and drew her right up next to him. I was glad she had some comfort.

"That's where they got him. They dragged him off the tracks and onto the farm to that tree beside the barn and hanged him. Marcell saw it all. And that's why Marcell drinks to forget. She surely does."

The evening settled down into night. Cicadas broke the silence. Brown Hound eased herself to her feet stretching with her head down and front paws out. She shook all over straightening her fur. I wanted to do that too; stand up and shake all over, throwing off the story like raindrops. Instead, I sat listening to the warm Carolina night.

"Go ahead and finish it Ben," Aunt Martha said, sounding tired.

"Lacy had a baby eight months later and it looked just like old man Elroy Simmons. No colored blood there. She'd blamed Ivis so Elroy wouldn't be found out. And Elroy let her do it."

"Jane?" Aunt Martha said, "Jane honey, you all right?"

"She's fine, Martha. Just going to take a little while for things to sink in. Now Jane," Uncle Ben leaned away so he could turn and face her. "You need to keep in mind that Cap'n Tom quit the Tigers years before when they started taking the law into their own hands. The men who hanged Ivis on Tom's farm did it as payback, that's what we always thought. Tom felt guilty about that. So that's why Miss Emily and Miss Jane keep Marcell on." Uncle Ben turned his head and looked at me. "And that's why Marcell hates dogs." He hugged Jane tight.

I nodded to him, letting him know I understood. I could see hating dogs from getting all torn up, but what I couldn't see was the part about the dogs chasing Marcell's daddy and then him being hanged from a tree. I was shaking inside and suddenly the night seemed mean.

Before, the night had been just fine. I liked the dark. When momma was asleep, I'd dance quietly around the house luxuriating in freedom from her gaze. It was also when I'd sneak out of the house and Brown Hound and I would sit on the picnic table glorying in the dark. But sitting on the cement porch beside Uncle Ben on this night, a cold, heavy feeling settled in my chest.

The plastic chair creaked. Suddenly, Aunt Martha kneeled beside me. And then she sat down on the cement. In her good dress. I never envisioned Aunt Martha in anything but a chair. I was astonished. Brown Hound gave a small bark and jumped off the porch. Aunt Martha put her arms around me and rocked me in the darkness.

CHAPTER 11

It was Wednesday morning, and we were back at the farm. Monday and Tuesday we'd stayed close beside Aunt Martha and Uncle Ben, playing in the yard, reading comic books and being quiet. It was like all four of us were tired. The only one with energy was Brown Hound, but even she seemed to feel our mood and didn't bark or mess with Aunt Martha's roses. Sunday night, Jane and I had cried a bit on the porch then were put to bed. Uncle Ben explained it pretty good, and there didn't seem to be much else to say. Now we knew why Marcell drank and hated dogs. It wasn't Brown Hound, after all. It was all dogs, and I didn't blame her. Every time I found out a secret, the world seemed meaner. If Jane and Aunt Martha and Uncle Ben were tired, I was extra tired from meanness. The silence and comfort of the two days were a blessing.

Jane and I were back doing chores. Miss Emily had us going to find a wandering mule. We walked down the road and cut over to the colored graveyard. The mule was standing in the shade, chewing grass. I grabbed its halter and hooked on a rope. Jane walked through the graveyard looking at headstones.

"There's Marcell's momma."

I walked over and looked at the headstone. Sophronia, Wife of Ivis, 1892-1910. Here was one of Marcell's ghosts.

"He's not here."

"Who?"

"Ivis, Marcell's father."

I closed my eyes and pretended she hadn't said anything.

"Did you hear me?"

"Yes," I said.

"Well, he's not here."

"Well, big whoop."

Jane stood in front of me, hands on her hips. I stared at her. She stared back. I gave in. "What?"

"That's why Marcell wants to be with ghosts. Her daddy's not here, and she's looking for him." Jane squinted her eyes, thinking. "Where do you think they buried him after they hanged him?"

"I don't know, and I don't care. I don't want to find what they did with him. I don't want to find out anything." The last few days came over me like a cloud of stinging bees and I ran, my misery trailing behind. Out of the colored graveyard, and down the road, I flew toward the farmhouse. "Brown Hound Brown Hound," I called as I ran to the front porch. I wanted my dog.

"Dog of yours in the swamp." It was Marcell. She was standing beside Granny Jane's rocking chair, offering the old lady a glass of sweet tea. I stumbled to a stop and looked at the colored woman. She'd been chewed up by dogs, seen her daddy chased through the swamp, and watched men hang him from a tree. And she was still alive and breathing. My own breathing slowed, and I looked at her in wonder. Maybe people could live past anything. I flashed on her drinking. Maybe they couldn't.

"Thank you, Marcell. Girl, come up here." Granny Jane dismissed Marcell. "Sit."

I did, hugging my knees, looking up at her.

"Been an active few days for you, hasn't it?"

"Yes, ma'am."

"Your Uncle Ben called. Said he'd told you and Jane a story."

Why couldn't anyone just leave it alone? "Yes ma'am." I lowered my eyes and picked at the porch boards. Granny Jane let it sit for a while. I felt bad I answered her so sharp, but I wasn't in the mood to talk. I wanted my dog. I wanted to bury my nose in her fur, smell her doggy smell, and hear her heart thumping.

"Where's Jane?"

I jumped at her voice. I'd been lost in longing. "Still at the graveyard. She's looking for Marcell's daddy's grave."

"Won't find it."

That got my attention. I looked up. Granny Jane nodded down at me, "Always been a mystery. When Tom went to take Ivis' body down and bury it proper, it was already gone."

I couldn't help myself. "Why?"

"Probably the coloreds didn't want to leave it

hanging there, the Tigers were known to come back and cut the body. So, they most likely hid it and never said a word. I clamped my hands over my ears and put my head down on my knees. Above me I heard her speak, "Won't help." The rocking chair gave a groan as the old woman stood up. "Come on girl, let's help Emily in the kitchen." I followed her inside.

I was pulling on my pajama top when I heard the dogs howling down by the train tracks.

"Sounds like they're going after a coon." Jane was hanging out of the window, looking into the night. She'd been edgy all day, late for dinner, barely touching the ripe sliced tomatoes, her usual favorite, skittering from one chore to the next. I settled on cleaning the chicken pen, a job she hated, just to get away from her. Supper hadn't been much better. Marcell had gone back home as usual, and the meal had been a strange affair with Miss Emily looking at Jane, then me, and Granny Jane arching her eyebrows and nodding her head. Silent communication flew all around the room, but I wasn't a part of it. And that suited me just fine. I'd had about enough communication for a while.

"Girls?" I turned as Miss Emily poked her head through the bedroom door. Jane yanked herself back in the window, pulled down the screen, and sat Indian style on the bed. Miss Emily came in, closing the door. Sitting on the edge of the bed she held out her hand to Jane. My cousin scooted over beside her. I climbed up with them and waited.

"I want to tell you both something. I know you've had a big shock about Marcell…" Jane started to interrupt, but Miss Emily put a soft finger over her lips and smiled, "Shhh. Now you just hush and let me talk. There's something I want to tell you both." I wanted to cram my hands over my ears, but Miss Emily gave me a smile that said this was going to be okay. I decided to trust her but kept my hands ready anyway.

She settled herself on the bed and said, "Your grandfather, Cap'n Tom was a good man. And yes, he belonged to the Grand Tigers, but quit once they started messing with the colored folks."

"Why'd he join in the first place?" Jane's voice held an edge.

"Because at the start the Tigers took care of things the law wouldn't."

"Like what? Chasing and hanging?"

Miss Emily put her hand on the top of Jane's head and stroked her hair. I sat still and listened. "No, Jane, things like making sure people helped each other out." I leaned past Miss Emily. Looked like Jane was refusing to hear a word. I bet Miss Emily thought so too, but she kept going.

"A long time ago when Cap'n Tom and I were first married, before Marcell was even born, there was a family living in the swamp near Miss Charity. The husband worked at the mill and drank up his money every Friday. He and his wife had a little boy that everybody called No Clothes." I laughed then smashed my hand over my mouth.

Miss Emily ignored me and kept right on. "They called him that because all he had was one shirt, a pair of pants, and no shoes at all. The other children teased him something fierce. One night your grandfather and the other Grand Tigers paid a visit to the man. Yanked him out of bed and scared him to death. They told him if he didn't start bringing money home for food and clothes for No Clothes, their next visit wouldn't be so friendly."

"What happened?" I couldn't help myself. I was feeling bad for No Clothes. I wondered if he had a dog.

"The next morning before work, the man went to the local store, and begged to borrow some shoes, and pants for the boy. Said he'd bring the money that following Friday."

"Did he?" Jane asked.

"Indeed, he did. And he kept providing for his family, too. So, the Grand Tigers weren't all that bad. Not at first." She moved to the edge of the bed. "I just wanted you girls to know." Placing her hands on her thighs, she pushed herself up.

I wanted to ask what happened that made Cap'n Tom get out of the Grand Tigers, but Miss Emily headed for the door. Her back was straight and stiff. Now didn't seem the time.

"You girls get to bed." She waited by the door until we settled in and pulled the sheet up to our noses. Smiling, she turned off the light and softly closed the door.

The night was warm and sticky. Jane thrashed under the sheet like a fish on a hook. I knew it wasn't because of the heat. She'd been thrashing all day since the graveyard.

"Where you think he is?"

I knew it. She wasn't gonna let it go. I tried to put an end to it, "Granny Jane said nobody knows where Ivis is."

"You asked Granny Jane?"

"No, she told me."

Jane wadded up the sheet and kicked it to the end of the bed. She sat up, and I knew I was in for a long night. Her voice was at its most demanding, "Well, what'd she say?"

I surrendered, "she said when Cap'n Tom came back to take Ivis down and bury him, the body was gone and they never found him. So, no one knows where he is buried. So that's that." I folded my arms over my chest and lay still, hoping she'd leave it.

"I think we should find him."

I looked at her. The moonlight slivered across her face and her expression surprised me. There was no daring in her eyes this time. No pirate grin. She was serious.

Jane uncrossed her legs then crossed them again. "Marcell drinks because she's sad and wants to be with ghosts. Now, when Granny Jane gets that sad look on her face she goes to the graveyard to have a chat with James Earl, and it makes her feel better."

I'd seen that with my own eyes and nodded my head in agreement.

"Anyway, I think if Marcell could go talk to her daddy, you know, be with his ghost, then maybe she wouldn't be sad and then she wouldn't drink."

I sat up slowly. What Jane said about Granny Jane was true. Maybe we could do some good for Marcell and….

"And…," Jane continued breaking into my thoughts, "if Marcell didn't drink then Miss Beulavine and the church ladies couldn't make me go live with Aunt Viola!"

My heart lurched to a stop. It was the answer. I knew about being sent away. I didn't want that to happen to Jane. She didn't have a dog. Thinking of life without Brown Hound clinched it. "How do we find him?"

Jane flopped back in satisfaction, and we stared at the ceiling. The cracked boards, glowing in the moonlight gave no answers. The dogs began baying again, farther away this time. Their singing drifted on the night and floated up to the stars. The curtains moved in a slight breeze then rested. Suddenly, Jane held her hands in the air and counted off possibilities.

"We can't ask Granny Jane. She'd wear us out with her cane plus she says nobody knows. Miss Emily would be upset and would forbid us to do it. Plus, she never wants to talk about anything. She probably wouldn't have told me about my momma and daddy if that Sunday School girl didn't." She continued to stare at the ceiling.

"Miss Charity Frazier?" I wanted to help.

"No."

I silently agreed. I'd had about enough of the conjure woman. I sighed and considered a name close to my heart. Uncle Ben. It made sense. He'd covered for us when he knew for sure we'd gone to the Freak Show. He'd saved Brown Hound by arguing with Aunt Martha. And he told us about Marcell and her daddy. He had to know more than he let on. I rolled over on my side facing Jane and explained.

Jane nodded her head. "But we can't let Aunt Martha know."

"That's true."

Jane looked at me. The pirate grin was back. "Uncle Ben," she said with firm satisfaction. She grabbed the sheet and pulled it up. I stared at the ceiling and listened for the dogs.

It was another week before we were able to corner Uncle Ben. A week filled with the normal adventures of playing hide and seek in the barn, and swimming in the creek under the railroad trestle. We didn't get bit by moccasins or rattlesnakes, so we took it as a sign our intentions about Ivis were righteous.

As for Marcell, she started nodding to us just like she did with Granny Jane. No more glowering or sharp speaking. I had been careful to keep Brown Hound out of her way. No more drinking, either. But then, as Jane explained when I pointed it out, she'd gone this long without having to be dragged out of a ditch before. I watched Jane this week, too. She seemed satisfied with herself and mostly went around with a small smile.

Sunday came. Jane and I planned to talk with Uncle Ben when he and Aunt Martha came out to the farm for dinner. We found him on the sofa in the living room by himself. Marcell had the afternoon off. Granny Jane was on the front porch napping in her rocking chair. Miss Emily and Aunt Martha were piddling around in the kitchen. Uncle Ben's head was tilted back and the sound of his snoring filled the room.

Jane tiptoed forward. "Uncle Ben?" She whispered as she put her hand on his arm giving him a slight shake.

He popped straight up. Seeing where he was, he settled down and rubbed his hands over his face. "Girls," he said tiredly.

Jane gathered her breath and jumped right in, "Uncle Ben, where is Ivis buried?"

He looked like he'd been hit on the head with a possum. He set his eyes on us and took a deep breath. "And just why do you need to know?"

"We figured, Gracie and me, if we could find where Ivis is buried, we could show Marcell. She could go and talk with him, then maybe she wouldn't feel so bad and wouldn't drink," She said it all in one breath. I watched her suck the air back in and then squirm. Jane didn't usually squirm and beg. It was fun to see.

"And that would make her stop drinking?"

Jane gave her reasoning. "When Granny Jane goes to the graveyard to talk to James Earl she comes back better."

"And you think if Marcell had a grave to talk to, she would be better?"

"Yes sir, just like Granny Jane." She added Granny Jane's name again to give weight to her request.

Uncle Ben smiled and said, "Now what you girls are saying makes a lot of sense. It just might do Marcell some good, but I'm afraid I can't help."

"Uncle Ben." Jane wailed.

"Girls, I truly don't know about Ivis." Jane opened her mouth again but was hushed by his next words. "There're only old stories about it." He looked at us and nodded his head. I could see he was telling the truth.

"Can you tell us the stories anyway? Just for fun?" Jane kept her eyes wide and tried to look innocent. I kept my eyes to myself and felt bad for Jane's trying to fool Uncle Ben.

"Well, I'll tell you one story and you'll see that it's nothing but foolishness." Leaning forward, he placed his hands on his knees and began. "One story has it that Elroy Simmons took him down and carried him to their big white house on the hill. They say he buried Ivis there because he felt bad about what he'd done." Uncle Ben gave a snort and shook his head. "Elroy never felt bad about a thing in his life. He was one mean cuss." He gave Jane and me a look. "And so there, you see? People say things just to be talking. Most likely none of them are true." With that, he sat back and picked up the paper.

I knew he wasn't going to tell us anything more.

As bad as Jane wanted to know where Ivis was buried, Uncle Ben was just as stubborn at holding his ground. Like he'd been with Brown Hound. I crawled up on the sofa and kissed his scratchy cheek. Jane stood in front of him and patted his knee. Quietly, we left Uncle Ben to his cigar and his paper.

※ ※ ※

"Well, so much for that." We were out in the graveyard sitting on the cement hump of James Earl's grave, picking at the worn spots. I gazed off into the distance. The late afternoon sun sparkled on the trees. I wondered what they would look like when frost came. Suddenly, I thought about school. I'd already been here over a month and summer was at its peak. The hot sticky days had flown by. Fall would come and paint the leaves all kinds of colors. Where would Brown Hound and I be then?

Suddenly with a chorus of barking and howling, Brown Hound, Black Jack and Sassy came tumbling out of the swamp. By the looks of them, they'd been chasing something that liked hiding in mud. They shook themselves so hard their feet flew off the ground, then trotted over. I stroked Brown Hound's head. Her eyes gleamed up at me. She was having a fine life here on the farm. There seemed to be a peace of sorts between her and Marcell now that I was keeping close watch.

I patted my dog again and the ripe smell of the swamp rose from her fur. The swamp. Miss Charity. We'd already crossed her off our list, but I decided to run it past Jane again. She shook her head back and forth, "No. We need to save her for when we really need her."

"Seems like we need her now," I said.

Jane stared at me. "You might be right. Maybe we can get her to put a spell on Uncle Ben, so he'll tell us more stories."

I looked at her in horror but saw she was kidding. I gave her a shove and she almost fell off the grave. I grabbed her shirt and hauled her back. She shrugged away from me but wasn't paying me much mind. She had something in her head and was chewing on it.

"Listen. Maybe there's something in her church. Like when they write in Bibles about who dies and who married who and so on."

"Marcell's church?"

Jane nodded. "The colored church."

"But if they'd it written down somewhere, then they'd of told Marcell, right?"

Defeat. Silence descended as we sat in the late afternoon heat. Jane tried again. "But maybe they know something. I mean something that's so bad they wouldn't want to tell Marcell."

I countered again. "But if they wouldn't tell her because it was so bad then why would they tell us, so we could tell her?" The noise of Aunt Martha and Uncle Ben's car starting and slowly driving away came through the air. We waved and they disappeared down the road.

Jane straightened up making a firm decision, "I think we should ask anyway."

"Who?" I sounded like an owl.

"The preacher at the colored church. I've known Uncle John since I was a baby. He'll talk to us." Jane hopped down from the grave and I followed.

CHAPTER 12

"Girls mighty quiet this evening." Granny Jane was wiping butter on her biscuit. Sunday dinner leftovers sat in the middle of the kitchen table, cold fried chicken, warmed up butter beans, reheated potatoes but new biscuits. Miss Emily never failed in the biscuit department. It was a good thing. We needed something in our stomachs after today's disappointment. Just as soon as we'd walked to the colored church we were walking right back. The preacher had been nice but brief. "No one knows what happened. If anyone does, it's Miss Emily. Cap'n Tom was her husband. You go on and ask her now."

Granny Jane asked me to pass the biscuits. I did and smiled up at her. She gave me an inquiring look and asked, "You hear from your daddy today?"

My smile faded. "No ma'am."

"Phone rang during my nap," said Granny Jane.

Miss Emily spoke up, "That was Viola."

"And she wanted exactly what?" Granny Jane took a bite from her biscuit just like she was taking a bite out of Viola. Jane and I cut our eyes at each other and tried not to grin. Miss Emily put the spoon back in the butter beans. She looked straight at us. "Viola called to say Jane and Gracie were at the colored church this afternoon."

How did Aunt Viola know? Was she everywhere at once?

Miss Emily's voice turned sharp. "I'd like to know what you were doing there. I've told you not to visit that church. You're getting too old to do that kind of thing. You have to quit giving people room to talk." She wasn't like the soft cloud I thought she was on that first day. She was a different cloud now. The kind that rained down on you hard.

Granny Jane's voice matched the crack of her cane as she punched it on the floor. "Answer your grandmother!" The cracking cane reminded me of Momma's broom. I shrunk down in my chair. Granny Jane turned to me. "Gracie?"

Usually, Jane had to answer. It was her house. I was just a visitor. But I could see this made no difference to Granny Jane. Pushing myself up in my chair, I answered, "We went to talk to Preacher John." The cane pounded on the floor again. I blurted, "We went to ask where Ivis is buried."

Well, that shut everybody up. Even the cane stayed still. The four of us sat at the table looking at the butter beans. Outside the biddies crooned and crickets began their evening song. Clacking dog toenails sounded on the back porch. Time for their supper.

"That so?"

"Yes, Ma'am."

"Jane?"

Jane looked at Granny Jane and nodded her head.

The old woman's attention turned back on me. "Ben told us you two had been asking about that. What'd Preacher John say?"

"He wouldn't tell us," I replied. Jane shot me a look that clearly said to shut up. Granny Jane was having none of that. The cane cracked again. I blurted, "and told us to ask Miss Emily."

"Well," Granny Jane leaned back, one hand on the head of her cane and the other on the arm of the chair. "Did he now?" This wasn't a question I was supposed to answer. Granny Jane's eyes fastened on Miss Emily. I was freed from the line of fire.

Miss Emily rose from her chair and headed towards the door. "Girls, clean up now."

Granny Jane pushed back her chair and headed after her. Jane and I waited exactly five seconds after the screen door slammed, then jumped up and dived at the table. I filled the sink and kept an eye to the window while Jane finished clearing. If we got done quick enough, we could follow. Suds flew, water splashed, and Jane's drying towel whirled through the air.

"They're out in the barn," Jane said as she stacked the dry plates on the counter. I nodded my head, let the dirty water drain from the sink, and mopped up the splashes.

"That's it. Come on." Jane grabbed the pan filled with scraps, I held the screen door, and we went down the steps into the yard. Brown Hound jumped up and patted my shoulders with her paws. I grabbed them for a minute and looked into her eyes. Happy girl. My heart gave a sweet thump.

"Let that dog go. Come on!" Jane headed to the barn. I quickly followed.

It was quiet as we approached the barn, the sound of our footsteps hidden by crickets singing and a mule crunching hay. Slowly we moved, hunching over like that was going to keep us hidden. At the barn door we sank to our knees and peered through the cracks. Granny Jane and Miss Emily were in the center, where Miss Emily whipped Brown Hound. I still didn't like that place no matter how much fun Jane and I had playing in the rest of the barn. Granny Jane sat on a bale of hay, leaning on her cane. Miss Emily stood with her back to the older woman looking out the opening to the field.

"Emily, what is it you know that you won't tell? What's bothering you so much? Every time Ivis is mentioned you freeze solid then snap at whoever's talking."

I blinked in surprise. Instead of slamming her cane and sharpening her voice to razors, Granny Jane spoke soft and low. Jane and I strained forward listening. Miss Emily didn't say a thing. She just kept staring out over the fields. Granny Jane rose from the bale of hay. Leaning heavily on her cane, she walked over. Putting a hand on her daughter-in-law's shoulders, she turned her around, so they were face to face. The words were quiet once again.

"Emily, the girls are going to keep digging until they know all there is to know."

Receiving no response, Granny Jane released her hold and turned to look out over the field herself. "You know, Jane and Gracie might have a point." She kept talking not looking at Miss Emily, but I could see she had gotten her attention. Granny Jane continued.

"Maybe it would do Marcell good to be able to grieve at her daddy's grave. We both know she has reason enough to drink. No child should have to run after her daddy and watch him get strung up. Maybe if there was a place where she could say 'there, that's my daddy and he didn't do anything wrong' it would heal a wound or two."

"For your information, I don't have a clue where Ivis is buried." Miss Emily's words were bitter and sharp. Not her usual way of talking at all. My knees were cramping, and I shifted to ease them out. Jane put her hand on my leg to keep me still.

"That so? Then why the fuss?" I could see Granny Jane begin to ease Miss Emily into confession.

Miss Emily turned to the old woman and spoke sharply "Why? Because it won't stop. The girls will want to know more, what Tom said, what Tom did. You think I should tell things better left unsaid just so those girls can go hunting clues about the grave?" Her voice was shaking. I'd never heard her talk like this. I glanced over at Jane. She was stone still.

"So, there is more to tell." Granny Jane reached out, but Miss Emily pulled back.

"Yes, there is." Miss Emily's voice was heated. "If Jane and Gracie keep stirring this up, the whole story just might come out. And you don't want that, you don't want that at all."

"That so?"

"Oh, yes. Because your son," her voice sounded like nails and pain, "your son helped hang Ivis."

There was complete silence. I didn't breathe. Jane didn't either. My eye pressed against the barn so hard my head hurt. If Aunt Viola found out, she would have more ammunition than ever. If Marcell found out she was working on the farm of the man who hanged her daddy, she'd drink even more. Everything would come apart.

I felt sick to my stomach. Why couldn't people just let things be? And then the answer hit me because Jane and I were stirring it up. I sat back hard on the dirt, the scene in the barn forgotten. It was my fault. I had wanted to help Jane by finding out about Ivis, but it was just like Momma said. No matter what I get into, I make it worse. My stomach clenched and I jerked to the side. Hot chewed butter beans, chicken, and biscuits came rushing up my throat. I gagged helplessly into the dirt while Jane hit me on the leg to be quiet.

Granny Jane had ears like a fox, and they didn't fail her now. Turning from Miss Emily, the old woman hot-footed it to the barn door and leaned out. Jane was starting to cry, and I was throwing up in the dirt. We made a sorry sight.

Granny Jane called out, "Emily, come here,

help me get these girls."

I felt hands on my shoulders and hunched, waiting for the blow. Instead, the hands gently moved to my waist and lifted me to my feet. I smelled the perfume. Miss Emily. Standing up I kept my head lowered and wiped vomit from my mouth. I didn't want to meet her eyes. I didn't want to see in them that I'd ruined everything. I'd made her tell a terrible secret. Maybe if I didn't look at her, she wouldn't yell.

She put her hand on my shoulder. I flinched away. She put her other hand under my chin. I fought to keep my head down. Releasing me, she wiped her hand on her apron and I heard her walk to the barn pump. Water splashed on the dusty ground, its sound mixing with the sound of Jane's soft crying. I saw feet. Jane's and Granny Jane's as they moved off toward the house. Then other feet came close. A cold piece of apron wiped across my mouth. I buried my head in the wet cloth and cried till I hollered.

Life wasn't worth this. Even with Brown Hound, I couldn't stand this. Not anymore. I always made things bad back home and now I'd made them bad on the farm. Grief rose up and devoured me. I slid sideways to the ground sobbing and hiding my face in my hands.

Miss Emily's words were firm but kind. "Stop it now. You're getting yourself all worked up for nothing. Hush." Even through my haze, I could hear the softness. I felt her kneel next to me. She began stroking the back of my neck and humming. Over and over, she stroked and hummed. Finally, I took a deep breath and shuddered to silence.

"No sense you getting all worked up about what happened in the past. It's not your doing."

At her words, I reared up on my knees and looked her in the face. The words burned out of me, and I couldn't stop them. "Is, too. It's just like Momma. No matter what I do, I make it bad and then everybody gets sick and gets hurt." I ran out of air, hung my head in exhaustion, and slumped back down. At least I'd said it before she had the chance to. She'd probably send me back to Virginia. That'd be best.

Fingers, firm from years of kneading biscuits, dug under my chin forcing my head up. I bore down, determined to keep my eyes to myself. Her other hand snaked out, grabbed the hair at the back of my head, and yanked hard. My chin popped right up.

"Child, look at me."

Staring into her eyes, I shrank way back inside of my head. Maybe if I stayed there, I could look at her and not die from it. So, I did and braced myself for what I knew was next.

"This isn't about you." I didn't believe her for a second. She gave a heavy sigh and let go of my face and hair. Settling herself on the ground, careful to avoid my puddle of vomit, she gestured me to her side. I moved to her and gazed out towards the house. This was better. Lowering her arm around my shoulders, she pulled me close. I let her do it but kept myself braced.

"Gracie, this doesn't have one thing to do with

you."

I kept my eyes on the house as I spoke, "Well, I'm the one who's bringing it all up."

"No, this was Jane's idea." I shrugged in the silence, letting her have this one. She continued, "You know, Jane is the one who lives here and knows how things are. She decided to try to find Ivis' grave, anyway."

I kept looking at the house trying to think of what to say, fighting to hold on to what I knew was true. "But I helped her do it. You had to tell your secret about Cap'n Tom, and everybody's gonna get hurt." My voice began to quiver, and I shut my mouth tight. How dare she say this wasn't true? This was always true. I shrank even further inside myself as the sun winked out behind the trees. Crickets continued chirping. Miss Emily and I sat in the silence. I had shut her up all right. I felt a small pleasure.

A dark shape came barreling around the corner of the house and the dogs appeared all in a bunch, Brown Hound leading the way. They were sniffing the sweet evening air and headed for their nightly rounds of the swamp.

"She's a fine dog."

I swelled with pride. Of course. Brown Hound was the best person in the whole world.

"You've had her since she was a puppy?"

"Yes," cautiously. I didn't know where Miss Emily was headed with this.

"Well. Let's see. You've had Brown Hound for

all these years and raised her from a puppy and she's healthy. And looks like she's happy."

I mumbled another cautious, "Yes."

"So, I guess that means you don't always make things bad or folks sick."

I sat completely still. Suddenly, I couldn't feel the ground underneath me. It was like when I went to the top of the Ferris wheel and there wasn't anything below. My stomach gave a flutter of hope, but then I tightened up.

"She's a dog."

"Your Aunt Martha and Uncle Ben aren't dogs. They love to have you around. I don't see them getting sick."

I thought for a moment about the fight they'd had about Brown Hound. I was there and they had fought. So there. My bottom felt seated firmly on the ground not up in that Ferris wheel. I started to open my mouth and tell Miss Emily just that when suddenly, I remembered the end of that fight. They'd fought, but were fine afterwards, hugging and laughing. I swooped back up to the top of the Ferris wheel. There didn't seem to be ground again.

"Now. Time you got this nonsense out of your head. You look at me, girl." Miss Emily's voice was sharp again like it'd been in the barn. She read my mind. "No, it's not you I'm mad at. It's some other folks. But you need to hear this right now and I'm speaking plain. Give me your eyes."

She didn't have to pull my chin up this time. I

made myself come to the front of my head. It made me squirm, but there was no hiding. Her tone of voice made it important. It was the same tone she used when she told the truth about Cap'n Tom.

"You did not make your momma sick." She said each word by itself. And then she repeated it with her eyes locked onto mine. "You. Did. Not. Make. Your. Momma. Sick."

I was at the top of the Ferris wheel, swaying. There was no ground below. I reached out and grabbed the front of her apron. Her hand shot out and covered mine.

The Ferris wheel began to turn. My stomach came up in my throat as I flew through air to a place I didn't know. I grabbed at Miss Emily with my other hand, and she scooped me up hard and fast onto her lap, hugging me tight. The Ferris wheel swooped downward, toward the bottom. But I had already landed. The breath knocked out of me but safe. And the ground was new.

We stayed sitting till dark covered us and the mosquitoes found our skin.

"Child, help me up."

I scooted from Miss Emily's lap. We stood and stretched like we'd been in a box for a year.

"Let's get some food in you." Miss Emily headed me towards the house. Looking up I saw the glow of light in the kitchen window. Shadows moved back and forth. Granny Jane and Jane were still up. We walked slowly to the house and up the back porch steps.

"Grab a plate. I warmed up the pie we missed for dessert," Granny Jane said, leaning down into the stove. Jane's back was to me, and she was busy at the sink. Miss Emily's lap had been firm ground, but I felt unsteady with the newness. Jane turned off the faucet with a yank and whirled around. Her hair was messy, and her eyes were red. I looked much worse. I gave a small smile. She gave a half-grin and said, "You look like a coon dog."

"You look like a squashed possum," I replied. Insults flew through the air.

Granny Jane cut us off right smartly. "Hush your mouths. Sit and eat." We did. As she and Miss Emily sat down to join us, she made her final demand of the evening, "While you're at it, why don't you girls give us that imitation of your Aunt Viola eating pie with her big teeth?"

We did.

CHAPTER 13

"Miss Emily says time to get up." With that, Marcell turned to head out of the bedroom then stopped at the door. Hearing her footsteps pause, Jane and I poked our heads out from under the sheets. It had been a restless night. After the pie and our performance of Aunt Viola's teeth, Jane and I were tossed into the tub and scrubbed within an inch of our lives. It was like the women wanted to scrub away the words that'd been said in the barn. No one talked about what had been said. Before we could blink, we were tucked into bed and the light put out. Exhausted and too worn out to talk, we listened to the murmur of the women's voices drifting in from the kitchen as we fell asleep. The jumbled sheets said it'd been on our minds all night.

Marcell walked back, stood at the end of the bed and said, "You went to my church. You girls old enough now to stop playing that way. Miss Jane, you know better." She paused and took a breath then stated plainly, "You have yours and I have mine. Don't cross into what's mine."

Jane and I looked at each other. Did we hear a shaking in her voice? We turned to her and nodded.

"Say yes."

Our nods hadn't been enough. "Yes."

"Breakfast's on." She left the room.

Jane turned to me and for a few minutes we stared at each other. She was the first to break the ice. "You think she was mad?"

"Sounded more like she was gonna cry than yell."

Jane shook her head and changed the subject. "You okay?"

"Yeah. You?"

She shrugged the sheet away and sat up, turning her head to look out of the window and replied, "I guess. Granny Jane says we have to wait for Miss Emily to tell the rest."

I didn't know what more there could be. Miss Emily said Cap'n Tom helped hang Ivis. That seemed pretty clear, but I kept my mouth shut. Jane pushed her way out of the bed and pulled on her shorts. I could see she wasn't gonna talk so I tumbled out of bed and silently dressed. I felt bad for Jane. I knew I should feel bad too, but today I felt different. Before last night, there was always a gray wave in the background, waiting to wash me into the sand. But now, it wasn't there. I stood still and tried to find it. It wasn't there. I closed my eyes and tried to see it, but it still wasn't there.

Jane headed to the kitchen. I followed, walking softly, afraid to disturb the wave. Maybe if I stayed quiet it wouldn't come back. Silently, I slid into my chair and began my breakfast.

"Marcell," Miss Emily said, "I have a hankering

for some watermelon. Sarah Tucker said hers were coming in by the bushel. You walk over to their place and get us one."

"Yes, ma'am." Marcell stopped what she was doing and headed out the door. Miss Emily watched her go then pulled out a chair and sat. I took one look at her face and checked to see if the wave was still gone. It was. Wrapping my legs around the chair rails, I waited.

"I owe you girls some explanation for what you heard last night."

I kept still and Jane kept her eyes on her plate. Her chin jumped up and down and she looked like she was going to cry. I felt my stomach churn. Miss Emily gave a heavy sigh. I heard the screen door and saw Granny Jane come in from the back porch. She pulled out a chair. Miss Emily looked at the older woman and smiled. My stomach released its hold.

"I know you girls heard me say your grandfather helped hang Ivis, but there's more to it."

Jane's fork clattered to the table, and she put her hands to her face crying. Miss Emily reached over and stroked her hair. "Just listen now. You need to hear this."

Jane raised her face and must have seen something in her grandmother's eyes. She wiped her tears with her hand, took in a breath, shuddered, then went still.

"Your grandfather quit the Grand Tigers when they started doing things for meanness.

"We know that," Jane's voice was small.

Miss Emily nodded her head. "Back then you just didn't quit and not pay for it. There were a few threats about barns burning and mules dying from bad water, but Tom kept his head down and ignored them. Things pretty much died down. And then Lacy Tillman came to town crying about being forced. Tom was in buying seed corn, heard about it and went to warn Ivis."

"So Cap'n Tom really did warn him?" Jane's voice was stronger.

"Yes. Later, he tried to talk the Tigers out of it. They asked if he had warned Ivis. He told them yes. And they laughed."

"Laughed?" I didn't think hanging was funny.

Miss Emily's eyes looked at the salt and pepper shakers like they had the answer. "They said since Tom warned him, he could just hang him. Tom tried to walk away, but they pointed a shotgun at him. Told him to keep in mind barn fires happen by accident all the time." The kitchen was silent. A drip splashed in the sink and sounded like a steel ball. No one moved. The air, heating up from the sun, drifted slowly through the screen door into the room. Jane looked at me. I looked back. Granny Jane's hand clenched and unclenched on the head of her cane.

Miss Emily kept on. "So, your granddaddy really didn't have a choice. The Tigers burned down the Smith's barn the year before when they tried bringing in outside help for the harvest. Isn't that right,

Miss Jane?"

Granny Jane nodded her head remembering. Suddenly she tilted her head up and pinned Miss Emily with her eyes and asked, "They say anything about the children? Sally was what, ten? And Robert was just a baby."

Miss Emily shook her head no and clamped her lips tight.

Granny Jane nodded her head with satisfaction. "So it was you they threatened Tom with?"

Miss Emily's eyes flashed hard at her mother-in-law "No need for the girls to hear that kind of thing."

We couldn't talk or even draw spit.

Miss Emily closed her eyes, opened them, and kept at her story. "Most of the men went to get Ivis. A couple of others kept the shotgun on Tom. They marched him through the fields to the tree out behind the barn and waited. The others caught Ivis, dragged him to the tree, kept that shotgun pointed, and made Tom knot the rope around Ivis' neck."

Jane started crying. I held my stomach.

"The Grand Tigers told your grandfather if he said anything, every last one of them would say truthfully that his hand tied the noose."

Granny Jane picked it up. "That was one part I never knew." Her eyes rested on her daughter-in-law, and she continued for our benefit. "After it was over Tom found Marcell near the barn and brought her inside for Emily to tend."

"Didn't she hate him?" I had to know.

"She saw the whole thing, Gracie, including the shotgun. Tom went back to take Ivis down to make sure the Tigers didn't cut up the body, but it was already gone."

"Where'd it go?" Jane asked.

I looked at her sharply. How could she be ready to play the game of finding Ivis at a time like this? I looked closer. She wasn't playing. She was caught up in the story. She wanted to know. She leaned closer to Miss Emily as if hoping to drag it out of her.

"Jane, please. I do not know." Miss Emily pushed her chair away and stood up. "That's all I have to say about this. I wanted you to know the whole story. Now it's time for you to leave this alone." She walked from the room.

I could see relief blossoming in Jane as she understood our granddaddy had been an honorable man. She took in a big breath and let it out. All last night's hurt went with it, but the gleam in her eye remained.

"Girls!'

I jumped a mile. Granny Jane's voice was sharp. "That's enough. You leave this be. If Emily doesn't want to talk about it anymore, it's her right. And it's our family's right not to want things dragged out in the open. Your grandfather was a good man and I think it broke his heart, what happened. He was strong, big, and healthy. Dead ten years later." She nodded to herself, "Took its toll. On everybody." She gave us a sharp look. "Now, you go on with yourselves.

Finish your breakfast." With a thump of her cane to emphasize her words, the old woman pushed her chair back and left the kitchen.

Jane and I were down by the creek near the train trestle, we'd gotten permission easily. I think Miss Emily was glad for us to do something other than ask questions. She'd packed us a lunch, we'd grabbed our bathing suits, and headed into the coolness of the woods.

It had been startling, walking from the hot, dusty backyard where the chickens and dogs had packed the dirt hard and dry, into the soft, deep green woods. The ground gave way under foot and the trees filtered the sun. But snakes loved the cool and damp too. I'd walked lightly.

The creek under the tracks held slow moving water. It hadn't rained for a week, so the water was low and clear. You could look down and see the bottom, a comfort considering the snake situation. We slipped into our bathing suits and entered the water. The cool silkiness slid over us. We didn't splash or try to dunk each other; we just kept quiet and still. After a while, we climbed out and let the dappled sun bake our backs.

"I still think we should find it." Jane just wouldn't give up. She turned to me with serious eyes and my words of protest died. She wasn't playing pirate. There was something different about Jane in the past two days. She was quieter, as if she had learned things that shifted who she was inside. I thought about that for a moment. I'd shifted some, too. The gray wave seemed to be staying away, but I felt a little bit lonely for it. Like a tooth that'd been pulled. You kept going back to the hole with your tongue, glad it was gone but missing the hurt.

"Listen, there's a bunch of reasons why we gotta do this." Jane held out her hand and began counting. "One, it would stop Marcell from drinking. Two, if she stops, the ladies can't say she's a bad influence and I have to live with Aunt Viola. Three, our granddaddy tried to help Ivis, so we should help Marcell.

I personally liked number three, continuing what our granddaddy started. It wasn't his fault Ivis got hanged and Cap'n Tom did his best to stop it. Now it was up to us to help Ivis' daughter. I looked Jane in the eye and nodded my head.

"Okay. You're right. But what if some of those Grand Tigers are still alive? They'd be really mad if we found Ivis and put him in a proper grave." I grabbed Jane's hand in fright. "And maybe they'd go head tell everybody that granddaddy helped with the hanging."

Jane said, "Yeah but then they'd have to say that they were at the hanging too.

Suddenly, the dogs burst past us in a flat out run, crashing though trees and raising a racket.

"I bet Miss Charity hates it when those dogs run through her place," Jane said.

The words hung in the air. I looked at Jane and shook my head 'no'.

Jane said firmly, "We have to."

I remembered hanging onto Brown Hound

like I was going to die while the conjure woman made Jane's spell. "What makes you think she knows where he's buried? And even if she did, it would be just like Preacher John. If she knew then so would Marcell."

I could see Jane grasping for a reason but coming up empty. She began to speak, stopped, got quiet, then made up her mind. "Well, least we can do is check Miss Charity off the list."

We changed into our shorts and Jane led the way, confidence once again flowing from her like a cloak of bravery. Jane pointed to chicken bones. We were coming close. As the sagging wooden cabin came into view, Miss Charity opened the door. Jane and I stopped a respectful distance.

"What you want?"

This was Jane's idea, so I stepped back. Jane's voice was at its most respectful. "We want to ask a question."

The old woman put her hands on her hips. "What?"

Jane took a deep breath. "Where is Ivis buried?"

Miss Charity stood as if she'd froze dead. Silence wrapped around us like the sticky air. I breathed softly, trying not to attract attention. Jane shifted from one foot to the other then back again. The pale dust puffed up around her feet. An ember cracked then fell in the fire under the pot. I jumped, but Jane didn't and neither did Miss Charity. Seemed like they were having a staring contest; the old woman looking at Jane like she could cut her in two with her eyes, and Jane looking back, protected by her cloak of bravery.

With a suddenness that surprised us, Miss Charity turned back into the cabin and slammed the door. Jane and I stood looking at the wooden slats.

"She knows about it." Jane nodded her head as if this would make the words true. "She knows about it and we're gonna find out."

I didn't like the sound of that. "Look, I bet she locked the door." I grabbed the back of Jane's shirt, tugging. "She's not gonna talk to us. Let's go."

Jane whirled around and clenched her fists. "Don't you dare stop me. I'm not gonna go anywhere. We have to find out about Ivis and make Marcell better." She sounded desperate but suddenly, her voice took on a taunting tone, "I'm not getting sent away like you."

The pain of her words made the world go black for a moment. I heard a gasping sound and realized it was me. The light came back, and Jane was standing in front of me, her hands still clenched. I jumped on her, punching, kicking, and biting. We fell to the ground rolling and tearing at each other in dead silence. I grabbed her shirt, and the buttons gave way, making hard popping sounds in the hush. Jane snatched a hand full of dirt and shoved it in my face. I grabbed her hair and yanked. She jammed her knee into my stomach. I tried to bite her shoulder. She seized the waistband of my shorts and twisted hard, cutting me in half. My head slammed into her face. She let go of my shorts and our arms wrapped around each other, trying to hit. We rolled in the dirt, silent, like two determined animals.

The switch stung our legs once, then twice. Miss Charity stood above us. We scrambled to our feet scampering apart, so she couldn't hit both at the same time. She paused, the switch at her side, taking us in with one deadly sweeping glance. Jane and I breathed heavy, not looking at each other, our eyes locked on the switch.

"Like dogs."

We kept our eyes on the switch.

"Wipe your nose."

Jane lifted her elbow and ran her arm across her face. A trail of blood streaked her arm and she glared at me. Miss Charity spoke.

"Bad things gonna happen to girls looking to stir up the past."

Jane looked up at the old woman defiantly, beyond caring. "We want to know."

Miss Charity paused for a minute then gave us a smile that looked like it had bones in it, slapping the switch on the side of her leg in time to her words. "All right, young misses. All right. You gotta know then you gonna know. I give it to you now, you carry this thing. It's on you, what you do with it."

"Old man Simmons buried Ivis on his farm." She stood watching like a snake at a mouse.

Jane took a breath. "He do it to say a proper burial and make peace?"

Miss Charity gave a hard laugh. "Make peace? Make peace when he stretched his neck 'til it broke? No, young misses." She tapped the switch harder against her leg. "No indeed, young misses. Story is he planted Ivis in the rose garden. So there be fence around him. And food for the flowers."

Jane and I stood as if struck by lightning. Which is how it felt. Miss Charity drilled us with her eyes. "Now get." She raised the switch in the air, and I stumbled back. Jane paused. Miss Charity took a heavy step forward. We turned and ran, finding the trail by sheer desperation. Without a word, we flew past the trees and leaped over the chicken bones.

After a few minutes we slowed down. The dogs crashed through the trees giving us a moment of terror thinking Miss Charity had followed. Brown Hound jumped up and put her paws on my shoulders. I grabbed her legs to push her down and saw a cut in her skin. I gave it a good look but it didn't seem too deep. I smoothed the fur, smearing the blood all over her leg. She dropped her paws and I knelt, hugging her neck. She licked my face then followed the others back into the woods. I stood up, brushed the leaves from my knees, and followed Jane towards the trestle.

Standing at the top of the train track, we stared down at the house. A car was parked under the oak tree. It didn't belong to Aunt Martha and Uncle Ben. It didn't belong to Aunt Viola and Uncle Will. It belonged to Momma and Daddy. Granny Jane had mentioned the other day in passing that Daddy called and said they might drive down again for a day. I'd figured it was just one of those things he did. Saying the right thing, so people would believe he was doing it and then not really having to.

Just then Miss Emily walked onto the back porch and saw us. She cupped her hands around her mouth and yelled, "Come on down. Gracie, your momma and daddy are here."

CHAPTER 14

Momma's voice floated through the screen door on to the back porch where we stood. "The girls in the garden club were just saying last week how they knew I missed Elizabeth Grace."

Miss Emily looked down at Jane and me and shook her head. With a firm grip on our shoulders, she began to steer us to the outside sink when Daddy called out, "There're the girls. Gracie, come on in here."

Miss Emily kept her voice calm. "The girls have been playing in the swamp. I think they want to clean up first."

"What kind of mother cares about a little dirt?" Momma stepped through the screen door and came onto the porch. "Come here, Elizabeth Grace and give me a kiss."

Miss Emily gave my shoulder a squeeze, let go of me, and I turned around.

Momma gasped, "Robert. You come out here right now." Footsteps hurried across the living room floor. "Robert! Look at her." Momma pointed a finger at me with her bright, red nails.

Daddy stared at us. We were a sorry sight. Jane with her bloody nose and ripped shirt. Me with my torn shorts and mud smeared cheeks. Both of us with red splotches from fists and tears.

"What in the world?" Momma's voice got harder, and she took a step toward us.

Daddy's hand came down on her arm. "Honey, looks like the girls have just been playing hard."

Momma yanked away from his grasp; her eyes glued to me. "Doesn't look like that at all. Looks to me like Jane has a bloody nose. As for Elizabeth Grace, just look at those new shorts I got her." She hadn't bought them. She was in bed having one of her spells when Daddy bought them. I kept my mouth shut. I'd been hit enough for one day.

Momma glared at him, "I didn't send Elizabeth Grace here to be a wild dog." She fixed her eyes on Jane. "And look, this one's turned our girl into a Carolina hick running around with dirty clothes and fighting. Fighting!" Her voice got louder, "Girls fighting! Low-class!"

"We weren't fighting." Jane's words were small but firm. I gaped at her. That cloak of bravery was a fine thing indeed. I listened for the lie I knew was coming.

Momma put her hands on her hips, "Oh? Then just what were you doing?" Her words sliced the soft, hot air.

"We were saving the dogs." Jane kept eye contact with Momma. I didn't know how she did it and not burn alive.

"Go on." Momma folded her arms across her

chest. This was a war of wills. I said a silent prayer for Jane. Momma never lost any of her wars.

"The dog got caught in one of the boards under the trestle and we had to get her out and she was hurt and fighting us. Gracie and I weren't fighting each other."

Sissy sucked in a breath. No one talked back to her. She unfolded her arms, and I could see her right hand twitch. I knew what that meant. I took a step forward to draw her fire.

"Momma, Jane's right. We weren't fighting."

Sissy's eyes flew wide. Her lips clamped together in a straight line. Slowly, she moved her eyes away from Jane and fastened them onto me. I went lightheaded.

"What. Did. You. Say?" The words dropped out of her mouth like poison toads.

Yelping interrupted us and the dogs bounded down from the train tracks into the yard. Momma's eyes narrowed, scanning the dogs for a moment. A sour smile crossed her face. "Miss Emily. I think a dog that would be so vicious when the girls were just trying to help would be too dangerous to keep around."

The dogs circled the backyard, sniffing and playing. Everyone on the porch stood silently looking at Brown Hound's bloody leg.

"And I guess we know just which dog that is." Momma's words shoved into the silence like a boogeyman lunging through a window at midnight. Jane looked at me in agony. She had lied to save us from getting in trouble for fighting but instead gave

Momma ammunition for Brown Hound.

"Sugar." Daddy tried to get the attention away from my dog. Momma wasn't about to let that happen. Jane had talked back to her and then unbelievably, so had I.

"Sugar, I think."

Momma interrupted him, "I think that dog's turned vicious, that's what. Miss Emily, don't you think something needs to be done to that dog? I didn't send Elizabeth Grace down here to get torn up."

"Sissy," Miss Emily's voice was soft, "she's not torn up. Her pants are ripped and her face is muddy. Nothing a needle, thread and a good bath won't fix."

Momma pointed her finger at Jane, "Well, a bath won't fix that." I didn't know if she meant Jane's nose or just Jane. I looked at Miss Emily. My grandmother drew herself up and gave Daddy a hard glance. He stood there frozen. He didn't want to upset Momma, but he was trapped by his mother's look.

"Now Sissy," he began haltingly.

"Don't you Sissy, me. That dog is a menace and needs to be shot."

Jane grabbed my hand and I went faint. I had defied Sissy, and this was my punishment.

"There's not going to be any shooting around here." Granny Jane's words preceded her through the screen door. Sissy whirled around and Daddy's shoulders relaxed. The old woman leaned on her cane. She was calm and steady as an autumn rain. "It'd be a shame to shoot such a fine dog as that."

I looked at Granny Jane like she was Jesus.

You could see Sissy thinking fast. "Miss Jane, you're right. I'm sorry. I was just upset about Elizabeth Grace. Of course, nobody's going to shoot that dog." She gave Granny Jane one of her card party smiles then said, "but could you perhaps get rid of the dog because she hurt the girls? Send her away? Surely you can do that?"

Sissy was determined to get at least that much punishment for me. What I didn't expect were Granny Jane's next words.

"We'll give her to Marcell. She lives alone. A guard dog would be good for her."

My mouth fell open. Jane's eyes bugged out. Miss Emily started to speak then clamped her mouth shut.

"Well, that's fine, isn't it Sugar? The dog will be gone." Daddy squeezed Sissy's shoulder then turned to me. "Gracie, you can go up to Marcell's anytime you want and visit her." He straightened up smiling.

I looked frantically at Granny Jane. She stood nodding her head, giving me a smile. I whirled to Miss Emily. She grabbed me before I could say anything and clamped a strong hand on my arm. "Well, that's settled. Let me get these girls cleaned up. Robert, Viola, and Will want to see you and Sissy, so they're coming to supper." With that, she pushed us in front of her like a dog herding geese.

Jane and I sat in the big washtub not making a sound,

listening hard. Jane had gotten out of the tub and cracked open the door. If we strained, we could hear Miss Emily talking hard to Marcell.

"It will only be for a day or two. Until they go back."

"Miss Emily, I don't want that damn dog around me."

"I know, Marcell, I know. But I really need you to do this for me."

Marcell's voice came low and sad. "Miss Emily, One gets too near I go right back to then. I don't want it near me."

"But Black Jack and Sassy…"

"They know to keep away from me. That other dog jumps up and won't mind. Miss Emily, you give that dog to somebody but not me."

Miss Emily's words came out softly, "Marcell, we both know you drink to get past the memories, and you know it'd be better if you faced them. Maybe having the dog around for a day or two would help. And there's no one else. Viola would never take her, and we can't ask Martha to take her again." Miss Emily took a deep breath. "Can you do this for yourself and do it for Gracie?"

There was deep silence. The bath water chilled our skin. Marcell would weigh how much she liked me against her fear and hatred of dogs. My stomach felt hollow. Suddenly, I remembered how Marcell had gotten Jane and me out of kissing everyone goodnight on Momma's last visit. And how Jane said Marcell hated Sissy. Hope flared.

"This a hard thing you asking." Marcell's voice flattened.

Miss Emily kept quiet and waited.

Marcell gave a sigh and said, "Miss Emily, I'll do this for you, for all you've done for me. If you want me to try and maybe help with the memories, I guess that makes some kind of sense. But I won't have that dog in my house. Best I can do is chain her out in the yard."

I gave a gasp and Jane shot me a look. I snapped my mouth shut. Marcell and Miss Emily walked into the kitchen. Tears flowed down my cheeks.

I sat beside the window looking out into the night. Jane slept quietly beside me, exhausted by the day. We had suffered through supper listening to Sissy and Viola. Sissy explaining about the dog and Viola promising to check to see that Marcell did her job by keeping it away from us. They'd kept referring to Brown Hound as 'it'. She was a 'she' and I wanted to yell that out loud, but Granny Jane kept her bird eyes on me. I ate in silence. After all, I had opened my mouth once too often today.

Jane and I had gratefully crawled into the bed, happy to be away from the adults. Jane had told me she was sorry. She didn't say what for. I think it was for the whole day. I'd told her I was sorry, too. Now, company had gone, the house had settled down and everyone was asleep but me. How could I sleep when Marcell had walked back to her house tonight with Brown Hound on a rope. My dog had bounded beside the angry woman thinking this was a new game. Marcell moved wide to the side every time Brown Hound got near. Gradually they'd faded into the night doing their dance. A yelp broke the silence. Black Jack and Sassy were headed on their usual rounds of the swamp. I wondered if they missed Brown Hound as much as I did.

I thought back over the day. I knew Jane feared Aunt Viola taking her away. Sissy let me go, but that was different. Daddy hadn't hung onto me the way I knew Granny Jane would hang onto Jane. And Miss Emily, for all her soft ways, would fight just as hard. I stared out the window some more. The only person back home who would fight for me was Brown Hound.

I could just imagine Marcell pulling my dog to her cabin. Brown Hound would plant her feet in the dirt and pull back. Marcell would drag her, twisting the rope like it twisted on her daddy's neck. I gave shudder. What if she wanted revenge? What if she wanted to hang my dog just like the Grand Tigers hanged her father? It would be revenge of the best sort. Marcell could say the dog tried to bite her. Sissy would win and my dog would be dead.

I shot out of the bed and yanked shorts over my pajama bottoms. Silently, I ran through the living room and out the front door.

The low moon lit my way as I trotted down the road; my bare feet making little puffs in the dirt. Trees loomed darkly beside the ditches. I didn't want to think of one-legged Confederate Johnny stumping down the road, his wicked smile half blown off by a minie ball. Instead, I kept my eyes on the road, looking for Miss Charity Frazier's conjure circles. I didn't want any more bad luck than I already had.

Suddenly, there was Marcell's cabin. I looked hard. No light. No sign of life. Nothing hanging from the tree. My heart eased a bit. A shape rose from beneath the tree and gave a yip. Brown Hound was alive! Feet flying, I ran to her, grabbed her snout to smother a bark, and kissed the top of her head. We sat in the dirt and looked into each other's eyes. I knew she had questions. I knew she didn't understand why she wasn't leading the pack through the swamp under the moon. Softly, I began to whisper to her just like I did when we were on the picnic table back home. Her tail gave a thump, and I knew she mostly understood what I was saying. But I also knew she was sad being tied up. I couldn't untie her. Not with Aunt Viola on the watch, not with Sissy's slapping hand just waiting, not with Granny Jane saying this was the law. So, I did the best I could. I pulled her paws out and gently pushed her down. Scooting up close, I curled around her furry body. My head rested on the dirt beside hers and she snuffled off to doggie sleep. I looped my arm over her and wiggled around to get comfortable. The moon drifted across the sky, and we slept through the night.

"Your momma gonna whip your tail." Marcell's words jerked me awake.

Jumping up, I squinted at the rising sun. Brown

Hound rose behind me stretching first her front legs, then her back, then shaking all over. I waited for Marcell's next move. She had my life in her hands. Brown Hound gave a yawn and a whine. Then, I saw a cracked bowl in Marcell's hand.

"Untie that dog. Bring her to the porch." I carefully followed the instructions. "Tie her here. She needs to be able to get under the house, away from the heat today." Marcell set the bowl of water next to my dog. "You gonna have to bring food and feed her. Miss Emily didn't say I had to do that."

I nodded my head, afraid to speak. Marcell took a step forward and I jumped a step back. Reaching out, she grabbed my shoulder, and all feeling left my body. Pulling me toward her she turned me around and began brushing the dirt from my clothes talking to herself, "No sense. No sense at all. That damn dog." I stood, shaking.

Letting me go, she gave me a small push. "Better get on back 'fore they get up. Don't want to get caught." Her voice tightened as she said, "No ma'am, don't want Miss Sissy to get all upset now, do we?"

I turned and met her eyes. We stayed that way locked. I'd never looked her square in the eye. It was all I could do keep from falling flat. Marcell slowly nodded her head once then tilted it towards my dog. Released, I stooped down and gave Brown Hound a kiss. Jumping up, I looked at Marcell again. Something had passed between us. I knew it and she knew it. I started to give her a smile. She took a step back and folded her arms across her chest. "Go on now. You hurry." I accepted it, the coming together and breaking away. Nodding my head, I turned and ran through the dawn.

I eased myself through the bedroom door and jerked to a stop. Daddy was sitting on the side of the bed. Jane was bunched up in the corner at the headboard, the sheet pulled up tight, looking like a trapped frog. I softly closed the door behind me and stood, waiting.

"Gracie, come here."

I walked over and he reached out and touched my hair, pulling a twig free. "You spent the night with that dog, didn't you?"

I looked at Jane and she shook her head. She'd guessed where I'd gone but she hadn't told him. Even after yesterday's fight.

"Yes, sir."

"Do you know how it will make your momma feel if she finds out?"

He didn't ask if I was all right. He didn't ask if Confederate Johnny had chased me down the dark road. He didn't ask if I had been cold sleeping in the dirt with my dog. A funny feeling started in my throat and moved down to my feet. Jane hadn't told on me. Marcell made me run home, so I wouldn't get caught. Miss Emily would be worried I'd been alone on the road at night. Granny Jane would ask how Marcell was treating the dog. Daddy could only think about how Sissy would feel.

All at once a great dividing came over me. It felt like I was on one side of a deep crack and daddy was on the other. Just like the Eskimos living on ice floes. As he kept talking, I floated a bit farther away. I didn't hear his words. I knew what he was saying anyway. It was about how I would make Sissy feel bad.

He kept talking and I nodded my head, unhearing. He reached across the great distance and patted my head. "Well then, get dressed and get the dirt out of your hair. We'll have a nice breakfast together then your momma and I will be on our way."

I smiled up at him from habit. He smiled back and walked from the room.

"I thought you were a goner!" Jane tore off the sheet and leaped up and down on the bed. "When he came in and you weren't here, I liked to died…" Her words trailed off as she noticed my face.

"Did you hear the stuff he said?" I asked.

"Sure. He was glad you got back early so your momma wouldn't raise a fuss."

I turned to Jane, "He wasn't worried about me. He didn't ask about Brown Hound; all he was worried about was Sissy."

We were both silent for a moment. Then Jane spoke in a reasoned voice, "Well, he saw that you were okay, and I guess he didn't much care about Brown Hound."

I could see her trying to make me believe this. She nodded her head up and down to emphasize her words. At that moment, I couldn't imagine ever fighting with her again. She was trying so hard to make things seem better and I wanted her to feel good. So I agreed when I really didn't. "Yeah. I guess you're right."

Jane beamed and jumped from the bed snatching up her clothes. Jamming her hands through her shirt sleeves, she demanded a detailed description of the night's events including Marcell's every move. Dressing slowly, I told her.

CHAPTER 15

The day passed easily. Nobody said a word about Brown Hound. Daddy and Sissy left without a fuss. I'd stayed on my ice floe but pretended to be nice. They didn't notice the difference. Miss Emily took Jane to a visitation and left me to myself. Now, Jane and I were changing into our pajamas, laughing and being silly.

"Doesn't seem to me like anybody's too sleepy." Miss Emily walked into the room. Covering us with the sheet she leaned over and gave us a kiss. "Get some sleep. And Gracie," she fastened her gaze on me and said, "sleep in the bed tonight and not with that dog."

Jane reached over and pinched me, "Brown Hound cooties."

I twisted over and jammed my pillow on her face.

"Girls!" We both stopped and looked up. "Go on to sleep. No more foolishness." Miss Emily frowned to give weight to her words, but we knew she wasn't really fussing. Turning out the light, she closed the door softly.

Jane bounded to a sitting position and looked down at me. "We have to have a look at that rose garden." I tried to pull up the covers. She snatched them down and leaned over, her face right above mine. I shoved her away. It didn't matter.

"Listen, tonight is the best. The moon is low, Miss Emily and Granny Jane are worn out from your folks' visit. Brown Hound won't follow you and bring along Black Jack and Sassy. It's now or never." Sitting there cross-legged, all she needed was a bandana around her head, a patch on her eye, and a knife in her teeth. I closed my eyes and wished her away. Jane was having none of it.

"Look. Let's just go ahead and do it. We can walk to the Simmons' easy."

Being on the road at night with Miss Charity's conjures and Confederate Johnny wasn't as fun as she thought. I told her so. She waved it off. "Oh poo. You did it last night and you aren't dead."

"No." But I was tired. Wrung out. The past two days had flattened me like a snake in the road. I began counting my excuses out loud when I noticed Jane had gone quiet and was looking out the window. I slid over to her and pulled at her pajama top. "What?" She shook me off, but I asked again, and she answered, keeping her eyes away from mine.

"Tonight, at the visitation, Aunt Viola came over and stood by me smoothing out my hair. She put her arm around me and was leading me all around saying hello to people."

I kept clutching her pajama top. "Miss Emily let her do it?"

"Well, she didn't say anything."

I eased back on the bed. If Marcell had one more drinking incident, Aunt Viola just might get Jane for real. We had to find Marcell's daddy for her. I looked up at Jane and knew she was thinking the same.

I gave in, "Okay. But what do you think we'll find? It's been thirty years."

Jane turned back from the window and tried to give me the pirate smile but failed. "They'll be something. Maybe a space all sunk in like the Indian graves in the woods next to the fields."

"Well, what do we do when we find it?"

"We'll tell Uncle Ben. He'll know what to do."

I wasn't sure I wanted to put the burden on Uncle Ben but looking at Jane's face, I was willing to give it a go. Anything to keep Aunt Viola from getting more ammunition. I slid off the bed and pulled on my shorts.

Jane and I stood beside the rose garden gate. We'd made it out of the house and down the road without either Miss Emily or Confederate Johnny grabbing ahold of us.

"What now?" I waited for instructions. Jane leaned against the white fence and looked over the territory.

"We go in and look for a sunken part."

"Then what?"

Jane punched my arm to get me quiet. I didn't think she had a plan after that, but I shut my mouth not wanting another bruise.

Clouds scuttled across the low moon. I looked at the woods near the property edge. Confederate Johnny might be waiting back in the trees, watching. Giving a shiver, I stepped closer to Jane. She shoved me back. We stood silent for a moment then Jane eased the gate open, and we were in.

Slowly, we walked through the garden keeping away from the roses. They were tall and mean with sharp hooking thorns. Jane sucked in her breath and stopped.

"There" she hissed, pointing to a shadow. Cautiously, we crept forward and sure enough. There it was. A sunken spot in a corner of the garden.

"Stay here." Jane was gone, melting into the night. I backed away from the spot and eased carefully between two rose bushes. Maybe Confederate Johnny wouldn't be able to see me here. The moon peeped out from the clouds and the hot humid air settled on my skin. So did the mosquitoes. I carefully slapped them away.

"Here."

I jumped completely out of my skin. Jane stood beside me with a shovel. I looked at her like she'd lost her mind.

"A shovel?"

"Got it from the old shed."

I didn't care if she'd gotten it from the hand of baby Jesus, I wasn't going to touch it. She gave me a dirty look and walked to the edge of the spot.

"I'll make it look like dogs were digging. We'll

leave the gate open." Jane had it all planned out. All I could do was look at the shovel.

"You're gonna dig him up?" I was aghast.

"We'll just look for clues. Then go tell Uncle Ben like I said."

I wondered if she knew those clues might be bones. It came clear to me she'd gone over the edge. Aunt Viola's escorting her all around tonight had snapped her brain.

She jammed the shovel in the ground. It went in one inch. "Hasn't been dug in a long time," she said. I kept my eyes on the shovel, too panicked to move. She tried again and then again. The red Carolina clay fought her. The shovel was in only two inches.

"Gonna have to jump on it." Placing the shovel's edge down in the dirt, she steadied herself then jumped on the top of the blade with both feet. Instantly, one leg whipped out toward the fence and one arm flashed high, fingers scrabbling the air. The shovel teetered once, twice, then Jane crashed to the ground taking the fence with her.

Silence. Then a light from upstairs. Seconds later, the back screen door slammed open. Boom! Birdshot flew over our heads. Jane was on the ground tangled in the fence and I was rooted on the spot like a hundred-year-old tree. I threw myself on the ground, hands covering my head breathing in dirt. Jane was kicking at the fence. But no more birdshot. Just clouds pushing in front of the moon and Confederate Johnny watching from the woods.

Jane untangled herself and duck walked over to me whispering, "Shhh."

Well, that was stupid. Of course, shhh. We got on our hands and knees and crawled through the garden keeping the rose bushes between us and the house. Near the gate, we flopped on our stomachs. Jane wiggled forward. Suddenly she jumped to her feet and ran toward the house.

"Miss Victoria! Miss Victoria!"

I jumped to my feet and followed. Stumbling to a stop beside Jane, I looked down. There she was. Miss Victoria laid out like she was at her own visitation. The shotgun by her side.

"She dead?" I was amazed my mouth worked. Jane squatted by her side. "No. Her chest's moving." Jane shook the old woman's shoulder. She just lay there breathing.

My mouth worked again "We gotta get Miss Emily."

"No!"

"Yes!"

"No! Wait!" Jane stood up and wrapped her arms around herself like she was coming apart. I knew I was.

"We can't just leave her here!" I yelled because I thought Jane was considering it.

Jane shook herself. "Okay look, you stay here with her, and I'll run in and call Miss Emily." She took flight.

I kept trying to breathe normal. I was glad

it wasn't me who had to tell Miss Emily we'd scared Miss Victoria to death. I wasn't happy about being left alone with the old woman. What if she died right this minute? Miss Victoria gave a rattled breath. She was still alive. For now, it was safe. I sat down beside her but kept my distance. I didn't know what I should be doing. I watched her chest rise and fall and thought about what we'd done. This was no cookie calamity. This was no bloody nose and torn shirt. This was real life and death. I looked at Miss Victoria's chest again to make sure I hadn't jinxed anything by thinking about death.

The sound of the farm truck cut through the night. I stood up to look for it but mostly to get farther away from the old woman. The truck rattled around the side of the house and jerked to a stop. Granny Jane and Miss Emily got out of the cab and hustled over. Jane came out of the house. The two women knelt over Miss Victoria, felt her head, felt her chest, and then put something under her nose.

"Get away! Get off!" Miss Victoria was coming around and swinging her arms. Granny Jane and Miss Emily leaned out of range.

"Victoria. You hear me? It's Emily, Tom's wife." The old woman gave another swing.

"She looks okay," Jane whispered to me.

Granny Jane shot us a glance then spoke to the patient. "Victoria, let's get you sitting up." The women coaxed and cajoled Miss Victoria until she was sitting, gave her a minute then got her up on her feet.

"Girls," Miss Emily spoke to us, "Go ahead and turn on more lights. Make sure the bed is turned down. We're going to get her upstairs then get the doctor."

Jane pulled me aside and whispered in my ear. "You go ahead. I'll get rid of the shovel." I was amazed that she could think straight. Jane took off into the night and I went inside to light the way.

* * *

Jane and I sat beside the bed with Granny Jane while Miss Emily escorted Doc Davis up the stairs and into the room. Miss Victoria was awake but groggy. Granny Jane snapped her fingers at Jane and me and we quietly folded ourselves out into the hallway. Silence filled the room broken only by the rustling of sheets and Miss Victoria's groans. Every time she let one out, I put my hands over my ears. What if we'd killed her? I didn't know how to keep breathing with that thought in my head. The doctor's words cut through the silence.

"No hospital. She'll be fine but someone her age needs to be watched after a shock. I'll call for some nursing.

"That's fine, Granny Jane said. Walking from the room she looked down at us. "Girls, let's start for home."

We dragged our feet out to the truck.

* * *

We were home. In the living room. Nobody was going to bed. Jane and I sat on the sofa. Granny Jane sat in her rocker lighting her pipe. Miss Emily stood by the door, leaning against the frame. Nobody said a word and exhaustion covered all of us like flypaper.

"Could have killed her." Granny Jane followed her words by blowing smoke in the air. "No great loss, but still."

"Miss Jane. That's not funny!"

"Not trying to be." Granny Jane kept rocking.

Miss Emily fixed her eyes on us and spoke, "She's right. About the killing part. A concussion can kill an old person." She paused and rubbed her head again. Looking up she quietly asked, "What you were doing there?"

Jane shrank into the corner of the sofa. I scooted in between the cushions like a small crab. Granny Jane watched us both through the smoke, her eyes like a cat's.

"Again." This time Miss Emily's voice wasn't quiet. "What were you doing in the middle of the night? In that garden?"

Jane looked at me. My mouth clamped shut. She answered, "We were trying to find Ivis' grave."

"Good God and Jesus Christ!" Granny Jane barked from behind the smoke. I'd never heard her take the Lord's name in vain. But I was hearing it now. Miss Emily looked at us like we were Martians.

Jane continued, "Uncle Ben told us there was a story that Mr. Simmons buried Ivis at his place and Miss Charity said it was in the rose garden."

"The rose garden?" Miss Emily.

"So, he would feed the flowers."

"Charity Frazier! Good God, she's got the devil

in her for sure!" Granny Jane waved the smoke away and leaned forward to get a better look at us. "And you two believed her."

"Yes, Ma'am."

The old woman paused, then sat back in her rocker. "Well, maybe it's true."

"That's not funny. He's not there and you know it," Miss Emily said.

"I don't know any such a thing. But seems like you do."

Miss Emily folded her lips together like she was pinching pie crusts. Granny Jane kept rocking. Jane and I sat on the sofa, our eyes flashing back and forth between the women. Suddenly, the focus wasn't on us.

The rocking chair went still. "Emily, these girls are going to keep getting into trouble trying to find Ivis' grave until it's settled. Now, if you know he isn't in that rose garden, where is he?" She reached through the smoke and pointed her pipe stem at us saying, "Not that it excuses what happened tonight. I'll get back to that later." She turned to Miss Emily. "Let's have it."

Miss Emily walked over to a chair and sat down. "There's nothing to tell. I already told most of it. I just didn't want the girls dogging me about it."

"Well, they're not dogging you, they're scaring the bejesus out Victoria and landing her in bed. Now let's have it."

Miss Emily nodded her head and began, "Tom came back for Ivis and he was still hanging there." Jane reached over and grabbed my hand. I stayed locked on

Miss Emily. She continued, "Tom cut him down and buried him."

"Where?"

"I don't know. Tom never told me." She shot us a look and repeated herself, "He never told me where. Never. That's the truth. And if you girls keep looking for his grave and getting into trouble, I don't know what I'll do about you." Her voice heated up and Jane and I tried to shrink back into the sofa. She was just getting started.

"I forbid you to look for Ivis' grave! I am at the end of my rope with the two of you. Running around, going to Charity Frazier, fighting, and getting Sissy all riled up and now! Scaring Miss Victoria half to death!"

Here she shot a look at Granny Jane who rocked in her chair and watched. "And all because you want to know where Ivis is buried." She looked at the two of us like we were spiders in the outhouse. "I am at my wits end. Honest to heavens, maybe Viola is right. I don't seem to be able to keep you two under control."

I couldn't breathe and Jane was having trouble herself. Miss Emily kept at it. "Now, the story is that you two snuck out and were playing down the road trying to catch I don't know, a hoop snake, and you heard the shot and came and got us. Do you understand?"

"Yes, ma'am."

She turned to Granny Jane "Miss Jane. Will you take it from here? I am completely worn out with these two."

"Oh yes. My pleasure. You go on to bed. Leave the girls to me."

Miss Emily left the room without looking at us. Jane and I kept quiet. So did Granny Jane. She just rocked and smoked her pipe. Now I really had made someone sick with what I'd done. What if she thought I needed to go back to Virginia? What if… my heart almost stopped. What if she truly agreed with Aunt Viola about Jane being too much to handle? I looked over at Jane and could tell she was thinking the same thing.

"What's this about finding Ivis' grave?"

Jane opened her mouth to answer and Granny Jane interrupted "Oh, I know you want to find it so Marcell can grieve and you think it will stop her drinking. Emily and I want her to stop drinking, too. But for us it's that she's going to kill herself if she doesn't. What I want to know is why it's so important to you two for her to stop drinking that you'd do an idiotic thing like dig in Victoria's rose garden."

It was my turn. Besides, Jane looked like she was going to throw up. I sat up straight and began, "Every time Marcell drinks and falls in the ditch Aunt Viola and the church ladies say that you and Miss Emily are letting us run wild and that Jane should come into town and live with her."

I heard the scratch of a match and waited through another pipe lighting. "Your grandmother and I know what Viola says. You think if Marcell gets better, they'll shut up?"

"Yes, Ma'am."

Smoke swirled again as the old woman

considered my answer. "Viola won't leave anything alone. She gets her mind set on something she never gives up." Granny Jane leaned forward to speak but stopped herself. For a moment, she gazed into the air then snapped her attention back to us and spoke, "You're both a sorry sight. Go on to bed."

Astonished, we stood up but froze as she continued, "Your grandmother and I will deal with Marcell and her drinking…" her words trailed off and I could see her thinking. I listened hard but she didn't say anything about Jane never having to go live with Aunt Viola.

She interrupted my thoughts. "For now, you're both to stay on the farm. You're not allowed to talk about Ivis to anyone. You're not allowed to look for his grave anywhere! That's final! And you are not allowed to pester Emily. Do you understand?"

We nodded and waited for our escape.

"If I were younger, I'd take my cane to the both of you."

We nodded again. She raised the cane an inch off the floor and we fled.

CHAPTER 16

Dog yipping floated through the air along with the rays of the morning sun. Popping up from under the sheet, I lunged for the window. Brown Hound was prancing in the front yard with Black Jack and Sassy. They were sniffing her rear end in greeting and she was taking it all in stride. Marcell had brought her home. I lay back on the pillow and smiled at the ceiling. Suddenly, a pillow crashed down over my face.

"What you so happy about?" Jane was crabby. Miss Emily's words from last night seemed to still hang in the air. I didn't want any part of bringing that up and changed the subject.

"Marcell didn't come wake us up." We gave each other a look, got dressed and headed to the kitchen.

Marcell stood with her hands on her hips looking at Granny Jane and Miss Emily. Jane and I stood smashed outside the kitchen door peering through the crack.

"I didn't say a thing yesterday what with that damn dog at my cabin and Sissy visiting. But I'm saying it now."

The two older women stayed silent. Marcell

continued, "It wasn't right. Asking me to take that dog. You both been good to me, letting me grow up here and stay and work. But that don't give you a right to ask me to do things like that."

Granny Jane looked up. "Marcell, it's got to stop."

"What?"

"Your drinking. You're going to kill yourself."

Marcel shrugged that off like a fly.

Granny Jane drew in a breath. "Marcell, you did good with taking Gracie's dog home. We just thought that if you started facing some memories, it might make you stronger and you might not have to drink." She paused and gave the colored woman a sharp look then said, "Marcell, forgive me. I thought you were strong enough and I see I was mistaken. I would never have done it if I'd thought it would be too hard on you."

I just about fell on the floor. Granny Jane apologizing. To a colored woman, even if it was Marcell. I looked at Jane and she shook her head. Guess she'd never seen that either. Granny Jane and Marcell stared at each other. Miss Emily stood to the side watching.

"Miss Jane, leave it be. I'm plenty strong and don't need that dog to prove it." Marcell turned. "Miss Emily, I brought that dog back and now I'm gone for the day."

My grandmother approached her and put her arm around the colored woman's shoulders, "Marcell, that's fine. We'll look for you tomorrow." They walked out of the kitchen and down the steps. Jane and I slipped back to our bedroom, pretended like we were just getting dressed, and went to the kitchen for the second time that morning.

✿ ✿ ✿

"Gracie, what's got you so quiet this evening?" Granny Jane sat in her chair pushing her food around her plate. All of us had been quiet and tired all day, even Brown Hound.

"Nothing."

"Well, you don't look so good. Swallow some of that water from the creek? It has worms in it you know."

Jane held her fork in the air and wagged it in my direction.

"Put that fork on the table or in your mouth," Miss Emily said, but I could see she was distracted. Jane shoved the fork into her mouth. Granny Jane shot her a look then took a sip of her iced tea.

"Girls, your Aunt Viola came over today while you were down at the creek," Miss Emily began. She was mighty upset about Miss Victoria." Neither of us took a breath.

Granny Jane stepped in. "She thought you girls did a fine job of coming to get us," she gave us a look, "but I can't say she had good words about you playing outside in the dark after bedtime."

This was leading somewhere. When Granny Jane wanted to get at you for misbehaving she could think of some powerful unpleasant things. I held my breath waiting for the ax to fall.

"You know there's a tent revival tomorrow night. Your Uncle Will can't accompany Viola."

Jane slid down in her seat. Granny Jane kept going like she hadn't seen. "I want you girls to go with her." Jane covered her eyes with her hands. Granny Jane kept at it. "I think it would be real nice for you to go with your aunt. And besides, I think you girls could use a bit of Jesus." She gave us a smile that wasn't a smile at all.

Jane's head was level with the table and still sinking.

"Sit up right now." Miss Emily's voice cracked through the air and Jane popped up like a rabbit in a field. Miss Emily's voice didn't sound like her. I gripped the sides of my chair. She sounded almost like Sissy. I pushed the thought from my head. She continued, "You girls are going to go with Viola tomorrow evening and show her how well behaved you are and that's the end of it."

Granny Jane nodded her head at us to emphasize Miss Emily's words. I looked at Jane. Maybe we could butter Aunt Viola down. Maybe we could show her we loved Jesus so much she'd change her mind about taking Jane away from the farm. It was a chance to be redeemed.

The next evening started with us trying to get into Aunt Viola's car without being eaten by Miss Garson. Our aunt waited for us with the car running, foot pressed in on the clutch, and white gloved hands gripping the steering wheel. We dived into the back seat avoiding Miss Garson's gnashing teeth. Aunt Viola tore out of the driveway, bounced over tree roots, wheeled onto the road, then raced to the edge of town to the revival.

We climbed down from the car soaked with fear and sweat. It was another one of those hot, clammy Carolina evenings where your clothes pulled at you when you walked, and the dust kicked up around your feet, fine and white. There hadn't been rain for a while and what moisture was in the air settled on your arms and behind your knees. Felt like you could wring yourself out to lay the dust on the ground. We made our way past the glaring yellow lights decorating the tent and into the doorway.

The air hummed as folks settled themselves in for the evening. Children ran to their parents, ladies waved fans and men loosened their shirt collars. The coloreds settled down with a soft rustle. I turned around, saw Marcell, and snapped quickly back to the front. Guilt gnawed at me. Here we'd tried to find Ivis so she would be better but all we'd done was about kill Miss Victoria and get Marcell so upset about my dog that she was at a revival.

Jane gave me a pinch and I snapped to. Suddenly, in walked the famous Preacher Giant Gerald. I sucked my breath. He was huge but walked soft like a boogieman creeping up to kill in the night. He placed his big hands on the pulpit, looked around with a loving gaze then roared, "I see a tent full of sinners! Sinners each and every one."

I jumped in shock. Jane had her eyes closed like she was standing in a strong wind. I sank in my chair. For the next hour Giant Gerald's voice thundered over the top of our heads telling us we were all no-good sinners and God was so disgusted with us he was ready to throw us into hell fire. I tried to keep my ears shut but suddenly his words came straight through and hit me like a Miss Charity spell.

"You could walk out of here this very night and get killed by a runaway car," he paused, "and if you aren't saved, you will be cast into the fires of hell forever."

My breath stopped. Aunt Sally and Uncle Dave had been killed in a car wreck. I thought about the mean girl in Jane's Sunday School class who'd taunted her that her parents died without Jesus. The next instant Jane was up, pushing her way past me and Aunt Viola. I jumped and followed.

The tent lights pooled on the ground but beyond them the night was black as tar. A sound caught my ear. I followed it into the dark.

"What's wrong?" I knew what was wrong, but I didn't want to say it in case I made a mistake.

"Nothing."

I tried for lightness. "Nothing poo. You ran out like Aunt Viola was gonna bite you with her big teeth." No response. I took a breath and tried again. "That preacher's stupid."

Jane kept quiet. I hoped this was a good sign,

so I kept going, "He's stupid 'cause if he was a good preacher, he wouldn't have to go around in a tent." I stopped in amazement. That had come out of me all by itself like magic. I opened my mouth in hopes of it happening again, "And he can't be right because of the Chinese babies."

Jane looked up at me and I kept talking. "Look, there's millions of Chinese babies born every year and they haven't had the chance to hear about Jesus and a lot of them die and I bet they don't go to hell."

"Yeah, well what if they had the chance and didn't listen?"

All I could do was keep talking and trust my magic mouth. "Well, I think if you get taken by surprise early, then you maybe didn't have a fair amount of time to know Jesus and I think God lets you off the hook."

"Giant Gerald said that isn't true."

"Giant Gerald's stupid." And I was immediately hauled to my toes by the hair on my head.

"I should wail you right here!" Aunt Viola shouted. Her free hand hovered in the air just itching to take a swing. Familiar ground. I clamped my mouth shut and tried to stretch my feet to the earth.

"Running out of that tent like a wild girl, saying bad things about the preacher! You two have no more idea how to behave than wild hogs."

"Miss Viola, you need help with these girls?"

Aunt Viola dropped me like a hot penny and whirled around. Marcell stood, her arms clasped in front of her, not quite folded over her chest. Aunt Viola paused, her breathing ragged from shaking me and being stopped from taking that swing. She gave the colored woman a hard look. "Good to see you here getting the word of Jesus, Marcell."

"Yes ma'am. You need me?"

Aunt Viola drew herself up and straightened her dress. "No. You go on back now. I'll get the girls home."

"I'll just stay here and help."

Shooting a scathing look at Marcell, and giving us a glare that would scare Satan, Aunt Viola stalked to the car, got in, and started it with a yank. Once again Jane and I dived for the back door. With a jerk Aunt Viola gunned the engine and we jostled across the dusty field away from the tent. The strains of the hymns and Marcell's watching eyes followed us through the night.

✿ ✿ ✿

"You girls have a good evening?" Granny Jane was in her rocking chair watching as we jumped from the rolling car. Her bird eyes followed Aunt Viola's car as it tore out of the yard. We sat on the steps. "And what did that fine preacher have to say?"

My scalp hurt. I had Miss Garson's slobber all over me. I'd about been killed by Aunt Viola's driving, and I felt bad for Jane. The words shot out of my mouth before I could stop them.

"That preacher's stupid and so is Aunt Viola." I guess my mouth stopped being magic.

"That so?" Frost came over the porch like a winter night. Jane jumped up and ran around the side of the house. "What's that about?" Granny Jane tilted her head. Water filled my eyes. I knew I'd probably get spanked, but I felt so bad for Jane I didn't care. Scrubbing the tears from my cheeks, I explained about the Chinese babies and Jane's parents going to hell. By the time I'd finished I was mad all over again. I looked up at the old woman. She reached down into her dress pocket and pulled out her pipe, beginning her usual loading and lighting.

"Nobody knows what Sally and Dave had in their hearts about Jesus."

"That's why Jane has to know the preacher is wrong about Jane's momma and daddy burning in hell." Granny Jane stared out into the dark. I knew I'd gotten to her.

"Think you're right, don't you?"

I flew to my feet. "I know I'm right."

Granny Jane began to smile.

"Don't laugh at me. Sissy laughs at me."

The pipe stem pointed at my chest. "I'm not Sissy."

I stood stock still, trembling with fear and courage. "Then why are you smiling?"

Granny Jane raised her hand and motioned me close. I stood still. She did it again. I obeyed. Reaching out, she grabbed my wrist. I was trapped.

"I wasn't laughing at you; I was smiling at your sass." I stood silent. She continued, "When you first came here you wouldn't say a thing for yourself. Only for that dog and even then, Marcell had to try to kill it before you'd speak up." She paused to take a puff of her pipe "And just now you're fighting for Jane, but you were fighting for your own view of things, too." She let go of my wrist and pointed to the steps. "Sit." I did.

"Gracie, here's the thing. Nobody's all wrong and nobody's all right. The preacher can be right about having to be a good person, but he can be wrong about the Chinese babies and people who die too quick."

"So, Jane's parents aren't really burning in hell for all eternity?"

"If you put that alongside those Chinese babies, I'd say you're right."

"But what about Aunt Viola?"

"What about her?"

I strained my ears for Jane, but she was probably long gone to the barn. Granny Jane had liked how I fought for Jane? She was gonna get more right now.

"Well so then what part of Aunt Viola's talking is right or wrong? She says you and Miss Emily are tired of having Jane around and too busy with Marcell. That you didn't have any choice when her parents died and you are stuck with her. That you'd be happier with her gone 'cause she's running wild. And it'd be better for everybody for her to come live in town." I strung the words all together like Christmas lights too hot to touch.

Granny Jane stopped rocking. "She say that directly to you and Jane?"

"No, but Miss Beulavine said it to us in church right before the baby shower. And we heard Aunt Viola say it to Sissy." I gave Granny Jane my best adult look. "And Jane tries not to talk about it, but I know she thinks about it a lot." I didn't want to betray my best friend, but it was a night for hard truths. I lowered my voice. "I think she's scared."

The old woman sat silently for a few minutes then leaned forward in her rocker and looked me straight in the eye. "You heard all about hell tonight?"

I swallowed dry air and nodded.

"Well, that's where I'll be before I'll let Jane live one day away from this farm."

A painful sob split the air. Granny Jane and I stared at each other. I jumped up, raced to the other end of the porch, and leaped down. There, huddled in the dark, hanging on to Brown Hound was Jane.

I popped my head up over the edge of the porch. "It's Jane."

"Of course it's Jane. Bring her here."

"I think she heard us."

"Of course, she heard us. Bring her here this minute."

Grabbing Jane's arm I tugged, but she wasn't coming. She had her face buried in Brown Hound's neck. Moving behind her, I put my hands under her arms and pulled. At first, she pulled back, then suddenly she shot up, throwing me backwards to the ground. Sitting in the dark, rubbing my behind, I heard Jane's feet run across the porch. Granny Jane's cane fell to the floor. The rocker give a mighty creak and begin rocking. I heard words but couldn't make them out. I didn't need to. Brown Hound licked my face. I got up and took my new truth-telling self around the back to the kitchen to find me and Brown Hound a biscuit.

CHAPTER 17

The morning dawned bright and hot. Jane had come to bed last night and dropped like a dead cow. This morning she smiled at the ceiling. Her leg snaked over and her toes scrabbled for purchase. I yanked my leg back then raised up on my elbow and looked out the window. Brown Hound was dragging a branch all over the front yard. Black Jack and Sassy were trying to get it away from her and she was having none of it. Just like I was having none of Aunt Viola. The thought filled me up. I felt like I could float right up through the ceiling and drift along in the clear bright air.

My foot eased over to Jane. Stretching my toes, I tried to pinch her. Jerking her leg away, she grabbed her pillow and jammed it over my face. I squealed, turned, and landed on her. Throwing her arms around me, she grabbed my pajama top and yanked it up over my head. We rolled on the bed wrestling and laughing.

"Quit cutting a fool. Breakfast's on." Marcell turned and walked out. Jane and I looked at each other.

Jane spoke, "We gotta do it. Now that I can never ever be sent away, we still need to make Marcell better for her own self."

I hopped out of bed and waved my pajama top

over my head. Jane joined me. Her face was shining. Because of my magic mouth and my truth-telling self, Jane was fine. Now on to fixing Marcell.

***

"Girls, your grandmother and I are going into town today." Granny Jane had finished breakfast as we took our seats. "Just the two of us by ourselves. We don't want to have to keep an eye on you." Her voice was sharper than usual. I looked over at Miss Emily for clues. She looked tired. Seemed like she hadn't quite recovered from Sissy and my father's visit the other day. Not to mention the Miss Victoria debacle. Doc Davis had called and said that the old lady was up and fine now. Probably nothing could kill her.

Granny Jane had her eyes on me. I smiled at her and she nodded her head then turned to look at Jane. Her hand opened and closed on the top of her cane. It was like she wanted to lift it in the air and crack it hard on somebody's head.

"You girls help Marcell. The house is mostly clean, so it should be an easy day." Miss Emily's voice really did sound as done-in as she looked. I turned my head and watched Marcell. She was moving slow. The last couple of days had tired her out, too. I felt bad for my part in that.

We finished breakfast, scraped our plates in the dog bucket, and cleared the table. Miss Emily had been right. The house was already clean. After Miss Emily and Granny Jane disappeared down the road, Marcell released us to go play. We could tell she wanted peace and quiet.

We were lounging on the living room sofa. "We're gonna find that grave." Jane's voice was firm. We'd promised Granny Jane not to look for it, but Jane was safe from being taken away and Granny Jane liked me for being a truth-teller. If we found it and only told the few people who needed to know, we wouldn't get into too much trouble. At least that's what Jane and I reasoned.

Jane continued, "If Cap'n Tom put Ivis somewhere in the woods he could've told Marcell years ago and things would've been fine. But he didn't tell so that means Ivis is buried somewhere he shouldn't be."

I had an idea. "What about the colored graveyard without a headstone?"

"No, that's too obvious and besides, Cap'n Tom could've told Marcell and Miss Emily with no problem."

I had another thought "Cap'n Tom couldn't carry Ivis' body around forever. He had to hide it fast. He wouldn't have time to dig a big hole."

"So, maybe somebody else's grave?"

"Yeah, but whose?"

Silence. We stared at the ceiling. The ceiling. The attic. "Newspapers!" I all but shouted.

"Shhh." Jane's hissed looking at the door, "What do you mean?"

I shook her hand off. "Newspapers. I bet they're old newspapers and clippings up there. Especially if somebody died that the family knew. All we have to do is figure out when Ivis died and then look for clippings about people who died near that time and find their grave."

"But wouldn't they already be buried in it?"

"Yeah, but maybe the dirt was soft and Cap'n Tom could dig it fast. He just put him on top."

Jane jumped up thrilled with the idea. "Let's go."

Silently, we tiptoed to the back hallway and climbed the stairs. The attic was the same as the last time we'd played up there. Hot dry air feeding into your lungs like sand. We moved toward the window and saw Granny Jane's trunk. It stood like a mystery; its dull brown straps coated in dust and the leather covering frayed at the edges. If there were clippings saved, this was a good place to start. I gave Jane the honors. Sweat dribbled down the sides of her face as she worked the latch.

"Let's open the window." My suggestion was met with a fierce wag of her head. She was focused on the trunk. And then a hard click. Jane sat back on her heels and grinned up at me. Rising to her feet, Jane lifted the lid, pausing when it creaked. I glanced at the door making sure it was closed. Stepping forward, I put my hands under the lid and we eased it open.

On top was the family album of Granny Jane and James Earl. Reverently, Jane picked it up and moved closer to the window to look. The first page was the wedding invitation. If James Earl had lived, they would have been married seventy-one years. Jane and I stood silently in awe that anyone might have spent that much time with Granny Jane and survived. Obviously, James Earl hadn't.

Jane closed the album and handed it to me. Taking out the top tray, she found newspapers and clippings piled in the bottom. Grinning in victory she said, "Uncle Ben said it happened when Marcell was about our age."

"Well how old is she now?"

Jane paused and I waited. Nobody knew things like that about coloreds, when they were born and their age. It didn't seem to matter. But it mattered now. I thought back over what Uncle Ben had told us. 1920. Then I thought about what Miss Emily had told us and I had another clue.

"Miss Emily said the Tigers burned the Smith's barn the year before they hanged Ivis. Same time of year, too." Jane dug into the papers. Grabbing a stack, she shoved them at me. "Get going!" I was standing in a daze of glory but quickly came to earth and started looking.

The attic was quiet as we shuffled through the clippings looking for dates and stories about the Smith's barn. Every so often Jane would pause and cock her ear towards the door. If Marcell was moving around in the house, we couldn't hear her. Sunlight pooled in through the windows and the dust danced. Jane sneezed twice but had the sense to bury her nose in her shirt.

"Here. Look." I spread a newspaper clipping out on the floor boards. Jane put hers aside and leaned over. Sure enough it was a story about the Smith's barn burning. Reading quickly, we found the fire was due to a lightning strike. We knew better. I had a feeling of satisfaction at being in on the secret, but it also made my stomach hurt. It was all really true. I looked up at Jane and saw the same thing in her eyes. I checked the date. 1919. "Let's look. Next year same time." We tore through the pile.

Dry, musty air swirled up to our noses and tickled. Jane finished first and, pushing her pile aside, leaned over my shoulder. I shoved her, "You're sweating on me." Jane leaned over farther and smeared her cheek on the side of my face. I reached up and grabbed her hair. She muffled a howl and fell over on her side. "Get up. You're tearing the paper." Jane bounced up and sat beside me.

"Look," I pointed to the torn sheet, "if anyone finds this, they'll know what we've been doing." I gave Jane a glare but she wasn't looking at me. Her eyes were glued to where the paper was torn.

"That's it." Her voice sounded funny. I pushed her hand away. It was an article about an event in town. Jane leaned over, placing the jagged pieces of paper together. She read in a quiet voice.

"April 18, 1920. The town of Kingston gathered today to dedicate a new memorial site. A long time in planning, this memorial celebrates the county's Civil War dead with The Grave of the Unknown Confederate Soldier. The memorial contains unidentified remains of soldiers who perished in the War of Northern Aggression. The Daughters of the Confederacy

are sponsors of this memorial for our forgotten heroes. Today's dedication included placing these warriors in the hallowed monument. Members of the volunteer committee include Mr. Benjamin Rouse, Mr. William James, Thomas H. Jones, …"

Jane's voice trailed off. She sat up on her knees. I kept quiet. The newspaper had been saved because it mentioned Thomas H. Jones. Miss Emily's husband, Granny Jane's son, and our grandfather, Cap'n Tom. He had helped build a monument big enough to hold a bunch of dead soldiers about a year after the Smith's barn burning. Two months before Ivis was killed. Our grandfather had put a colored man in a monument for Confederate soldiers.

I looked up at Jane. She stared back. Wonder filled her voice. "That's where he is."

"Can't be." I denied what was right in front of my face.

"Well, where else? It fits."

I said the first thing that came to mind, "Aunt Viola's gonna swallow her teeth."

Jane howled with laughter and fell sideways smashing into the floorboards. I clamped my hand over her mouth.

"Shut up. You want Marcell to hear?" I pushed off of her and she sat up.

"Cutting a fool?"

We jumped to our feet, pushing each other, trying to stand over the clippings.

"Miss Emily gonna wear you out if she finds you was up here. Look at this mess." Marcell pointed to the scattered newspapers. "And from Miss Jane's trunk. Clean it up right now. I'm gonna stand here and watch." She folded her arms. Quickly, we gathered the clippings, being careful to keep the page about the Confederate Memorial out of sight.

"Come on now. In front of me." Silently, we made our way down the stairs. Reaching the back porch, we asked Marcell if we could go swimming in the creek. She shrugged her shoulders and headed towards the kitchen, glad to be rid of us.

"She didn't even tell us to be careful," Jane said as we walked through the yard.

"Probably hoping we'll drown."

Jane kept walking towards the creek, but I stopped in the yard to say hello to Brown Hound. She had only been at Marcell's a little while, but it had felt like years. I grabbed her behind the ears and rocked her head back and forth. She smiled at me, gave a happy yip then dropped back down, trotting off with the other dogs.

The creek level was still low. I entered the water, digging my hands in the sandy bottom for anchor. Jane held on to an exposed tree root, stretching her arms out, letting the slow current keep her afloat. After a while, I climbed up onto a rock and let the sun burn me dry. Neither of us talked about what we found in the attic. We were keeping it in, chewing it over.

Jane had chewed enough and asked, "You think I'm right? You really think he's there?"

"I really do." But knowing where Ivis was

buried didn't solve anything at all. There was no way on God's earth we were gonna tell Marcell her father was buried with a bunch of Confederate soldiers. And we promised Granny Jane and Miss Emily to not look for the grave.

"First off, we've gotta make sure he's there." Jane drifted calmly in the water.

"And just how"

"Uncle Ben."

"What?"

"Uncle Ben. Let's tell Uncle Ben. I bet he'll help."

I loved Uncle Ben and didn't want to get him involved. "Not on your life!"

"Why not? Look, he took us to the carnival and you know he knew we were gonna make straight for the Freak Show."

"I don't care. I don't want him to get in trouble."

Jane gave me a look of superiority. "Nobody's gonna get in trouble."

I glared at her snotty self. I hated it when she gave herself airs. Jane unhooked her fingers and slowly began to drift downstream. I sat, fuming. I hope she drowned. Well, not really, but there was no way I was gonna let her ask Uncle Ben for help. Jumping from the rock, splashing over to the edge of the stream, I gathered my clothes and towel, and walked back to the house by myself.

"These girls help you today, Marcell?" Miss Emily sat

down to supper. Marcell gave a nod. "That's good." Our grandmother smiled at us, but I could tell her thoughts were somewhere else. Granny Jane came home from town and went directly to bed. She was fine, Miss Emily told us. Just tired.

My thoughts were elsewhere, too. I was mad at Jane and trying not to show it. I could see she was still feeling snotty. I wanted to yank her hair out, but then we'd be asked what the fuss was all about. If I tried to lie Miss Emily would see right through it. Jane might be safe and Granny Jane might like me, but there was still a chance they'd send me back to Virginia if I was making too much fuss.

I sat for a moment wondering about going back to Virginia. Summer was getting near the end and nobody'd said a word about me going back. But they would. I knew they wouldn't forget about me like Sissy and Daddy usually did. The time was coming and it made my stomach twist. Maybe they wouldn't want me back. All Sissy ever did was complain about me and Brown Hound. And Daddy had made clear the night I slept in the dirt with Brown Hound; Sissy would always come first. Maybe he'd be glad to let me stay here. I pushed the thought away.

After supper we helped Marcell, then still not speaking to each other, went early to bed.

CHAPTER 18

Jane and I were in the back of Aunt Viola's car again with Miss Garson snarling by her side.

"I don't wonder Miss Jane is still in bed. I don't blame Emily for sending you two to Martha and Ben's for a night or two. Getting you out from under their feet. It's wearing having you girls around. Those women need a break. It's enough they have to deal with Marcell."

Jane closed her eyes. Aunt Viola continued to yap about Marcell. I piped up to break the flow.

"Well, Marcell was nice to my dog."

"I heard all about that. Your mother is a good woman, having mercy like that. I'd have shot that dog on sight. It's no wonder Marcell and your dog get along."

I sat back and wished I could fold my ears up around my head. I missed Brown Hound already but had agreed with Miss Emily that Aunt Martha and Uncle Ben had seen enough of my dog. I didn't want to push it in case there was another emergency.

Jane stared out of the window. I knew she was planning and plotting. This trip was getting her where she wanted to go. She was holding firm in her belief that Uncle Ben would help us with Marcell's daddy's grave. I was just happy to be at their house. It was like having grace said over top of your head, flowing around you like a warm light.

"Just look at those flowers sagging in this heat. I'm gonna call Beulavine." Aunt Viola fumed as she drove through town. We turned to see what flowers she was talking about and our eyes landed smack on The Grave of the Unknown Confederate Soldier. There it was in all its glory with wilted gummy flowers at the base. Aunt Viola continued to fuss. Jane and I sat straight up, pretending we hadn't seen. A few turns and we were pulling into Aunt Martha and Uncle Ben's driveway.

"Here we are!" Aunt Viola sang out as she yanked on the brake. Uncle Ben stood on the steps. "Girls. Glad you're here."

Jane and I jumped from the car and ran to him, hugging him around his waist. He patted our heads. "Viola, you go on in. Martha has some sweet tea and she just made those butter cookies you like." Aunt Viola hurried into the house. Uncle Ben plucked our overnight case from the car and slammed the door on Miss Garson.

"Don't know that we have anything exciting planned for you girls this time." We followed him up the steps and into the front bedroom. It was just like always. White curtains, white bedspread, and smelling like beeswax and lemon. I closed my eyes and took a deep breath. When I opened them, Uncle Ben was looking at me, smiling. I smiled back. My feet felt like potatoes planted solid in the summer ground. Uncle Ben chuckled.

"I don't know what's got into you, Gracie. You're looking different each time we see you. Could be you're growing up?"

"Ha! She's still a baby. I'm three months older and I'm growing up faster." Jane pushed her way into our smiling circle and I let her do it without a fuss.

"That so?" Uncle Ben patted our heads again and left the room. Jane opened the overnight case and we put our fresh underpants and pajamas in the dresser.

"We're here. It's all gonna work," Jane nodded her head as she spoke. I still didn't like it.

"I don't see how we're gonna do anything at all."

Jane ignored me. "First step is to check the territory." She had the pirate look in her eyes and it made me uneasy. It was all right to talk about finding proof Ivis was in the Confederate monument, but it was another thing to do it.

Jane waved her hand in the air. "You just leave this to me." Turning, she sashayed to the kitchen and I followed.

"And it's a shame, that monument looking so bedraggled." Aunt Viola was ferociously chomping cookies and washing them down with gulps of iced tea. Aunt Martha leaned against the sink drying her hands on a tea towel.

"Girls!" She didn't have to say anything else.

The tone of her voice told us how happy she was to see us. We gave her a hug and sat. Uncle Ben pushed the cookies toward us. Aunt Viola gave a frown. Jane put her plan into action.

"Aunt Viola," she began, her voice dripping with sugar, "we know how upset you are about those flowers on the Confederate grave. So Gracie and I thought Aunt Martha could help us pick some flowers then we could go up to town and replace the old ones."

Aunt Martha looked pleased. Aunt Viola continued to chew. Uncle Ben looked at us like we were bugs needing close examination.

"Girls, that's so nice of you. We'll do it as soon as your Aunt Viola leaves."

Aunt Viola gave a frown. I couldn't figure if it was about us doing a good deed or her having to leave the cookies.

"Well, Martha, that's fine." Aunt Viola brushed the crumbs off her lap and stood. "Seems like these girls are beginning to understand how to behave. Just look at how they helped with Miss Victoria. Even though they were out playing when they should have been in bed."

Aunt Viola waited for backtalk. Getting none, she pushed her chair under the table, and gave one last look at the cookies. "I'll just be going now." Uncle Ben walked her out. Aunt Martha rummaged in a kitchen drawer and found the shears.

Jane and I walked down the street by ourselves, Aunt

Martha having declined to join us in the noon-time heat. The gray monument loomed in front of the courthouse, reminding everyone of the soldiers who'd died in battle. Ivis had died in a battle of sorts, so it kind of made sense Cap'n Tom had buried him here. The more I thought about it, the more I believed our grandfather had truly done just that. Stepping over the low fence, we walked around the square of grass examining the monument from all sides.

"Where do you think the grave is?" Jane whispered.

"In the ground, where else?"

Jane gave me a pained look. "Of course, it's in the ground. I mean where in the ground. For a moment her resolve wavered. "You don't think they sat the monument on top of the bodies, do you?"

Our gazes traveled to the top of the six-foot monument. We hadn't considered that. If the bodies were under it, Ivis couldn't be buried here. We weren't gonna find anything.

"I'll clean these flowers up. You keep looking if you want." I wished I could clean and hold my nose at the same time. The flowers stank and clung to the stone like dripping fingers shedding skin. Hunkering down, I used my thumbnail to scrape the decaying petals. I moved from the front to the side and then to the back where people had been lazy and shoved older flowers. My thumb was getting raw and my legs were tired from crouching. Jane had gone to the courthouse to get more water for the flower bucket. I sat back on the ground and looked at the monument wondering about the dead soldiers. I thought about what it must have felt like to get shot, then have your bones shoved into a monument. Suddenly, I froze. Where did that thought come from? About putting bones inside the monument instead of under it? I focused my eyes and realized I'd been looking at the back of the monument where the sun was reflecting.

I moved closer and stared hard. There, at the base of the monument was a metal plate. It was painted to match the concrete, but it was there. Raising my hand, I traced its edges. It was about the size of a sofa cushion, maybe a bit smaller.

"Here's the water."

I shot into the air then plopped down in front of the metal plate.

"You look like you've seen the dead soldiers!" Jane snorted as she sat the bucket down. Reaching over for the shears, she pulled the new flowers to her and settled on the ground. After cutting the first three, she looked over at me. Her hands got still. "What?!" She tossed the flowers to the ground "What?!" she demanded.

I didn't say anything. She followed my eyes and looked. Getting on her knees, she reached out and traced the metal plate. Then she sat back and just stared. We both did, lost in our thoughts.

"How you girls coming along?"

Jane and I flew in the air like frogs in hot grease. Landing on our feet, we gaped at Uncle Ben.

"Getting spooked being around a grave?" Our uncle's eyes twinkled, but I could see he was busy wondering what we might be up to. He chewed on his cigar and watched the Sherriff walk over.

"Afternoon, ladies, Ben," said the sheriff. "I was coming from the courthouse and saw you girls. You cleaning up the monument for us?"

"We were just," Jane began. I interrupted, "just scraping the flower drippings off." Uncle Ben nodded his head. I thought we looked guilty. I hoped the sheriff couldn't see through us. Maybe if I told about finding the metal panel and made it seem casual, they wouldn't realize something was up.

"And I got to the back here and its metal not stone. I'm afraid of scratching the paint off." That sounded just right, nice and relaxed. I shot Jane a look of triumph. She glared at me. I glared back. I was doing the best I could.

"Well now, good I came along, said Uncle Ben. "We wouldn't want anything scratching this fine monument. Let me see if I can help rub those flower traces off the metal for you."

Jane and I backed up and made room being careful to avoid the sheriff. Uncle Ben squatted, pulled out his hankie, wet it with spit, then gently rubbed at the flower stains. "Wouldn't want to call attention to it."

"Why not?" Jane ventured a question.

"It's the door to the grave."

"Bodies are in there?" Jane asked. Uncle Ben

creaked up to standing and tucked the stained hankie back in his pocket.

"That's right. The panel opens to the hollow part. That's how we put the soldier's remains inside."

"Why didn't you bury them under the cement?" Jane was doing all the talking now.

"We thought there might be a few more soldiers discovered after a time and wanted to be able to include them."

"We who?" Jane was keeping at it.

"Me, your granddaddy, your Aunt Viola's husband, Will, and a few others."

"Did you know who the soldiers were?" Jane was pushing too much. I interrupted, "Why else do you think they call it the 'unknown' grave?"

Uncle Ben smiled, put his hands on his hips and arched his back, looking up at the blue Carolina sky. "No, we didn't know any of them. Most were just bones and a few buttons."

"If they were just bones, how did you know they were Confederates?"

Uncle Ben stopped in mid-stretch. The sheriff bared his teeth in a smile at Jane and said, "Lots of questions, girls."

Jane started back peddling, "Oh, just passing time." She reached down, picked up the fresh flowers, and started examining them.

Uncle Ben studied her. He turned his eyes to me. I smiled and tried to look like I didn't know anything. Rubbing his chin, he said, "I'll be on then. I'm picking up ice cream for dessert tonight. Y'all come on home once you're finished."

"You girls be good, now," the sheriff said.

"Yes, sir," we answered and watched them walk away.

Jane collapsed to the ground.

"You think they know?"

"No, but you've got the brain of a chicken. The only reason they didn't figure it out is because what you want to do is so stupid, they'd never think of it!" I knelt back down and started scrubbing on the last side of the monument.

Jane sat up and continued snipping the new flowers. "You know, if the Confederate soldiers are just buttons and bones, then anything else in there has to be Ivis. You know, something more, maybe with clothes on it."

I tried to ignore the image and kept scrubbing.

Jane got huffy. "Well, you could at least say something."

I sat back on my heels and looked at her. "No matter what I say, you're still the one with chicken brains. What if Ivis's really in there? What're you gonna do, pry this thing open and look inside without anybody seeing you? And if you find something with clothes on it, how you gonna know it's Ivis?" I leaned back toward the monument and continued scrubbing. My thumbnail finally gave a tear and I popped it into my mouth sucking the blood. If anyone wanted the rest of the stains off of the monument, they could doggone well scrub it themselves. I pushed to my knees then stood up. Jane finished with the flowers and we arranged them in front of the monument. For a minute, we stood there looking at it, knowing old, dead soldiers were jammed in the space behind the panel.

"Well. Now isn't that nice." We swirled around. It was Aunt Viola out running her errands and checking up on us. Bet she thought we'd brought the cookies.

"You arranged those flowers just right. And you even scrubbed the stains off." She put her hands on her hips. "Who knew that Emily and Miss Jane had time to teach you seeing as they have to spend most of their time pulling Marcell out of ditches."

I thought about Marcell falling on the porch after Brown Hound had sent the cookie tray flying and then how she didn't want to take my dog home but had done it anyway. And how she'd stood in front of Jane at the revival. I swallowed and kept my mouth shut. Aunt Viola was on Sissy's side. It wouldn't do for her to call Sissy and tell her I was talking back. I didn't want them coming down here.

A cold wave went through my stomach. I sank to the back of my head and looked at the thought. I didn't want them coming down anymore. All I did was feel bad when they were around. I heard my name and looked up. Aunt Viola was talking to me.

"Elizabeth Grace, I'm sure this is your influence. That momma of yours is a lady in every respect. And Jane, if Miss Jane and Emily would let you come and live with me, I'd have you made into the perfect little lady in no time." Her words dripped with honey. Jane smiled, knowing she was safe.

"We're pleased to do this, Aunt Viola. We know all about flower arranging. Marcell taught us how to do it," Jane said.

The woman threw Jane a glare. Turning, she gave me a pat on the head. Ignoring Jane, Aunt Viola walked on down the street.

Jane reached over and swiped her hand over the top of my head where Aunt Viola had touched. "Brushing off cooties."

"Yep," I replied.

Aunt Martha and Uncle Ben spoiled us with too much ice cream and letting us stay up as late as we wanted. Once in bed, we pulled the covers over our heads and began plotting. Plans were built and plans were destroyed. And then Jane's eyes gleamed in the dark.

"Let's get some bones and say they're a dead Confederate soldier. Uncle Ben will put them in the monument and see Ivis."

"What about the others?"

Jane chewed this for a minute and answered, "Since it will be us who finds the bones, we'll request a family member place the remains." She finished like a queen granting favors.

I marveled at her brilliance. She continued, "That hole is small and when he opens it up, he'll see Ivis. You know Uncle Ben. He's not gonna say anything until he's chewed it over a bit. So he'll put the bones in, close it up. He knows about Ivis. He'll put two and two together."

"But why would he tell us what he saw?"

"We'll be there when he puts them in. We found the bones and want to see them treated proper."

"How will he know for sure that it's Ivis?"

"Well, he won't. And we can't tell him about Cap'n Tom taking Ivis away, but once Miss Emily knows, she'll see how important it is to Marcell and she'll figure out how to tell."

That sewed it up. Jane had an answer for everything, I nodded my head in agreement.

CHAPTER 19

We were back at the farm and headed to the old Indian graveyard next to the far tobacco field.

"They have to look old and busted up," Jane said firmly.

"And they have to be human," I added. We walked quietly as if the bones could hear us coming and run away.

"Least we got the minie balls and buttons." This was the dazzling part of the plan. In the barn loft, Jane had a glass jar filled with arrowheads, clay minie balls, and some Confederate uniform buttons that she'd picked out of the fields after each spring plowing.

"Here." Jane stopped at the edge of the field. A little ways in to the woods were oblong hollows in the ground where graves had caved in. Under them were dead Indians. Jane was acting like the grand queen for figuring out the plan, so it was up to me to do the work. I took a big breath and stepped into the woods. One more step and I was down into one of hollows. The sun slanted through the trees and lit patches on the fallen leaves. Slowly, I moved around, hoping to find a bone on the ground. Nothing. Taking a deep breath, I knelt to push away leaves, sticks, and small branches. Each one felt like a bone and made my heart stop. I pushed more leaves away and suddenly, there it was. A bone. I brushed the rest of the leaves and dirt away. Maybe part of an arm? My stomach rolled over. It was just a bone I told myself, like the ones Brown Hound dug up all the time. Why some of the bones the dogs dragged back were probably Indian bones. And anyway, the Indian was in the happy hunting-grounds and didn't need his bones anymore. I felt better. I reached over and grabbed ahold of it. I knelt there for a minute just looking at it.

"You ok?"

Jumping to my feet, I waved the bone over my head like a flag, "Got it." And scrambled out of the grave.

"Heard you girls were a big help with the Confederate monument." Miss Emily handed the mashed potatoes around. I grabbed the bowl and took a big scoop. Her mashed potatoes were heaven on a plate.

"Yes, ma'am."

Granny Jane motioned for me to pass the bowl. I handed it to her and looked at Jane across the table. She gave me a smile. The bone was hidden in the rafters of the barn so the dogs wouldn't get it.

"Ben said you did a nice job and your Aunt Viola was impressed with how you arranged the flowers."

Jane piped up, "I told her Marcell taught us how to do it."

Granny Jane gave a snort and Jane asked, "Granny Jane, that monument. Where did they find all those soldiers?"

"Here and there." She was busy spooning gravy all over her potatoes. Looked like she was going to use it up before I had my chance.

"They ever find anybody here?"

"On the farm, you mean? No. Nothing around here. Emily, you ever hear anything?"

"No." My grandmother buttered a biscuit then set it down on her plate thinking and tapping her bottom lip with her knife. "There weren't any battles right around here as I remember tell of."

"But what about all those minie balls and things in the fields?"

Miss Emily nodded her head, "Now that's a thought. Maybe they did have a skirmish out there. I never thought much about it. You, Miss Jane?"

Granny Jane was busy eating and not paying too much attention. I was glad because I didn't want her thinking back to this evening's conversation once Jane and I announced our amazing discovery. So nobody really knew if there'd been a battle here or not, but there was evidence from the minie balls. That was enough. Now we just had to put the arm bone in the field. I looked down at my plate. I pushed the chicken wing to the side.

�֍ �֍ �֍

The end of the summer was passing in a blur of hot days and anxious anticipation. Jane and I had to wait for rain to "find" the bone. It stayed dry all week. We kept a close eye on Marcell. Now wasn't the time to upset her and make her drink. Granny Jane's idea about her facing the past seemed to be working.

It was Sunday afternoon, Marcell was gone, Granny Jane was napping on the porch, and Miss Emily was resting in her room. Pressure from thunderheads building in the distance made her head hurt. The heat drove the energy out of everybody but Jane and me. We were living on high hopes, and dreams of Marcell being happy forever.

We were in the barn loft going over the plan when thunder rumbled in the distance. Jane and I lifted our heads.

"It's time." Jane hissed. We packed up the bone, minie balls and a few selected buttons. Climbing down, we peeked out the barn door. No one. We streaked around to the back and made for the woods. Thunder rumbled again. It was closer. That was good. Finally, we were getting the rain that would disguise our tracks. We made it to the tobacco field. We stopped to catch our breath. Thunderheads rose up like dark mountains. The air was heavy and damp.

"Come on," Jane's voice had an edge to it. She grabbed my hand and sped along the side of the field, thunder and darkness closing. It felt like something was chasing us. Reaching the half-way point, Jane turned and headed out into the field. I was close behind trying to grab onto her shirt. Thunder clapped and I leaped into the air. I didn't want to be anywhere near a field when lightning started snapping.

"Here," Jane said and stopped suddenly. I almost ran her down.

"Why here? Let's put it more in the middle," I said.

"People have been running over this field with tractors for years. Bone would be mush. It's better near the side where the tractors might've missed."

We stood looking at the ground.

"How deep should we bury it?" I'd never found a bone before.

Jane looked at the arm bone and then back to the dirt. "Not too deep. The rain has to wash it up, so we can see it." I knelt and dug down an inch or two. Laying the bone in the dirt, I looked at it for a minute. Thunder clapped again and fat drops began to fall from the sky. The wind turned chilly.

"Come on. Let's go." Jane was dancing. I patted the dirt over the bone and stood up. The rain began to fall harder and Jane turned to run.

"Hey," I screamed "Hey! The buttons."

Jane wheeled around and digging into her pocket, she pulled out the minie balls and buttons. "Here." She tossed them. I snatched them out of the air and scattered them around. Looking up, I saw Jane hauling fast. Just then lightning slammed the air nearby and my feet grew wings. We raced back to the barn.

Thunder shook the old tin roof. Jane and I lay back on the hay basking in safety. A spear of lightning screamed out of the sky and slammed into a tree in the swamp. You could hear the sizzle all the way to the barn. Granny Jane said sometimes a swamp tree would burn for weeks when it'd been hit. Sounded like this would be one of those trees. Another slice of lightening ripped the sky and landed nearby. Jane grabbed my hand and smiled.

"Gracie, wake up." I untangled myself from the covers. Miss Emily was in the doorway instead of Marcell. I looked at Jane. She was still asleep, face smashed into the pillow, and hiney stuck in the air. The light from the window was hazy and soft. It was early.

"Come on with me. Your daddy's on the phone."

My stomach flipped then cramped. Miss Emily shook her head. "It's nothing bad child. Your daddy just wants to talk with you. Seems like every time he calls, you and Jane are out playing or staying with Martha and Ben."

I slid out of the bed. The floorboards were cool against my feet, but I could feel the day starting to gather heat. I followed Miss Emily's gown tail. She was getting a slow start today and no surprise. Jane and I had waited in the barn for the storm to stop, but it hadn't. We'd finally flown through the back yard to the house, swearing it was a miracle we hadn't been fried alive. The storm pounded through the afternoon then pulled back and waited until full dark. It pounced again late in the night and kept at it until almost dawn.

"Here." Miss Emily held out the phone. I reached to take it. The plastic felt sticky, but I knew

Miss Emily's hands were clean. It was me who was sweating.

"Hi, Daddy."

"Hello, Gracie. I'm sorry to be calling so early, but I wanted to talk to you before I left for work. Seems like when I call later, you two girls are off on some adventure. Don't you ever stay in the house?" I searched for a smile in his voice and found it. Miss Emily was right. No one was fussing. No one was telling me to pack for home. I shoved the thought away and answered, "We're usually off in the woods playing."

"But not getting into trouble?"

"No, sir."

"Well, that's good. Listen honey, I just wanted to tell you that your momma is doing fine. I don't want you worrying about her." I felt a flame of guilt. I hadn't thought about her at all except to feel how good it was without her.

"What do you think?"

"Sir?" I hadn't heard a word he'd said.

"Gracie, get the wax out of your ears and listen. I said I thought maybe your momma and I would wait a little while longer before we come down to see you again."

I felt a small pleasure "Yes, sir. That'll be okay." Then I told the lie. "Tell Momma I miss her."

"That's a good girl. She misses you too. Now let me talk to your grandmother. You be good. Don't get into any trouble."

"Bye, Daddy." I handed the phone to Miss

Emily and walked back to bed.

"Where you been? You're didn't go find the bone without me!" Jane rolled on her back and waved her legs in the air, spreading her toes as far she could.

"You look like a frog. Stop it. No, I didn't." My words ended in a yell as Jane flung her legs over on me and pinched my calf with her toes. "Stop it. Ow. Quit!"

"Jane, stop. Gracie, I want to talk to you."

Jane pulled her legs back. Miss Emily gave her a look. Jane switched around and gazed out of the window. I know she was hoping Miss Emily hadn't heard her words about the bone.

"Gracie," Miss Emily began as she sat on the side of the bed. I scooted over to give her room and she patted my leg. "Gracie, I know what your daddy said. I'm sorry they aren't coming to see you soon. I know you must miss them."

"I don't mind. I don't think about them much anyway."

Jane and Miss Emily went still. The curtains moved, but that was about all. I had no idea what I should say next. It seemed like it was right to be honest. After all, I was a truth-telling person now. I looked up at Miss Emily. She leaned over and kissed me. Jane seemed to take this for a signal to breathe.

"Miss Emily, you having to fuss with these girls already this morning?" Marcell stood in the bedroom doorway, her arms folded across her chest, her eyebrows cocked at us.

"No, Marcell. Just having a little talk."

"Uh huh." Marcell stepped back to let Miss Emily out, then stepped back in. "Better not be bothering Miss Emily with your mess. Now get dressed." She swung the dish towel at us in a deliberate miss. We scrambled out of bed.

※ ※ ※

It was a fine morning and we couldn't stand it any longer. That bone called out to us from the back field and we couldn't stick with anything we tried to do. We cleaned the chicken yard in fits and starts. We cleaned up branches in the front yard that had fallen from the storm, working under Granny Jane's supervision. We made it through lunch, but only because Miss Emily complained we had ants in our pants and made us take our food out to the back porch.

"We're gonna go see if any trees came down last night," Jane said after we'd finished eating and taken the plates to the sink. We sauntered through the door and out of sight. Then like a flash, we were off.

"It was about here," I said looking out at the field.

"You sure?"

"I think so."

Jane reached out and gave my arm a slap. "You should have marked it."

I yanked away from her. "Yeah, then someone else could have come and wondered why there was a stick pointing to a buried bone."

Jane gave me a glare, walked into the soft field, and sank up to her ankles. I laughed. She pulled one foot out with a soggy pop and then put it down with a bigger squish. Bracing her knees, she began to pull the other foot up when suddenly it flew into the air and waved like a flag. She sat down hard. Mud splashed everywhere. I yelled with laughter, "You look like a mudpuppy!"

Jane glared at me then suddenly grinned. "Come on"

"No. You're the one's dirty. You go on and find the bone."

Jane sat for a moment trying to think of a way to get me into the field.

"Listen. If I come back muddy and you don't, they're gonna wonder why you just stood on the side when I thought I saw something." She smiled and leaned back against her mud-caked hands. I waited a minute. She was right. I'd never stay on the side and just watch.

"Hey, the dogs!"

Things had been stirred up by the storm and they were out surveying the new smells.

"Brown Hound, Sassy, Black Jack." Jane bellowed and one by one they slid into the field, mud flying and tails in the air. It was enough. With a whoop, I headed for the middle of the pack. Soon we were running and chasing, the dogs trying to grab our shorts, us trying to grab their necks. We were rolling and yelling. They were barking and having a fine time. Five minutes later, we were coated with mud and breathing hard. The dogs panted, gave us a few licks, then bounded up shaking off the mud.

"Who looks like a mudpuppy now?" Jane started scraping mud off her knees and laughed at me.

"Marcell's gonna wear us out!"

"No, everybody's gonna be too excited about the Confederate bone and the buttons we found playing with the dogs."

She pointed and I looked over. There, gleaming in the sunlight, sticking out of the mud was the bone. Jane looked at me and grinned. Any reservations fell away like dead leaves. It was a sign. We were doing the right thing.

❈ ❈ ❈

"Miss Emily, come here. These girls need wearin' out for sure." Marcell had her hands on her hips watching us run up to the house.

"Look what we found!" Jane and I yelled together.

"Lot of trouble is what you found." Marcell shook her head at us as we slowed and approached the porch. "Don't you step up here. I'm not gonna sweep your mess off the boards. You go on out to the barn and get in the trough and wash off."

"Girls?" Miss Emily came out to the back porch followed by Granny Jane.

Jane waved the bone in the air. Miss Emily gave a start. Jane yelled, "It's a bone. We found it in the field." Marcell took a step back and folded her arms around her waist. She looked sick. It hit me and I stopped in my tracks. She thought it was her daddy's bone. I jammed my hand in my pocket and yanked out the mud-caked buttons and minie balls.

"Here!" I yelled too loud, "Minie balls! We found buttons, too!" I held out the treasures like they were Sunday communion.

"Bring them over. Let's wash them off." Miss Emily walked to the big iron sink she used for vegetables and chopped-up chickens. Marcell backed up and gave Miss Emily plenty of room. She didn't mention the mud as we climbed onto the porch. Jane laid the bone in the sink and I placed the buttons and minie balls, so they wouldn't go down the drain. Jane primed the pump and the cold water splashed over our booty.

"It looks like a human arm," Miss Emily said bending over the sink. Jane shot me a triumphant look then quickly lowered her eyes.

"It's probably from the old Indian grave yard." Granny Jane said in a firm voice.

"No." My voice was high and it cracked, but maybe they'd think it was excitement. "We got it from the back field when we were looking for trees and stuff that fell during the storm. The dogs were playing with us and we found it." I was talking too loud and Jane gave me a look to shut up.

"Let me see." Granny Jane took her turn at the sink. Reaching in, she poked the buttons and minie balls with her fingers. "Give me a few more pumps." Jane worked the pump and water splashed again. Granny Jane picked up a button and washed it off, turning it over and over. "Emily, take a look"

Miss Emily moved closer to examine the button. "My gracious." Jane and I waited. "Girls," my grandmother began, "this looks like a Confederate officer's button. Look here," she took it from Granny Jane so we could see, "it has the eagle with its wings spread and a shield. And see the tiny stars around the edge?"

We looked at it like it was a rock from the moon.

Miss Emily continued pointing to the sink. "Those are minie balls. And this," she turned her eyes to the bone "is most likely part of a Confederate soldier." Her hand went out as she ran her finger down the length of the bone. I started to feel bad for the dead Indian but then looked at Jane. She was beaming. I felt better.

"Marcell," Miss Emily said still looking at the bone, "wash this all off and then wrap it in flannel. I'm going to go call Ben." She stopped and turned. Marcell was gone. Granny Jane and Miss Emily passed a look. Granny Jane shook her head then spoke, "Girls, you go clean up at the barn."

Jane and I jumped off the porch and left them at the sink. As we trotted away, I looked over my shoulder. Granny Jane watched us all the way to the barn.

"We did it!" Jane stood on the edge of the mule trough, naked as a jay bird. Holding her nose, she pretended to take a huge jump but just landed in the water up to her knees. Laughing, she plunked down and let the water rise to her chin. Shucking my clothes, I joined her. We sat, letting the cool water seep into our pores. I watched as mule slobber drifted by. Jane picked up some floating straw and flicked it out.

"You think Marcell was upset?"

"You showed her the buttons right off," Jane replied.

"Yeah, but she walked off the porch."

Jane said, "Well, she'll be better when she knows about Ivis." I could see her trying to convince herself. I wanted to be convinced, too. Jane pulled me away from my thoughts.

"I bet Miss Emily's talking right now to Uncle Ben about putting the bone in the monument." Jane scrubbed the mud from her arms and continued, "I bet they're already planning a ceremony." She grinned, pinched her nose, and sank under the water.

She came up sputtering with triumph on her face. Her cloak of bravery was wrapped around her and I marveled at her place in the world. Her feet belonged on this farm as sure as the sun rose each morning. I lifted my leg out of the water. My feet didn't seem to have a place anymore. Things were in the air just like my foot. I didn't really belong to the farm as much as I wanted to. But I didn't belong back in Virginia. I was coming to know that more and more as the summer passed. Daddy and I were on different ice flows. His concern would always be caring for Sissy.

Jane's foot flew up and pressed against the sole of mine. I pushed back. She pushed harder. I scooted down and raised my other leg. Her other leg sprang out of the water. Our ankles locked and soon we were trying to flip each other over, turning, splashing, and yelling for help.

"You two clean now?" Granny Jane stood watching and we stopped mid-flip.

"Yes, ma'am."

"Then dry off and come back in. Bring your clothes." She draped two towels over the barnyard fence and walked off.

We were dry, in clean clothes, our wet hair plastered to our heads, sitting in the living room with our hands on our laps, knees together. Excitement cracked around us like the lightning from yesterday's storm.

"I just got off the phone with Ben." Miss Emily began, "He said from what you girls found, it looks like a Lieutenant Colonel strayed from some battle."

Jane inched forward on the sofa. I could see her busting to ask when the bones would be put in the monument. I slid my foot over to hers and gave it a nudge. She settled back, but I could see it was an effort. Miss Emily stood up from her chair like she'd finished talking. Jane and I looked at each other in astonishment. That was it?

"Girls, I'm going to need help with supper. Marcell's gone for the day."

We stood up and followed.

CHAPTER 20

Jane and I cut our eyes at each other over breakfast. The kitchen was quiet. Miss Emily and Granny Jane ate their eggs and bacon without a word. Marcell was nowhere to be found and we weren't about to ask. The idea that she might've thought the bone was her daddy's made my stomach hurt. All last night Jane and I agonized about how to bring up burying it in the monument. I asked Jane if she thought Marcell might be drinking. She didn't answer. We went back to plans for talking to Uncle Ben.

A familiar putt and sputter drifted through the kitchen. Aunt Viola's car. Tires bumped over driveway ruts, then the engine struggled to shut down. Miss Emily sighed. Placing her napkin beside her plate, she rose from her chair like she was under water. Granny Jane got up, as well. Both women walked from the kitchen without a word. Jane and I bounded after them at a safe distance.

"Stop that! Jane, Emily!" Aunt Viola hollered over the noise of yapping dogs. Brown Hound, Sassy, and Black Jack were paws up on the car door trying to get at Miss Garson. The ratty dog was giving it right back, barking and smearing the window with yellow, chunky dog slobber.

"Girls, get those dogs," Miss Emily said, knowing we were behind her without having to look. We ran down the steps and began yanking at dog collars.

Aunt Viola straightened her dress and walked forward, "I suppose I don't need to tell you why I'm here." An air of satisfaction drifted around her like old sour perfume. Jane and I shoved at the dogs and they trotted off. Our eyes locked on Aunt Viola. She was smiling, her big teeth flashing in the sun like the foil on Juicy Fruit gum.

"Will was going into Kingston for the auction this morning and he found Marcell in a ditch halfway between here and town." She looked at Miss Emily and Granny Jane like they were candy she was going to eat. "He took her to her cabin and laid her on the bed. I made him take his clothes off before he came back in the house."

I thought about Uncle Will standing naked at the back door begging Aunt Viola to let him in. I'd have laughed out loud if I hadn't been so scared.

"Please give Will our thanks. Is there anything else?" Miss Emily's tone was as formal as church.

"Anything else?" Aunt Viola swelled up like a dead cat in the sun. "Anything else? You'd better believe there's something else. We're about to finally have an understanding about my niece being raised around a drunk colored woman!"

The words knifed through my head. That wasn't Marcell, that wasn't who she'd become.

"I'll not have family raised around Marcell. It's a crime the way she behaves, falling in ditches, dragging into town bothering people." She paused for a breath then continued, "I can't understand why you two, God-fearing women keep her around. Neither can any of the ladies in our Dorcas class."

"Your Sunday School class has nothing better to do than talk about Marcell?" Miss Emily's voice sounded like it had bits of sharp glass in it.

"Well, of course we do. It's just that Marcell's behavior has been brought up once or twice." Aunt Viola shifted on her feet. "And anyway, people talk."

"Do they talk about exactly why she drinks?" Miss Emily folded her arms across her chest and waited. Jane and I held our breath.

"No. Well, no they don't."

Granny Jane leaned on her cane. "They don't have to talk about it, Viola, because they know the truth. And the truth is, their fathers are most likely the ones who chased Marcell's daddy through the night and hanged him."

Aunt Viola swelled up even bigger. "Now Miss Jane..."

The cane punched down on the hard dirt. Jane and I jumped. Miss Garson threw herself at the car window.

"Don't you 'Miss Jane' me, Viola. I've known you since the day you were born and you've never been able to keep your nose where it belongs. Those women wouldn't be talking if you weren't stirring things up."

Aunt Viola drew in a breath. I could see she wanted to take Granny Jane apart piece by piece but thought better of it. She smoothed down the front of her dress to gain time.

"I'm just worried about Jane. She's the last of our family and I want her to be raised right."

"What about Gracie?"

Aunt Viola turned and looked at me. Granny Jane gave a satisfied nod. "Both Gracie and Jane are the last of the family."

"But Gracie's in Virginia," Aunt Viola began.

"Not anymore."

The words caused so much noise in my head I couldn't hear. Not anymore? Did that mean 'anymore' like 'anymore' forever? I tried to hold onto anything that made sense, but it was like grabbing at clouds. Aunt Viola's voice cut through the noise.

"My point is, Miss Jane, it is past time for you and Emily to get rid of Marcell. You know it. I know it. And everybody in the county knows it. Things here are going to change if I have my way, no two ways about it."

Wheeling around she stalked to the car. Seeing Aunt Viola's approach, Miss Garson threw herself once more at the window, lost purchase on the vinyl seat, and cracked her head hard on the glass. With a slam of the car door, Aunt Viola drove off in a fury, dust swirling behind her like a bad dream.

"My head hurts." Miss Emily rubbed her hand on her forehead.

"Not as much as that dog's."

The two women gave small smiles. Jane and I waited, unsure what to do. Things had been said that made me want to ask questions but I knew better.

"Come on, girls." Miss Emily held out her hand. Granny Jane eased up on her cane and walked back to the porch, taking her seat in the rocking chair. We followed. Miss Emily leaned against the railing and Jane and I sat down quietly. Looked like we were going to be included in the women's talk.

"She's not going to let this drop." Miss Emily pushed some hair from her forehead.

"I know." Granny Jane's answered. She looked at us. "Girls, this is about more than Marcell."

More secrets. Granny Jane began, "Viola only had one baby. Little Bess. She died when she was about three months old. Viola just about lost her mind. Didn't get out of bed for months. Cried all day and night. Will was about ready to have her sent to the mental ward." The old woman paused and looked at Miss Emily. Our grandmother took up the story.

"About nine months later, Sally had you, Jane. And then Sissy and Robert had you, Gracie. It was like a knife in her heart. And she never did have another child. I guess that knife just keeps turning."

I asked, "So she wants Jane because she doesn't have little Bess?"

Granny Jane shook her head. "Yes and no. Meanness has been part of her nature since she was born. I think her wanting to take Jane away is twisted up with jealousy and hatefulness." The old woman gave a sigh. "Having Jane wouldn't help her one bit, not that she stands one chance in the good Lord's Earth of that happening."

Jane and I gave each other a grateful look.

"But Miss Jane, she's pulling more and more people into it now," said Miss Emily. "You know how much power she and Will have in the church. She's liable to have the preacher out here next. And then who knows where it will go."

"Well, the Lord himself knows we've tried with Marcell. I thought her having that dog for a few days might help her start coming to grips…"

The two women continued to talk, but Jane and I didn't hear a thing. We looked each other straight in the eye. The time had come to act. It really was up to us. We turned back to the conversation.

"You think church women would be more charitable." Granny Jane's voice was grim.

"I know. The only thing holding them back is they're afraid we'll talk about how their daddies had part in Ivis' hanging."

The dogs came trotting up the porch steps and drew Miss Emily's attention down to us. "You girls go on and clear the kitchen. I need to go and see Marcell."

Jane leaned against the sink. "We have to call Uncle Ben and tell him what happened today."

"With Aunt Viola?"

"Yeah, and that we need to get Aunt Viola and her Dorcas class thinking about something other than

Marcell. And we have just the thing!"

I chimed in. "We tell him the bone needs a ceremony and the Dorcas ladies can arrange it. The whole town will be there and everybody will be talking about that instead of Marcell's drinking."

We grinned at each other in fierce satisfaction. It could work. And the best part was that it was Aunt Viola who gave us the excuse to call Uncle Ben. Jane went back to the dishes humming a song.

A tea towel slapped my butt. "Come on, let's call Uncle Ben."

"Uncle Ben?" Jane's hand held the phone in a death grip. I stood, wiggling my knees back and forth, too excited to sit. Jane started right off telling him about Aunt Viola. I grinned. Jane was making Aunt Viola sound like Satan himself.

"Yes, sir. Well. I guess you're right." Suddenly her words seemed like the air had squashed out of them. "I know. I love you Uncle Ben. Bye." Hanging up the phone, she turned to me.

"What?"

"He said it was a good idea and that he'd get on it right away."

"What else?"

"He said we needed to get it done so you could be part of the ceremony before you went back."

Jane and I hadn't talked about it before now. We'd just ignored it. We'd been too busy with Marcell to talk about summer ending. We just thought it never would.

"Granny Jane said something to Aunt Viola about me not being from Virginia anymore. Maybe she meant I was going to stay."

Jane knew I was grabbing at straws. "Yeah, I guess." She was going to put it away so she wouldn't have to think about it, just like she did with her parents. I shoved it aside, too.

"So, what else did he say?" I tried to change how my voice sounded.

"Said he was going to talk to the preacher, and the committee. Next Saturday afternoon would probably be the day to do it."

"Do what?" Granny Jane opened the screen door and walked into the living room.

"Uncle Ben's going to have a ceremony at the Confederate memorial to put in the bone and buttons. He wants to do it next Saturday." Jane announced.

"Called him up and asked, did you?"

"Yes, ma'am." Jane looked her great-grandmother straight in the eye. Granny Jane looked right back. I could see she was thinking. She cocked her head and gave a small smile.

"Well, that's fine. Just fine."

She headed for her bedroom. Jane looked at me astonished. I watched Granny Jane's back disappear down the hallway and turned to Jane.

"Something's up."

CHAPTER 21

The week flew by like sticks in a storm. Miss Emily worked her usual magic and Marcell came back acting like nothing had happened. Granny Jane told us it was the shock of seeing an arm bone and thinking it belong to her daddy that drove her to drink. That type of thing would make anybody fall in a ditch, Granny Jane said. Jane and I felt guilty, but knew that no matter what, it would all be better when she knew where her daddy was.

The newspaper sent a man to talk with us and take a picture. They were calling the bone 'the sacred remains'. Marcell quietly watched the fuss and washed our good Sunday dresses. Wednesday evening, Uncle Ben came out to talk about Saturday.

"I just dropped by to tell y'all everything's set. It'll be at four, that way it's before supper but after most of the heat. The girls will carry the bone and buttons. Will is making a box for them. I'll say some words and the preacher will say a prayer. The Dorcas ladies will bring iced tea, lemonade, and cookies so folks can stand around and talk. That sound all right to you?"

"And the flags?"

"All three of them." By that he meant the

American flag, the North Carolina flag, and the Confederate flag. "And Charles Major is going to blow taps on his horn."

"Sounds like a fine show," Granny Jane said.

Uncle Ben smiled at us. He turned to the women to talk more about the ceremony. My smile faded. I loved Uncle Ben and felt bad about him having to find Ivis' bones right in front of a bunch of people.

Suddenly Granny Jane's words jerked me back. "...and Gracie's parents are going to be so proud."

I looked over at Miss Emily. She looked startled. I turned back to Granny Jane. The old woman nodded her head at Miss Emily as if to say, 'so there' and smiled like a fox. Miss Emily sat silent. Uncle Ben slapped his hands on his knees and stood up.

"That's settled then. Girls," he turned and gave us a big grin, "you be sure to wear your good Sunday dresses. Everybody's going to be watching!"

Silence followed him out the door. It lingered in the air for a minute then Miss Emily spoke, "Miss Jane, I don't remember us discussing inviting Robert and Sissy down here to the ceremony. You know how she's..."

"Girls," Granny Jane interrupted, "go put the hens in the pen and shut the coop."

"Yes, Ma'am." We had no intention other than going one foot out the door and listening in.

"Miss Jane..."

The old woman interrupted, "Emily, it's a good opportunity to talk to Robert about Gracie and how happy she is here."

Jane and I looked at each other. So that was why Granny Jane had looked like she'd had a secret this past week. Miss Emily's voice cut through the air.

"What are you trying to do Miss Jane?"

Granny Jane's voice sharpened, "What do you think I'm trying to do? I'm trying to take care of my own flesh and blood. And that means rescuing that girl from her mother."

"Miss Jane!" Miss Emily raised her voice, but Granny Jane firmly overrode it.

"Emily I love you like a blood daughter and I know you love that son of yours, but he's married to a spoiled brat and dances to her tune. In Virginia, Gracie was dying on the vine. Just look at her now."

There was dead silence. Jane and I crouched by the door as still as stumps. Marcell came out of the kitchen onto the back porch. She opened her mouth to yell but took one look at our faces and stopped. Silently, she walked across the porch and stood over us.

Miss Emily broke the silence. "Don't talk to me like that Miss Jane. I love Gracie and know how hard it is for her to be with Sissy."

"I'll talk any way I want to. This isn't about Sissy. God and all his creatures know that woman's not going to change. I'm talking about Robert." There was a pause. She continued. "He's my grandson and I love him but Emily, you're not blind. I know you've seen what I've seen all this summer. That child has blossomed like a flower in the sun. She came here scared to death and hanging all over that dog. Now, she's running around happy as a small pig. The farm's healed her."

"I know. But Robert loves her and wants…"

"I don't give two cents what Robert wants!" The cane thumped on the floor. "If you ask me, he has exactly what he wants. And that's Sissy, though God only knows why."

Miss Emily's heavy sigh drifted through the screen. "I know. It's hard to see him so blind about her."

"Emily, you know as well as I do that Robert only wants Gracie home because Sissy doesn't want to look like a bad mother."

Jane reached over and touched my shoulder. I shook her off.

"Miss Jane, she might do just as well back home. I think I've finally got her convinced she's got nothing to do with Sissy's craziness."

"Convinced is one thing. But living it day to day is a whole other matter. Dear lord, Emily, she's a child. I know you love Robert and want him to be happy, but he's made his choice. Gracie hasn't got any choice."

A hard silence poured through the screen door.

"What if it was Jane?" Granny Jane's voice held a satisfied note. "What if Jane hadn't been able to live here at the farm with us after Sally and Dave died and was with Sissy and Robert? What then?"

The two women were silent. Jane and I strained toward the screen door. Marcell's hands clamped down on our shoulders and pulled us quietly to standing. She backed us up and hissed, "Not for your ears. You come on or I'll make a fuss."

Jane and I backed farther away from the door then turned around. The dogs ran up looking to play. Neither of us felt like it. We headed out to the barn.

"Young ladies, I brought you a treat!" Uncle Ben arrived Friday afternoon and waved a copy of the local newspaper. Grinning, he nodded to Granny Jane and sat on the porch steps. Jane and I crowded around him. There on the front page in black and white was a picture of Jane and me, sitting on the sofa, holding the sacred remains and grinning like monkeys. Black Jack, Sassy, and Brown Hound sat at our feet.

"You look like a cootie." Jane punched me in the arm.

"You look like Black Jack's momma."

Granny Jane gave a chuckle. "You girls made the paper just like movie stars."

"Yeah, like Trigger."

"Yeah, like Cheetah."

Jane and I traded insults again, pleased as punch.

"I hear Robert and Sissy are coming for the ceremony." Uncle Ben said to Granny Jane.

"That's a fact. They're driving down tomorrow morning and will be here in plenty of time." Her voice was firm and ended that part of the conversation. "You like to stay for supper, Ben?"

"No thanks, Martha's expecting me back. I just wanted to drop by and make sure you got an extra copy of the paper."

Grinning, he said his goodbyes, kissed the tops of our heads, then drove off. Granny Jane rocked and looked out over the fields. We left her with her thoughts and went to help Marcell with supper.

At the table, nobody had said a thing about Daddy and Sissy coming. That was fine by me. I remembered pressing my teeth into my bedroom window sill the night before I left. I wondered if I'd see those marks again. I didn't want to. I was holding tight to the hope Granny Jane could scare Sissy into leaving me here.

"All right, young ladies," Miss Emily was smiling through her stern words, "you get those pajamas on and get into bed." Jane and I'd decided to wear the same pajama top. We were fighting and tussling and falling all over the bed trying to get it away from each other. Miss Emily shook her head.

"You're going to be too tired for the ceremony tomorrow if you don't stop this foolishness." Jane and I popped up out of our tangle and grinned at her. She smiled back. She knew we were a hopeless cause.

"You girls are making us mighty proud. Tomorrow's going to be a fine day. Now just settle down." Miss Emily turned out the light and pulled the door to.

Jane's foot sneaked over and I swatted her for trying to pinch me with her toes. She laughed and smoothed the sheet over her body. The night settled, muted and soft. We heard the scratch of paws prancing across the yard. The dogs were trotting off to the woods tonight. I let my mind drift.

What would it be like for Brown Hound to trot into the woods when it was cold? When the air bit her nose, and fluffed her tail? What would it be like to lay here snuggled under quilts with the cold moon overhead and the grass tipped white with frost? How would it be to march down the driveway with my books under my arm and climb in the school bus with Jane? My heart gave heavy thumps of excitement. I tried to push the feeling down. I didn't want to think like that. Not while there was a chance I would go back to Virginia. Not while Sissy was coming. Not yet.

I looked up at the ceiling. I'd sent so many wishes through those white boards up to God. I wondered if He'd heard them all. Marcell hadn't stopped drinking. Sissy hadn't acted any better. But that was okay. Everything would be fine if he would just give me this one wish. If he would just give me Jane, Granny Jane, Miss Emily, the farm, and Aunt Martha and Uncle Ben. I drifted off to sleep, counting my wants.

CHAPTER 22

We were up before Marcell for the first time. Pulling on our play clothes, we ran to the kitchen to help. Marcell turned from the stove with a snort, "Looks like trouble, you two up this early. You ready for them Sunday dresses?" We grinned back at her. She didn't know that today her life would be changed forever. She would find her daddy and quit drinking and be happy. She turned back to the frying pan, "Go set table."

Jane and I ran over to the cabinet, grabbing at the plates. It was like if we hurried, we could make the day go by faster.

"Up early and helping. That's my girls." Miss Emily came into the kitchen, tying on her apron. She gave us a smile but looked worried. I reminded myself that today was going to be a big strain on her. She was gonna talk to Daddy about my staying.

"Marcell, take a plate in to Miss Jane, please."

We froze in our tracks. Granny Jane not at breakfast? We looked at Miss Emily. She smiled again but looked worried. "Miss Jane was up most of the night with some pains in her chest." Marcell stopped dishing up the eggs, her hand in mid-air. She had the same look on her face as us. Stricken.

"You best call Doc Davis then." Marcell tried to make her voice sound normal. I could hear it shake. Jane and I didn't have any voice at all.

"Nothing to worry about. She said it was just supper trying to come back on her. Just some indigestion, that's all." Miss Emily's voice sounded calm and firm, but if it was just nothing then why'd she been up all night with Granny Jane?

"Go on Marcell, dish up that plate. Girls, set table. Let's get breakfast done before Robert and Sissy get here."

She moved to the stove to take Marcell's place. My throat was so dry I didn't have spit. Granny Jane sick? Granny Jane not here to do battle with Sissy? I could barely breathe. Jane looked as strangled as I did.

"Go on now. She'll be fine with some breakfast and some more rest. You know she's had spells before."

Jane and I ate quickly then cleaned up breakfast so Marcell and Miss Emily could spend time checking on Granny Jane. We didn't say much. It was like if we said anything then the words being in the air would make it true. I looked at Jane as she washed the dishes. Her face was white and she kept folding in her lips. Suddenly, I felt selfish. Here I was worrying all about me when Jane had been with Granny Jane all her life and didn't know any other way to be. I reached out and touched her on the arm. She shook her head at me and didn't say anything, just kept washing. I guess she didn't have any spit either.

It was time for lunch when the dogs started barking. My parent's car jostled down the driveway and pulled up under the oak tree in a cloud of dust. Brown Hound, Black Jack, and Sassy jumped at the car doors as Jane and I made our way down the porch steps.

"Gracie, call the dogs." My father stepped out of the car shoving Black Jack aside.

The dog danced away then reared up and got a hard knee in the chest. Yelping, he backed away. Brown Hound jumped at Sissy's door but retreated when she heard Sissy yell.

"Gracie," Daddy repeated, "get those dogs away so Sissy can get out of the car." His voice was on edge. Jane and I dragged them around the side of the porch, patted their heads, and shoved them towards the backyard.

"Where's the welcoming committee?" My father's voice was trying to be light as he helped Sissy out of the car. The screen door banged. Miss Emily walked across the porch, down the steps and went to give hugs.

"Sorry, I was in with Miss Jane."

"Is she sick?" My father asked.

"No, just doesn't feel right and needs to rest a bit."

"Well, she's certainly old enough to be sick." Sissy pulled off her gloves. She was dressed up in her high-class ladies lunch clothes.

"Elizabeth Grace, give me a kiss." I reached up on tiptoe and kissed her cheek. She headed to the house, pushing herself out in front, as usual.

"Let's go in out of the heat." Miss Emily held the door open and we walked into the living room.

❀ ❀ ❀

Sitting at the dining room table, Jane and I picked at the food.

My father smiled and said, "Gracie, you and Jane are pretty quiet for such an exciting day."

"They're excited, but I think they're worried about Miss Jane." Miss Emily gave Jane and me a smile.

"Well, they'd better get used to the idea of her not being around. She's old enough to die any minute." Sissy leaned toward the kitchen door and called out, "Marcell bring me some more of that tuna fish salad." The rest of us sat quiet. There didn't seem to be anything to say after that. Miss Emily closed her eyes, my father rearranged his knife and spoon.

"Here, Miss Sissy." Marcell leaned over Sissy's shoulder and dropped a big splat of tuna fish salad on her plate. Beads of mayonnaise juice flew through the air.

"Marcell!" Sissy's voice reached to the ceiling.

"Sorry, Miss Sissy. It fell off the spoon before I could get it to the plate." I kept my eyes on the tablecloth. I was glad we were going to get Marcell's daddy back for her.

"Gracie, tell your parents about finding the bones." Miss Emily turned the attention to me. I began the tale. It took us through the rest of the tuna fish salad and on through dessert.

After lunch, my father and Sissy retired to their room for a rest. Jane and I cleaned up while Marcell went to see about Granny Jane. After a few minutes, Miss Emily stuck her head into the kitchen.

"Girls, come say hello to Miss Jane." Jane and I dropped our tea towels and ran. Skidding to a stop at her door, we opened it and quietly walked into the room.

Granny Jane sat in bed; a white sheet pulled up to her lap. She had on her nightgown and looked smaller than when she sat on the porch.

"What trouble are you two into now?" She was gruff, but glad to see us. Jane ran to the bed and threw her arms around the old woman. Granny Jane patted Jane's back, then motioned to me to come over. "You too, girl." I sat on the bed beside Jane and we both started asking questions at once. Granny Jane held up her hand for silence.

"I'm fine. Just some of last night's supper coming back around for a visit. I wouldn't miss your ceremony for all the tea in China."

We heard a humph at the door and turned. Marcell stood with her arms crossed over her chest. "Miss Jane, you should stay here and rest."

Jane looked at our great grandmother with a worried frown on her face, "Maybe Marcell's right. Sissy said you could die any minute."

"Did she now?" Granny Jane looked over our heads at Miss Emily. "Well, I reckon she better watch out, too. Any one of us can die the second the good

Lord decides to take us. Just like that Confederate officer you found in the field." Her eyes twinkled. Jane and I leaned over for another hug.

"You come on now. Miss Jane's tired of your mess," Marcell waved us out. "Time to start getting ready."

Jane and I raced each other to our bedroom. Flinging the door shut behind us, we ran to the bed, and jumped up and down. Granny Jane was gonna be fine. The ceremony was almost here. We were gonna be heroes. We were about to explode with excitement.

"Get down right now." Miss Emily was at the door and her voice had a sharp edge to it.

We jumped down and stood still our hands behind our backs.

"Get dressed and stop your mess." I walked over and hugged her around the waist. Her hands stroked the top of my head. I knew she was just tired from staying up with Granny Jane and having my parents here. We got dressed.

Jane and I were in the back of Daddy's car. Granny Jane sat in the middle. She thought we needed to be separated and she was right. Jane kept leaning over and sticking out her tongue and my fist itched to smack her. We were all wrung up and ready for the afternoon to come. Marcell and Miss Emily were in the farm truck carrying the dogs.

The sun was burning low in the August sky. The slightest movement drew sweat. Jane and I jumped from the car before it stopped and danced impatiently. Sissy got out, smoothing wrinkles from her dress. Daddy helped Granny Jane from the car.

"I'm fine, Robert. I can walk," Granny Jane fussed. I guess the heat and the supper that wouldn't go away were making her snappish.

"Miss Jane?" We turned. Uncle Ben stood with the sheriff. Granny Jane leaned on her cane and looked from one to the other. "Something wrong, Ben?"

"Miss Jane, we need to speak to the girls before the ceremony."

A hand clamped down on my shoulder, nails dug in. I looked up. Sissy's eyes were as hard as her voice. "What have you done now?"

"If we could just…" the sheriff began, but Sissy cut him off, eyes locked on me. "Oh yes, let's do talk to the girls." She moved her eyes to Jane. My cousin stepped close to Granny Jane. Uncle Ben raised his voice just a bit.

"We just need to take care of something before we start the ceremony. And we'd like to do it in private." He tilted his head toward the crowd gathering in front of the memorial.

People had stopped work on their farms early to come to the ceremony. Men had on their nice shirts and the women wore dresses they used for church. Children ran around the square shouting, jumping, and playing hopscotch. Over to one side, the Dorcas church ladies were setting the tables with pitchers of iced tea, lemonade, and plates of cookies.

The sheriff turned and walked away like there was a fire on his heels, his back straight and tight. His words shot back to us. "Let's go into the courthouse. Shouldn't take long."

Sissy let go of my shoulder, put her hands on her hips, and smiled at my father. Her teeth were like bits of glass.

Granny Jane spoke. "Robert, stay here. Tell Emily and Marcell to come along to the courthouse. I want everyone together." She turned to follow the sheriff. "Girls?" Jane and I walked on either side of her. Sissy and Uncle Ben followed behind.

❊ ❊ ❊

The inside of the courthouse it was dim and cool. The sheriff stood at the end of the hall beside an open door. As we walked toward him, my father hurried up behind us saying, "Mother and Marcell are going to join us a soon as they make sure the dogs are settled." No one answered.

The sheriff pointed through the door. We filed in. On a large table sat a metal tray draped with a bath towel. The sheriff shut the door. I stared at the small lumps under the towel and knew it was Ivis. I closed my eyes. Jane moved so her shoulder touched mine.

"Robert," Sissy began in a sharp voice.

Granny Jane cut her off. "Hush, Sissy. Ben, Sheriff, what's this about?"

Uncle Ben rubbed his face. His hand drifted to his shirt pocket searching for a cigar. The sheriff cleared his throat, gave Jane and me a hard look and started talking.

"Ben and I opened up the monument earlier today to practice and check that things were in order." He stopped and shook his head. "You could say we found more than we expected."

Granny Jane shifted impatiently. "Ben let's get this going. I'm tired and the girls are wrung up enough as it is."

"Well, Miss Jane," the sheriff said stiffly, "I'll just cut to the end. We opened the monument and found these." He pointed to the towel-covered tray.

Uncle Ben cleared his throat and spoke, "When we first interred the remains, the soldiers' bones were in an oak box that I'd made. These," he nodded at the tray, "were laying beside it. They weren't there when we closed the monument up back in the 20s."

Words flew out of Sissy's mouth like striking snakes. "You've done something. I know it. What have you done?" I had nowhere to go and Jane was beginning to shake.

"Now just hold on, Sissy." Uncle Ben stepped closer to Jane and me. "Nobody's saying the girls had anything to do with this."

"Then just why'd you bring us here?" Her words made me catch my breath. How dare she talk like that to Uncle Ben? I felt Jane stop shaking and tense up. I could see Uncle Ben struggle to answer in a civil tone.

"The sheriff and I saw the girls arranging flowers at the monument and he wanted to know if they noticed anything unusual."

Granny Jane gave a heavy sigh. "Ben, couldn't

this have waited until after the ceremony?"

The sheriff stepped forward and explained, "No ma'am it could not. These bones have clearly been hidden. This is foul play. And these bones take precedence." He hooked his hands in his belt. I waited for Granny Jane to whip his head off with her cane. Instead, she leaned toward the table and used her cane to flip back the towel. Everybody stepped forward at once. Pieces of bone lay there, musty, and old, with scraps of cloth and a thin necklace mingled in. Thirty years had done their work. There wasn't much left.

Granny Jane gave a grim laugh. "These bones are old as the hills. When you find the killer, you're going to have to dig him up to put him in jail." Her cane pushed the bones around on the tray as she spoke. "You're wasting our time and upsetting the girls." Her voice stopped mid-sentence as the necklace fell into full view. She staggered back a step.

"Miss Jane," Uncle Ben said.

The door opened. In walked Miss Emily and Marcell. Granny Jane looked up and lifted her hand, palm facing out like she could stop them. But she couldn't.

"Marcell," Granny Jane tried to speak. Marcell walked over to the table and stopped still, her eyes widening, then dropped to her knees. Then slumped sideways like she'd been hit with an ax. Uncle Ben pushed past the sheriff, ran to Marcell, and crouched down and felt for her pulse.

"She's fainted. Robert, come here. There's a

sofa in the room across the hall. Let's get her off the floor. Miss Emily, hold her head." The room was quiet as they carried her out. Suddenly the silence split.

"Your daddy and I came all the way down here for this ceremony and what happens? It all goes to hell in a handbasket and guess who's in the middle of it." Sissy reached for my arm, but Granny Jane raised her cane and pointed it at her.

"Stop."

Startled, Sissy stepped back. The room filled with silence. Granny Jane lowered her cane. All eyes turned back to the table. We waited until Daddy and Uncle Ben walked back into the room. Miss Emily stayed with Marcell. Granny Jane's voice punched through the air.

"Ben, I know who those bones belong to. See that chain and cross?" She nodded toward the tray. "I'd know it anywhere. It's the one James Earl and I gave to Sophronia when she and Ivis got married." She stopped for a moment then continued. "After Sophronia died, Ivis put that chain on and never took it off. Said it would go to Marcell when he died, so she would always have a part of her mother."

"Good God!" Uncle Ben leaned over and pulled the chain from the bones. The small cross dangled in the air.

Sissy turned to me, "Don't stand there like you're stupid. You know something about this and I want an answer."

Uncle Ben took a deep breath and shared a

look with Granny Jane. My father stood silently. Sissy's hands whipped out and grabbed me. My head jerked back and forth.

"You and Jane knew something about this. I don't know how. But you did and you planned to cause a scene at the ceremony! Wanted attention? I'll give you some attention!"

I knew that tone of voice. It was the one that made me hide in Brown Hound's doghouse. Her hand dug into my shoulder. I closed my eyes and waited for the slap.

Sissy screamed and I opened my eyes. Jane had flown through the air, fists swinging and landed straight on her.

"You dirty child!" Sissy yelled. "You piece of trash. Get off me!"

She let me go to shove Jane. Jane lowered her head and dived forward. Daddy grabbed her, swinging her around, and dropped her to the floor. Jane bounced up, Granny Jane reached out and yanked her away. I jumped behind them. My father's eyes flashed from me to Sissy. Uncle Ben stood ready, watching hard. Sissy wiped at her hands and looked at Jane. Her mouth twisted.

"That girl needs a beating for sure. No wonder Elizabeth Grace is in trouble with the sheriff." She paused for breath then looked at her husband. "Robert, you go start the car and take Elizabeth Grace with you. We're going to the farm and pack her up. She's coming home with us right now."

Words burst out of me that had a life of their own. A life that came from Granny Jane telling stories so I'd know about my family, from Miss Emily believing that I hadn't made Sissy sick, from sleeping with Jane, from Marcell fussing then making sure our dresses were clean.

The summer came together like a sparkling wave. It crashed over me, washing me clean.

"I'm not in trouble with the sheriff. Jane's not trash. And I'm not gonna go back with you." Sissy and Daddy stood speechless. Jane shook off Granny Jane's hand and stood up straight. I walked to Uncle Ben and held out my hand.

"Please."

Uncle Ben dropped the chain and cross into my palm without a word. I looked over at Jane. I could see her cloak of bravery. As for me, I had all the bravery I would ever need.

"Young lady, you're coming back with us right now!" The words exploded in the air and tried to suck the breath from my body. Sissy stood, arms folded across her chest, eyes on me. "Isn't that so Robert?"

Granny Jane leaned on her cane and looked at Daddy. He spoke up.

"Miss Jane, Sissy and I were talking on the way down. It's getting on time for Gracie to get ready for school and she needs…"

Sissy broke in. "She needs to quit running wild. I don't know what in the world you've done with her this summer."

"We've given her a home." Granny Jane's voice

had nails in it.

"She has a home back in Virginia." A hard satisfied look came on momma's face. "What she needs is to get back up there where I can remind her of her manners.

"Sissy," my father started to speak. Sissy ignored him. Keeping her eyes on me she snapped her fingers.

"Elizabeth Grace, let's go." I looked at those red nails flashing in the air. They matched the flashing in my head. The clean feeling from the sparkling wave had disappeared and I wanted it back. I knew I wouldn't get it back by sitting on the picnic table with Brown Hound after one of Sissy's spells. I'd get it back by staying right where I belonged.

"I don't want to go back. I'm staying on the farm." I kept my eyes steady on Sissy, but my insides were shaking hard. I felt Granny Jane's eyes on me. Jane nodded her head as if she had a say. I squeezed the necklace meant for Marcell. The cross cut into my palm.

"Gracie honey, now come on," Daddy began. My eyes stayed on Sissy as I answered him.

"No. I'm not coming. I'm staying on the farm." The cross cut in a bit deeper.

"Right now, young lady. Right now!" Sissy started forward, her voice raising the hair on my arms. I moved closer to Uncle Ben. Out of the corner of my eye, I saw Miss Emily come back into the room. Sissy's voice rose higher as Daddy grabbed her arm.

"Robert, she's coming with me. Right now!"

"Sissy!" Miss Emily's voice cut the air. "Behave yourself! This minute! Robert, let her go." Everybody stood like they'd been turned to rocks. Even the sheriff. Miss Emily was breathing hard. I pulled my eyes from Sissy and looked at my grandmother. She didn't share Granny Jane's blood, but this second, she looked just like her. Granny Jane had a small smile on her face. Miss Emily caught her breath. The words continued to snap out of her.

"Sissy, what do you mean acting like this in front of the sheriff and Ben? You should be ashamed of yourself. You're acting worse than the girls ever did."

"Momma, Sissy can't …"

"Can't what, Robert?" Miss Emily turned to her son, "Can't help it? I think she can. I think she can help it plenty." She turned back and stared at Sissy, "I think she chooses when to help it and when to not." My father opened his mouth, but Sissy pushed herself forward.

"You don't know any such thing."

"I know plenty, Sissy," Miss Emily's voice softened, "I know you have a hard time and I understand when you get sick," she paused and her voice got harder, "but I also know you pitch a fit when it pleases you. And right now, it pleases you."

Sissy gasped. The sheriff took this moment to slip past Miss Emily and out the door. "I'll just go and check on Marcell…" his voice trailed off. No one was listening to him.

Miss Emily continued, "Right now it pleases

you to browbeat Robert into taking Gracie back to Virginia when she doesn't want to go." Everybody turned to look at me. I was frozen with hope. Jane's hands clasped in front of her like she was praying.

Miss Emily kept talking. "What I want to know is why do you want your child to be unhappy and go back to Virginia when she wants to stay here with us?"

"Because she's been ruined this summer that's why. Just look at this." Sissy threw her hand out toward the table.

"Yes, let's look," Granny Jane interrupted. "Looks like Gracie and Jane found Marcell's father for her. And now she can grieve." The old woman smiled and said to both of us, "I'm not so old I don't remember every one of your questions."

My father turned and began, "Sissy, if Gracie wants to stay so bad maybe…" Sissy stilled, her eyes darted between Daddy and Miss Emily. Her face appeared to crumple.

"She wants to stay here because she hates me. And you're going to let her do that. They're all taking her part, Robert, and so are you." Sissy wiped her eyes and gave Daddy a sad look. He stood, hands hanging at his sides. Giving another sniff Sissy looked around and saw Miss Emily, then Granny Jane. She moved her eyes to me, and they narrowed. The tears dried up. The hard satisfied look came back on her face.

"You just stay here with this wild cousin of yours. You just do that. I'll tell everyone you went wild digging up bones, getting in trouble with the sheriff. So wild you had to be kept down here where they could deal with you." She tossed a scornful look at Miss Emily and Granny Jane. "Real ladies can't be expected to deal with such a ruined child." She nodded her head and her lips twisted in a half smile. Her eyes threw knives at me, and then at Jane. We shook with the blow but stood firm.

"Sissy," Daddy held out his hand. She refused it and, turning her back on us, pushed past Miss Emily and stalked out of the door. My father turned to Miss Emily. "Momma."

Walking forward, Miss Emily put her arms around him and patted his back. Pulling away she grasped his shoulders and looked him in the eye.

"Robert. Give your daughter a kiss and go on to your wife." Daddy looked sick to his stomach. Miss Emily continued, "Virginia's no place for Gracie. Not until Sissy gets straight and you know it." She let go of him and one hand reached up and gently patted his cheek. "You let us take care of Gracie. She'll be fine. You go on now and take care of Sissy."

Daddy nodded his head, gave her a kiss, then turned to me. I ran past Uncle Ben and Miss Emily and hugged my daddy around his waist.

"Thank you, Daddy."

"You want to stay here that bad?"

"Yes, sir."

Daddy gave a sigh and leaned down with a kiss. "We'll come and see you as much as we can. We'll try this for the school year and see how it goes. Maybe

Sissy will be better after that."

"It's okay, Daddy. I'll be fine." I smiled up at him. He smiled back then lifted his head.

"Ben, Miss Jane." He nodded to the them. We watched him turn and slowly walk out of the room.

"Girls." We looked at Granny Jane. "You were old enough to start this," she waved her hand toward the table. "You're old enough to finish it up."

I walked over and looked out of the door and down the hall where Daddy had gone. I felt my stomach get tight, but I couldn't tell if it was from being sad or happy. I thought it might be both. Jane came over to me. Silently, we crossed the hall to the room where Marcell sat on the sofa. We came to a stop in front of her. Jane poked me with her elbow, and I began.

"Marcell, this was your daddy's." The colored woman looked up at me and didn't say a word. I held out the chain and cross. She took it. Jane and I sat down on either side of her. She placed the chain in her lap. And slowly, softly, she placed one hand on Jane's knee and the other on mine.

CHAPTER 23

Jane edged close and hissed in my ear, "You get to stay!" I tried to keep the grin from my face but failed. We stood in front of the monument and listened as the preacher said a prayer and Uncle Ben read from the writings of Robert E. Lee.

The ceremony was a success. Uncle Ben had taken charge of Ivis' remains, squared things with the sheriff by reminding him there were folks right outside who would not care to have the circumstances of Ivis' death brought front and center. Everything went on without a hitch. The dogs behaved except for Black Jack who howled when they played Taps. The sacred remains were interred, the lemonade and cookies were served, and before we knew it, we were back at Aunt Martha and Uncle Ben's sitting on the sofa, exhausted. Aunt Martha came in from the kitchen with a frown on her face.

"Ben, those dogs are going to tear up the yard."

"Martha, they won't be here long. Miss Jane and I just want to get a few things straight with the girls before I drive them back to the farm."

Jane and I let that sink in. I was beginning to wish we'd ridden with Miss Emily when she took

Marcell home but knew the colored woman didn't want the dogs or anyone else around.

"Girls, why don't you start at the beginning." Granny Jane cocked her head with interest. Jane went first.

"Well, Marcell drinks because she's sad. That's what Miss Charity said." Aunt Martha closed her eyes and made a sound. Jane plowed ahead, "and we knew that was true because of what happened to her daddy."

Granny Jane looked at Uncle Ben and he shrugged his shoulders "You agreed they were old enough to know." I picked up where Jane left off.

"So, we thought if she could grieve over her daddy's grave like Granny Jane does with James Earl, she would stop drinking. And Aunt Viola and the church ladies would stop talking." Granny Jane gave a laugh. Aunt Martha shook her head with a smile.

Uncle Ben changed the conversation and asked, "Was that truly a confederate bone?" Jane looked at me. It was my turn again.

"No sir. We got it from the Indian graveyard." Granny Jane gave a bark of laughter.

"Oh girls," Aunt Martha whispered.

I continued. "And Jane had some buttons and minie balls in a jar."

Uncle Ben shook his head and asked another question, "How'd you know where Ivis was?"

Jane plunged in. "Miss Emily told us all about what happened with Cap'n Tom that night."

Granny Jane's voice broke in. "Careful." Jane knew the part about our grandfather helping with the hanging was to be a secret forever. I could see Jane thinking about her next words.

"Granny Jane told us Cap'n Tom wanted to leave the Tigers. They said they'd burn his barn like the Smith's."

Aunt Martha went still in her chair and Uncle Ben drew in a breath saying, "I always knew there was more to that story than you and Emily let on."

Jane continued. "Cap'n Tom couldn't stop the hanging, but he did steal Ivis. We figured he didn't have time to dig a hole big enough." She explained about the attic newspapers and our plan. She finished and the adults shook their heads.

"Ben, their hearts were in the right place," said Aunt Martha coming to our defense.

Granny Jane nodded, satisfied that Jane had told just enough. She turned to Uncle Ben. "You've taken care of the sheriff?" He nodded his head. She gave a grim smile. "Didn't think he'd ask too many questions. Hits too close to home." She paused and finished up, "And now, I'd like to go back to the farm." She smiled but looked tired. In the excitement, we'd forgotten about her supper coming back on her from last night. We rushed to her side. She patted Jane's head and gave me a smile.

"I'm fine. It's just time for us to go home."

The word floated through the air like a wisp

of cotton candy. Home. Jane grinned. Aunt Martha smiled. Uncle Ben led us to the car.

⁂

Jane and I were in bed. A small breeze had settled in, a fine relief from the August heat. Miss Emily sat talking with us.

"Marcell wants to thank you, but right now I don't think she can."

"That's okay, but she's all right?" Jane asked.

"She's as fine as she can be with just now finding her daddy and all those bad memories coming up. It's a start. And for now, she's not drinking." Miss Emily gave us a serious look. "You know this might not stop that completely?"

We nodded our heads.

"Uncle Ben is getting Ivis put in the colored graveyard?" Jane asked.

Miss Emily smiled. "Yes. There's going to be a funeral and all the family will attend."

"Even the dogs?" Jane asked.

"Only if you put bows on them." Miss Emily replied. Jane and I hollered with laughter, happy to break the solemn mood. Miss Emily shook her head and looked at me.

"Gracie."

"Yes, Ma'am?"

"You sure this is what you want, staying here? You won't get homesick for your daddy?" She didn't mention Sissy.

"No, Ma'am. I've got Brown Hound."

Jane laughed and snaked her leg over to pinch me with her toes. Miss Emily shook her head like she knew I hadn't given her a straight answer. But I had.

The breeze blew the curtains around the window. Jane slept hard, her arms flung out, the sheet tangled around her legs. I heard a soft yip and crawled over to look out the window. Black Jack and Sassy trotted across the front yard with Brown Hound leading the way. Another night in the swamp. I moved back to my side of the bed, straightened the sheet, and pulled it up to my chin. The curtains flapped again. The breeze flowed over my face. In my bed, in my home, I drifted into sleep.

READERS GUIDE

1.   Gracie is being sent to her grandmother's farm for the summer. How does she, her daddy, and her mother truly feel about this?

2.   How did Brown Hound's actions influence events in the story. How did these actions encourage Gracie's growth?

3.   Great Granny Jane is always there, comforting, and telling hard truths. Why did the author include her? What is her purpose in the story?

4.   The setting is 1951 North Carolina. How does this setting reveal the prejudices and injustices of that time?

5.   Marcell changes during the story. Does finding Ivis help her? In 1951, how much will she actually be able to resolve?

6.   Gracie goes alone to see Miss Charity. What happens to bring about the courage do this?

7.   Several characters vie for 'least liked'. Which is your choice? How might these characters be redeemed?

8. Several major turning points change Gracie's view of herself. Name at least two and talk about the impact.

9. The story ends with the soft summer night and safety. Is this temporary? How do you think she will navigate the coming year?

10. This story is told by 10-year-old Gracie. How would the story be different if it was told by Marcell?

About the Author

Author, broadcast journalist and freelance writer Karen Jones is the author of *Up the Bestseller Lists! A Hands-On Guide to Successful Book Promotion, Death for Beginners*, and *The Highland Witch*.

Jones has fifteen years of experience in television news as an on-air anchor and feature reporter where she wrote and produced the Associated Press Award winning series *The Haunting of Virginia*. She co-directed the Chesapeake Writer's Conference, was an advisor to The Bay School of the Arts, and is a member of the National League of American Pen Women, and the Authors Guild.

She has taught writing seminars at the University of Richmond, Christopher Newport University, LSU and CNU. She has held week-long intensive writing camps for adults on Ocracoke Island, NC and will be holding her next writing camps in Virginia's Blue Ridge Mountains.

Jones lives beside the Atlantic Ocean with her amazingly tolerant husband who has just given a big sigh, because she is beginning to write her next book. She can be reached at her website: kjwriter.com